TO BE CLAIMED

BOOK THREE

WILLOW WINTERS

WALL STREET JOURNAL & USA TODAY BESTSELLING AUTHOR

From USA Today best-selling author, Willow Winters, comes a tempting tale of fated love, lust-filled secrets and the beginnings of an epic war.

Never in my life could I have prepared for what fate had in store for me. Or for any of us.

Our tales are intertwined and destiny saw fit to give me to a beast of a man who would die for me. He longs for me and I for him, but my past is riddled with a darkness and our present with deception and the whispers of war.

Everything warns me that my life will change forever. That the world will crumble and burn. I don't know what will happen or what will become of us. All I know is that, in his eyes, I belong to him.

This is book 3 of the To Be Claimed Saga. Wounded Kiss is book I and should be read first

PRIMAL
LUST

PART I

SCARRED MATE

CHAPTER 1

GRACE

My palms and knees roughly scrape back and forth against the grass, my nails digging into the dirt as my body pushes forward with every pleasure-filled thrust. Every nerve ending in my body is sensitized and even the moans that slip from my lips seem to add to my insatiable desire. My head hangs low, then rises with a desperate need to cry out as I take the punishing fuck. Devin's grip on the curves of my ass is so powerful that I wouldn't be surprised to find bruises later. His sharp fangs graze the tender skin on my neck, causing my blood to heat and rush through my veins with intense need. Arching my neck for him, I give him easy access to bite me, to claim me as his.

Every move is achingly natural and primitive; dark and seductive under the full moon.

"More," I say, whimpering my plea. His hips pound against mine as his pace quickens. Devin's thick girth stretches me fully, giving a hint of pain to the waves of pleasure crashing through me. It's instantly forgotten as overwhelming heat builds in my core. It spreads slowly through my body as my toes numb. *Yes, yes!*

As he slams into me, the force of his powerful thrusts pushes my body forward, nearly knocking me to the ground. Strangled moans escape me as he continues to pound into me without holding back, the beast in him taking over, fueled by the full moon. It's all so intense and my head thrashes as I fight the urge to pull away.

Too much. Too much.

I almost cry out for him to stop but I hold myself back, clenching my teeth and submitting to the overwhelming and all-consuming haze of passion, loving his fierce desire to claim my body with his.

Devin gently kisses my back, a move that's at odds with his forceful motions. Again his fangs glide across the skin of my neck, threatening to pierce me, to mark me and scar me forever as his. I groan in approval at the thought. I desperately want to be his. I *need* to be his. I moan my pleasure into the chill of the air, knowing I'm his to claim.

He owns me: my body, my heart, my future.

The unrelenting heat threatens to burn me as he pistons his hips harder and faster. I whisper the words "I can't," as he nips my ear, sending a fresh wave of pleasure to my throbbing core. Refusing to slow his pace, a low growl rumbles in his chest. I gasp for air as my body gives out and he slams into me to the hilt. His fangs finally give me what I've been wanting. They pierce into my sensitive skin, and I let out a scream at the agonizing sensation.

A sharp pain attacks my body, making every inch of me shake violently. Fire courses through my veins, blistering my skin and threatening to choke me. Just as I register the pain, a soothing wave of unmatched pleasure rocks through me, easing the burn and forcing me to tremble with sated desire.

"Mine." Devin licks the deep marks on my neck. Devin's hot tongue soothes the claiming bite. The intensity subsides as the cool wind caresses my exposed skin. "Mine."

"Yours. I'm yours." I say the words quickly as I try to catch my breath. His long, warm exhale against my skin causes goosebumps to flow down my shoulders as he licks his mark again and then nuzzles into the crook of my neck. His strong arms pull my feverish body into his muscular chest.

"I love you, Devin." My eyes refuse to open as I nestle into his embrace and sigh with contentment. I am his mate. Feeling overwhelmed with the emotion consuming my every thought, I leave kisses on his chest, his neck—every inch of him. I don't know how it's possible to feel this kind of love so quickly, so assuredly.

"I love you, Grace." Hearing the tender words spoken in his deep voice has my heart swelling in my chest. My limbs continue to tremble as he holds me tighter.

A small smile pulls at my lips until the heat in my veins slowly returns, demanding attention. I struggle not to pull away from my mate, my Alpha.

The sensation tightens my throat with a fire that's unsettling.

"It feels like I'm choking." I murmur the words, writhing in his grasp. He doesn't react except to pull me closer to him. As if he didn't hear at all.

I need air. I need this burning to stop. Every inch of my body feels superheated, growing hotter and hotter with every passing second. Fear latches on to me as I push away from Devin. The cold ground calls to me, promising me respite from the unrelenting heat. His arms tighten rather than loosen and I struggle against him. "I'm too hot." I can barely push out the words. The feeling of my breath against my face is too much. It's too hot. My hands shake, and my muscles tighten all at once. I try to push away again, but a dizziness overwhelms my body. Anxiousness washes over me. I'm not okay. Something's wrong. Something's very wrong.

"Shh, sweetheart. It'll be over in a minute. I've got you." His words are a soothing balm, and paired with his dominance, I'm able to settle for a moment. It's a much-needed reprieve. Devin rubs soothing circles on my back as he licks his mark. His touch calms me and his tongue soothes the burn. I manage to take one deep breath, and then another. The burning slowly wanes, starting at my neck and cooling in small waves down my body. The cold sweat that's left makes me feel even more tired. I lie limp in his arms, knowing I'm safe. Knowing he can comfort me and heal my pain.

It's only then my racing heart seems to steady and beat in tandem with his.

"Why?" I don't have the strength for more words, but I know he won't need any more. He'll tell me what I need to know.

"The essence of my wolf is claiming you. It will scent you as my mate." Devin gently pulls away from me to look into my eyes and I whimper from the loss of his calming touch. "Everyone will know you are mine. Only mine. Forever."

With his hand around my throat, he lowers his lips to mine and kisses them lightly. Before he says the word, I feel it, I hear it even, just a moment before. "Mine."

Exhausted, I lie in his arms, feeling the heat turn to warmth as my body slowly comes down from the high and adapts to the effects of his mark. My eyes close as he kisses my hair, murmuring words of love and devotion.

At the sound of a sob, my brow furrows and I pick up my head, immediately on alert. *Lizzie?* Brushing Devin aside, I whip around to my right to find her somewhere in the dark. "Lizzie?" I whisper as I try to creep from Devin's lap. His stubble gently scratches the shell of my ear as he shakes his head.

"It's not her, sweetheart." His voice carries a hint of anguish. Oddly, I feel it. That worry, that knowing concern, in a way, is present deep in the pit of my soul. I glance up at him and then follow his gaze to the gap in the tree line where we entered the clearing. Off to the left I make out the tall form of Veronica. She's alone and another sob rips through her as my eyes focus in the dark. She's hunched on the ground and crying. I scan the area for Vince, but he's nowhere to be found.

"He left her?" First disbelief, then anger runs through me, awakening my senses and energizing my limbs. How could he leave his mate crying? She must be in pain! The very thought she's suffering from his bite, from that unbearable heat, has me nearly in tears. *How could he leave her alone to suffer?*

"It's not what you think. She's not in pain. She's not human, so she won't be feeling the same as you. She may not even feel anything at all."

"How could she not feel anything? How could she not feel *that*?"

He chuckles and my instinct is to strike him for it. A member of our pack is broken down and alone. "She needs us." He must hear the insistency of my comment because his grip tightens and his voice lowers to a serious timbre.

"They're working through other things right now. It's best to leave them be."

My head shakes of its own accord. "She needs someone." My whispered plea begs him to understand. Regardless of whether or not she felt the pain of Vince's mark, she's obviously hurting from something. "I want to go to her." I've already started to stand as I make the statement, but Devin's powerful arms constrict around my body.

"It's best not to interfere." His words are hard and his tone is absolute.

How can he be so cold? A moment passes and she sobs again, crying out for Vince.

"I can't sit here and do nothing. She needs someone." His eyes soften at my words and his grip loosens. He doesn't say anything, merely gazing into my hazel eyes before nodding his head and releasing me.

As I step out of his hold and walk toward her, I'm suddenly very aware of the fact that I'm naked. Cold and naked, to be exact. With my arms crossed in front of me, I gather my courage and set the thought aside. They're shifters, they don't care.

Well, she's a vampire, but I doubt she'll mind.

Another soft cry for Vince is barely heard in the distance and any thought of modesty vanishes.

She needs me. I feel a pull to her. A pull to my pack as I get closer to her. It's a strange sensation that I haven't felt before, almost like a pressure in my chest is pushing me forward, urging me to comfort her. My hand rubs at the hard knot growing in my chest as the pain becomes impossible to ignore.

I approach slowly until I'm able to see her more clearly. Streams of blood leak down her face. Tears? She blinks and the whites of her eyes return to normal before clouding with the dark red liquid yet again.

The terrifying sight is both shocking and frightening, and I gasp while taking a hesitant step back. At my reaction, Veronica's head pulls up in a nearly violent fashion. My heart pounds and I can't control the natural instinct. When her eyes catch sight of me, she immediately rises, and in a blink, she's gone. Nothing but a blurred vision.

She vanishes so quickly, I don't believe it at first. I question my own senses. Did she run? *Holy shit.* How is that possible? I'd heard that vampires were fast, but to see it is something else entirely. Something eerie and startling.

I swallow a scream as Devin's hand comes down on my shoulder. My beating heart slows once I realize it's him.

"She ran." I don't know what else to say.

"I saw. I thought she would. Like I said, it's best not to interfere. It's complicated, Grace."

My head shakes at his words. "No. She's not okay. She needs someone. I need to help her. I felt a pull to her."

His tone changes at my admission. "You felt a pull?" He turns me in his arms to look at me. "You felt a pull?" he repeats. I nod at his question. That's exactly what I felt. I rub my chest remembering the slight pain and growing knot. That's all but gone now. "I felt a physical need to go to her."

Devin lips turn up slightly into an asymmetric grin of pride.

"You were meant to be an Alpha, sweetheart. Fate has

given me a strong mate."

"An Alpha?"

He nods his head. "An Alpha feels the needs of his pack. And sometimes those who aren't even his responsibility. You," he says as his hand cups my chin and lifts my lips to him for a sweet, soft kiss, "you are an Alpha." I smile against his lips, his words warming me with satisfaction.

Pulling back slightly, I manage to remember Veronica through the needy haze of my heat returning. "Where do you think she went?"

"I'm not sure. Vince is going to her now, though." My confusion at his knowledge dissipates as I remember their ability to communicate even at long distances.

"But how will he find her?"

"He'll always be able to find her. She'll never be able to run from him. Not now that he's claimed her."

I look back at the direction she ran. "But what if she doesn't want him to find her?"

He shrugs. "I suppose she'd have to keep running. Vampires are much faster than werewolves. She could outrun him forever, but she won't." I look back into his silver gaze questioningly. He gives me a small smile and a peck. "She may want to run now, but she needs him. And she knows it just as much as he does."

CHAPTER 2

GRACE

My body is so damn sore as I walk down the hall to Vince and Veronica's room. Every movement makes me ache, but there's also a deep sense of satisfaction knowing it's from being claimed by my Alpha. A simper slips across my lips as my fingertips graze the wound on my neck. The moment I touch it, as if to check that it's still there, I wish I hadn't. I wince from the gentle touch. *Fuck*, it hurts.

I remember being stunned this morning when I first looked in the mirror. My entire neck is bruised and his mark looks horrendous. It's going to take a week or more for it to heal. Devin spent most of the morning licking and kissing it. A familiar heat rolls through my body at the remembrance and the pain is so easily forgotten.

The sigh of contentment is met with regret as my gaze settles on Vince and Veronica's door. Taking a moment to shake out my hair, I wipe the grin off my face. This isn't what Veronica needs. I can already feel the venom she would give me if I were to prance in with puppy love, no pun intended, written across my expression.

An image of her disheveled and broken appearance last night flashes in my mind and my heart drops, although my pace doesn't slow. I have no business going to her with my happiness so damn evident. I clear my throat and compose myself before knocking hesitantly on the door.

Thump, thump, my heart is only given a single second before the doorknob turns.

Veronica opens the door slowly and raises her brows when she sees me. Given how well vampires hear, it's obvious she's not surprised to see me. Just surprised at the sight of my condition judging by how her gaze travels over my plain white V-neck tee and dark gray sweatpants. I was a bit too sore for jeans.

"Well, that beast didn't take it easy on you, did he?" She steps away from the door, holding it open and allowing me to walk through.

My eyes widen at the sight of her in a deep burgundy satin robe. I nearly gape at her appearance. She looks just the same as she did yesterday—not during the ceremony, but before.

The way she always looks, which is stunning. Her tanned skin is completely unmarked with the only exception being a very faint silver scar along her shoulder. I have to squint to make it out. *Seriously?* I look like shit, like my mate mauled me, and she gets to go back to looking like a runway model? *Not fair.* Swallowing the petty thought, I enter the room and feel slightly uneasy as she shuts the door behind me.

It's only when I clear my throat to speak that I notice how sore it is. If I had to put money on it, I'd bet Veronica's throat isn't hurting either. As I part my lips, I note how casual she appears while she makes her way to the window. She doesn't seem to be in distress like she was last night. She's entirely composed. There are so many questions that beg to be asked. So many thoughts filled with compassion and empathy that stay lodged in the back of my throat. Nothing is as I thought it would be.

Devin was right when he said it's complicated, and that's in addition to the significance and difficulties Veronica being a vampire already brings.

Before I can speak, she gestures to a high-back chair in the corner of the room by a desk. "Sit."

A brow of mine cocks up of its own accord. I hesitate and narrow my eyes, not liking her tone or the use of the word "sit." Flashbacks of my first night with Devin run through my mind.

With a corner of her lips pulling up, she adds easily,

"Please," while gracefully lowering herself into the desk chair. She crosses her long legs, which causes the slit of her robe to fall open slightly, exposing even more of her. I glance around the room before taking my seat.

"Where's Vince?" My posture mirrors hers, both of us resting our hands on the arms of our respective chairs. Suddenly, it feels claustrophobic in here even though it's just the two of us.

I'm alone in a room with a vampire … although Veronica's lips perk up again, no doubt at the sound of my racing heart, her dark eyes contradict her countenance. Her gaze holds a sense of mourning in them that I wish I could ease.

"I heard you were coming, so I asked him to get us coffee." I don't miss how she relaxes her posture, appearing far less dominating.

"You must've heard Lizzie and I are practically caffeine addicts." I grin, but Veronica simply stares back without any trace of humor. "Thank you, though." I'm quick to add, "That's really sweet of you." At the word "sweet," her crimson lips curve upward and a small huff of a laugh leaves her.

"Yes, I can be very *sweet*." The way she speaks makes me uneasy. Any semblance of ease vanishes. She stares back at me as though I'm her prey. I shift uncomfortably. She doesn't seem to want my company, and I find myself regretting my decision to comfort her. She obviously doesn't need it. I start to get up, but then that knot in my chest forms again. My hand flies to the center of my chest and I press on it to try to ease the discomfort.

"Are you all right?" There's a trace of concern in Veronica's voice.

Nodding my head, I plant my ass firmly back down in the seat. "It's funny you should be asking me that, because I came here to ask you the same question." As the words leave my lips, the hard pain dissipates, granting me freedom to breathe normally. Rubbing the spot, I'm amazed at how quickly it left me. I make a mental note to talk to Devin about what the hell just happened.

It's similar to the pull from last night. Something has changed and it demands attention.

In the silence, my eyes find Veronica's dark gaze. Her lips are pressed in a hard line.

"I'm fine. I was mistaken about something last night."

"Mistaken?"

Her eyes narrow and I hold my ground as a flare of anger passes through me. She was more than shaken last night, so beat down, yet she refuses to acknowledge it. It's none of my business, except that she's my pack and this damn restlessness prods me to push. Just like I have to with Lizzie.

My eyes widen at the realization that Veronica's pulling the same shit Lizzie does. I narrow my eyes right back at her and repeat the single word incredulously, "Mistaken?" She seems to be shocked at how brazen I am, but I'm not going to back down. This pull inside of my chest demands action.

My voice is tighter than I'd like when I ask, "Why were you crying?"

Veronica clicks her tongue while searching my eyes before she purses her lips. "Why does it matter to you?"

"I hurt for you. You're a member of my pack and I want to help you."

"I don't need help, little human." Her wicked grin returns and her hard mask resurfaces. "How could you possibly help me?"

"I can't answer that question until I know what the problem is." I stare straight back at Veronica, unaffected by her arrogant tone. She's not going to fool me any longer. We all have walls we build, brick by brick, to keep ourselves protected. Hers have tumbled down and I'll help her rebuild them if she needs, but only if that's the boundary she needs. My teeth sink into my bottom lip wondering if I should push her, and if so, how much harder.

Her shoulders relax and she leans back in her chair while tapping her bloodred nails on the desk. "I didn't like last night." Her cool expression and flat tone are at least a bit more genuine. I'll take the small opening she gave me.

"You didn't want him to claim you?"

She shakes her head gently. "It's not that. I'm honored to be his mate. I really am." She takes a deep breath and adds, "I didn't know fate would give me a mate at all."

"I don't understand. Don't you all have mates?"

Her response is to give me a soft smile that doesn't reach her dark brown eyes. "No, only werewolves, dear." She watches her fingers tap along the desk for a moment before continuing. "Other shifters too, I suppose." She breathes in heavily before meeting my questioning gaze. "Not vampires. We don't have mates."

"But you have Vince?"

"Only because Vince has me as a mate. Fate's a cruel bitch." She snorts a laugh although there's no humor in what she said.

"Why is it cruel?"

"Well, for starters, she gave Vince a bitch for a mate. And then for me …" Her voice trails off and she straightens in her seat before staring into my eyes. "Fate decided to give me a mate. One person to love for my entirety. I will love him with everything I have, but I will live much longer than he will. I will watch him grow old, while I am ageless. I will hold his hand when he dies, yet I will live." Red tears brim around her eyes as she smirks.

"Like I said, fate's a bitch. I never planned this." She huffs that same humorless laugh. "I never wanted this. I never thought I'd have someone to love. And now that I have it, I'm not sure that I should. I wasn't made for this. It's not what I am." Her voice turns hard at the end and it makes my body stiffen with fear. She's a roller coaster of emotion ranging from disbelief to sadness and ending in anger. At first I'm taken aback by her honesty, but then I focus on what she said.

"You never thought you would love?" She can't truly mean that. "Do vampires not have the ability to love?"

She laughs, with real humor this time, and leans back in her seat while wiping away the blood rimming her eyes. I grimace inadvertently at the sight and unfortunately she sees my reaction.

"You don't know much about vampires, do you?"

"No. I'm sorry, I didn't—" She cuts me off before I can fully apologize.

"I've been a vampire for nearly two hundred years and I still despise some aspects of our species." She wipes her fingers on a tissue and places it on the desk as if she knows she'll need it again before trashing it; the bright red is vibrant against the stark white. "If I could change it, I would."

"You're two hundred years old?" Holy fuck. I don't have enough self-control to contain my shocked expression.

"Something like that." Her voice is flat. Then she tilts her head and a glint of happiness sparkles in her eyes. "Would you like to know how I came to be immortal? How I was changed?" Her smile widens, revealing her sharp white fangs. "I wasn't always like this." She shakes her head. "Vampires are a capricious species."

I clear my throat. From what I learned of vampires in school, that sounds about right. But then again, humans in general don't know much about them.

"Tell me." She quirks a brow and I suppress my smile. "Please." Her grin grows as we share a knowing look.

"I was a little older than twenty. I don't remember what day my birthday was because it's been so damn long. I was unmarried because I had been raised religious and thought I would become a nun. The day everything changed happened sometime around summer. I know that because there was a big thunderstorm that had just passed through our area, and where I lived the rainy season began in June." She rocks gently, glancing out the window as if watching her recollection playing out before her like she's watching a movie.

"I was in the rainforest foraging for my grandmother. She sent me out all the time to gather things. My mother and father had both passed away when I was a baby, leaving me alone with my grandmother to raise me by herself. She was in good health for her age and took care of me as any mother would." A sad smile pulls at her lips. "She always said I looked like my mother." That humorless huff of a laugh erupts from her throat. "I don't remember her at all. I used to be able to, but it was so long ago that I can't even picture her face anymore." Veronica falls silent as she tries and fails to recall her memory.

"I'm sorry." My voice brings her back to the present. Her dark eyes find mine and her grin returns.

"Don't be, dear. My first twenty years were good years.

Even if I suffered loss, I was still grateful for my life." She visibly swallows. "At least until that day." I settle into my seat as I watch her pull her legs into her body. "I was gathering pandan leaves in the rainforest when I found some mangoes. They were delicious; I remember that well. They were nearly overripe but I'd cut one open to taste it. Fruit is best when it's almost too sweet, don't you think? It was a little treat for me. A reward for going out for my grandmother."

Her smile fades and her voice drops as she continues her tale. "I traveled to my usual area, where I knew I'd be able to find most of what she'd asked for. I was at the last pandan plant with only half of my basket full. I knew she'd need more leaves, so I went out a little farther. There was a large clearing and on the other side I spotted more bushes. The storm the previous night had left downed trees and broken branches in its wake, but somehow this clearing had been spared. It was so pretty. Undisturbed with dewdrops clinging to everything and sparkling in the light. So pure. I almost felt bad crossing through it to get to the other side." She gently shakes her head again and swallows. "But no one lived close to us and I didn't think I'd ruin it for anyone but myself. So I continued into the other side until my basket was full." Her lips pull down in a frown. "I knew my grandmother would be grateful. She would've been so happy to have a full basket."

Leaning forward in my seat, I clasp my hands. A hard pit forms in my stomach and my blood chills. I can tell I'm not going to like what I hear next. She clears her throat, but her dark eyes stay focused on her nails, tracing over the grain pattern in the walnut desk. She nods her head slowly. "I knew something bad was going to happen when I got back to the clearing. I could see so many large footprints in the dirt. They came from the left. I remember thinking there may have been four of them." The red tears brim in her eyes and spill over, trailing streaks of blood down her light brown skin. I part my lips, but before I can speak, she continues. "They were werewolves. I saw them shift in front of me. Well, two did. Two didn't." Her breath hitches.

"I don't have to tell you everything they did. But know that I didn't value my life afterward. I wished they'd just killed me. Instead, they left me mangled and damaged after they'd had their way with me. I was covered in bruises and bleeding out from the injuries they'd inflicted on me. Some of the plants I'd gathered had medicinal qualities; I used them to staunch my wounds. I still don't know how I made it back without dying. It was the longest journey of my life. Part of me wanted to stay and just succumb, but I was so scared they would come back."

"Where did you go?" I whisper the question, not sure I want to hear more but knowing I have to.

"Back to my grandmother's. Where else could I have gone? It was two hundred years ago. There were no phones to call for help. We lived in such a remote area, there were no hospitals nearby. The shamans in our area had all left due to religious persecution. There was no one but her." Her sad smile returns and she laughs before she tells me, "She scolded me. When she heard the door open, she yelled from the kitchen that I'd scared her and to never do that again. And then she came out and saw me.

"She looked so broken when she saw me. When she saw my bruised body and she realized what happened. I was barely clothed and covered in blood. My grandmother was a truly devout Catholic. She said the church would help us, that they would know what to do." She reaches across the desk for the crumpled tissue and regains some of her composure before continuing. "It took forever to reach the local priest, but he accused me of making everything up. That I must have imagined what I saw and experienced because werewolves would never do such a thing." She straightens and faces me. "They were supposed to protect us. We had a pact with them. Apparently they were allowed to do whatever they wanted so long as the vampires were kept at bay. What happened to me was nothing more than a small sacrifice in exchange for the security they provided." Her dark eyes harden as she spits out, "That's what the priest told me. 'It was a small sacrifice to pay!' That's the day I started to hate everyone. My grandmother was the only one who wanted justice. No one else dared to confront the wolves." She calms herself and wipes her eyes again. I can't even fathom her pain. To live through something so monstrous and survive, only to experience a horrible betrayal—my heart breaks for her with the injustice of it all.

"She died a few weeks later. I think the church's refusal to intervene was too hard on her. She was so angry at everyone else and felt like she had failed me, even though there was nothing she could have done differently. Her heart just couldn't take it. So I was left on my own, on the outskirts of the town. I lived in fear that the shifters would come back. One night I thought they did. I thought they'd come for me again." A wicked glint shines in her brown eyes. "But it wasn't the wolves." Her dark red, plump lips form an evil smirk. The look on her face is one of a scorned woman who's reaped her revenge. "No, it was three vampires. They'd come to kill everyone." She tilts her head and I hear her neck crack as she reclines in her seat and crosses her legs. Her characteristic collected facade replaces the emotional woman who I'd just been sitting with.

"They were going to kill me. Most of the town had already been slaughtered. They decided to punish everyone who'd sided with the wolves. Not that we had much of a choice in the matter of what the werewolves did. Obviously. When they saw me, they smiled. Like we were old friends. They'd heard what the wolves had done and offered me a choice: death or the chance to have vengeance. If I'd been smart, I would have chosen death. But then again, fate wouldn't have been able to curse my poor pup had I died all those years ago."

"You'd rather have died than become a vampire?"

She shakes her head and purses her lips. "Not now, no. But the things I did, all out of hate and to get revenge ..." Her dark eyes narrow as she meets my stare. "There can be no forgiveness for all the innocent lives I've taken and all the times I sat back and watched as my coven ravaged villages for sport."

"Does your coven still ..." I swallow hard, not able to get out the rest of the words.

"My old coven, I'm not sure. If they do, then they must be keeping quiet about it. The Authority has no use for those who make messes they have to clean up."

"So your old coven is the one who trained you. Natalia?"

"Natalia's a bitch." Her voice is hard and dripping with spite. "She was there when I was made a vampire. She taught me some things, although she's not as good as she thinks she is. Hate motivated me for decades, but when the years pass like days, you learn to let some things go in the name of self-interest. Natalia's still fueled by malice. I've no idea why, but I tired of her antics long before I'd even left that coven."

"What about your current coven?" Part of me is intrigued, wanting to meet more vampires and hear their stories; the other part is terrified.

"They're ... vampires. There's not much to say beyond that truth." She stands up and heads to the door, opening it just before Vince enters. "You took your time, didn't you?"

He only huffs a humorless laugh, each hand holding a coffee. Vince's silver eyes find mine and he smiles, although it's subdued. "Hey, Grace," he says. Veronica may seem the same as she did before last night, but something has shifted in Vince. Something darker, something more careful.

Veronica asks Vince to give me my drink and holds the door open, telling me, "You can go now."

"I was really hoping to talk to you a bit more." Glancing between the two of them, I'm left feeling like an intruder.

"I'm happy you came to see me, sweet mate of my Alpha, but Vince will take care of me." Vince looks up from setting her coffee on the dresser and gives Veronica a semblance of a smile.

"I've got her, Grace." I feel the need to pry and protect Veronica, even if she doesn't think she needs it, but something in me settles and I know that I can leave them be. Something deep inside me is telling me that Vince will heal her. He is her mate. As I head back to the east wing of the estate, I expect the knot to form in my chest, objecting to my leaving. I rub my chest as I walk back to my room, waiting for the pull, but it never comes.

CHAPTER 3

DEVIN

"What does your coven want with the blood bank?" My hardened and blunt tone doesn't seem to bother Veronica. Good. I'm glad she's taken to her position in the pack easily enough. Unlike my mate, who's still finding her feet and second-guessing herself. She's doing well, though.

It's not until Veronica answers that I realize my thoughts have drifted to Grace yet again. Even with treachery at hand and the threat of war, all I do is think about Grace. *I'm an obsessed wolf.*

"There isn't nearly enough blood to sustain our coven. We don't venture into human territory much and we don't reside near wildlife." Her nose scrunches in distaste. "More than that, purchasing blood from the Authority costs far too much for far too little." Her sharp nails tap on the counter once before she adds, "It seemed wiser to go directly to the banks."

"You have to order the blood for the coven?" It's difficult to keep my expression impassive. Much about vampires remains a mystery, even to other supernatural species. So long as laws aren't broken, they aren't required to divulge any information regarding any aspects of their way of life. There are plenty of whispers, though ...

"We don't *have* to order blood. But most of the humans won't sell theirs and like I said, our sources for acquiring it are limited."

"What about having a personal ..." I leave the remaining words unspoken.

"Drinking from humans? From their necks? It's been outlawed, as I'm sure you know."

"And your coven abides by the law?"

She swallows thickly, her gaze dropping for a fraction of a second before she nods.

"I see." When I see him, I'll be sure to ask Alec about the blood they sell to the covens. If they're drugging blood from the humans' blood banks, then I'm certain they'd be tainting the blood they sell to the covens as well. A tic in my jaw spasms. Thank fuck we don't drink that shit, but Veronica might.

"And do you plan on drinking the blood from the banks?" I don't miss that her body stills and tenses. "I *need* to know."

Not only for her protection; I need to be sure she isn't a part of this scheme to poison other immortals. I'm fairly certain she has nothing to with it, but the way she glances at Vince and instinctively touches her neck where his claiming bite is, has my stomach knotting. As if she thinks being his mate will protect her if she's a part of anything as fucked as tainting blood.

Drawing herself to her full height, Veronica responds loud enough for Vince to hear, "If you'd rather I didn't drink from him—"

"Fuck that! What the fuck, Devin?" Vince's aggression takes me by surprise but as always, my face stays expressionless. My eyes narrow as they meet his and he backs down, no doubt feeling my anger.

"I want her to drink from me." His hands fist at his sides, but he relaxes them, reining in the initial indignation.

"He's your Alpha." Veronica's hushed words seem to relax him a bit. As Vince comes closer, sidling up to the counter in the kitchen, Veronica's hand gentles on his arm. The touch is light but meaningful.

"This has nothing to do with her drinking from you." A look of relief flashes across Veronica's face. It appears she was only worried I'd make her stop drinking from Vince. Instantly her posture relaxes.

"Good. I want her to," Vince answers and then slides out a stool, the legs of it scraping against the floor as he does.

"So, you two are breaking the law?" I allow a little lightheartedness to enter my voice so Vince will calm the hell down.

Vince nods, letting a smirk grace his lips as he nods at me. "I'm a rulebreaker, Alpha," he jokes, but Veronica is less flippant.

"My entire coven is breaking the law. Most are pissed about the decree, but Natalia is essentially an inquisitor. She regularly visits our queen and the heads of the other covens. I was sent to observe members of the Authority after the queen's son was taken and punished for disobeying Natalia."

"He drank from a human?"

She nods. Vince's attention is focused on Veronica now, the reality sinking in hard that the Authority may step in. His anxiety and anger mix into a cocktail that's practically fucking palpable.

"Where did they take him?"

"To the Authority. To their dungeon. He was given a thousand lashes."

"A thousand?" The surprise is evident in Vince's voice. "A thousand silver lashes?"

She nods once and adds, "He was nearly dead when Natalia brought him back."

"For drinking from a vein?" How the hell is that reasonable?

"He did it in front of Natalia. The bitch had two enforcers take him in the middle of the night. Had they been seen, it would have been war. When she returned him, my queen nearly sent the entire coven to exact vengeance on the Authority. But she put her emotions in check, realizing it wouldn't have been wise. Not when we're so greatly outnumbered."

Vince's pulse still races. Not from fear of lashes, but from the danger his mate is in by staying at a coven clearly on the Authority's radar. His thoughts race but I silence them with a wave of my dominance as his Alpha.

"They allowed this?" I can't fathom that Alec would allow such violence. A thousand lashes just for drinking from a vein. Before she can reply, I ask, "The person offering the vein, they were willing?"

"She was willing. She's his partner. What's even more offensive is that Natalia violates the law herself. She only drinks from a vein, I know she does." I consider her words as she shakes her head.

"How do you know?"

"I've seen her do it for over a century now." Vince wraps his arm around Veronica's waist and pulls her closer to him. She leans into his touch, her hip nestled against him. A smile threatens at the sight of the two of them on agreeable terms after last night, but I hold back.

I don't know what happened between them, but she didn't run like I thought she might.

Perhaps she feels more for him than she lets on. Or perhaps her coven is truly in need.

Desperate times and desperate measures ...

"So that's why your queen sent you. Because her hand is being forced by the coven?" She nods once at my question. "And is it solely Natalia that's pushing the issue?"

"Mostly, but she has the backing of the other members. When they came to collect and imprison Stephan, she brought nearly a dozen other vampires with her."

"Was Alec there?" I hesitate to ask, but I have to make sure before I go to meet with him.

"No, only the vampires of the Authority." If I remember correctly, there are fourteen who are members of the Authority. That's more than most covens.

"Thank you, Veronica. Vince."

He immediately responds, "Yes, Alpha?" That's a much better tone, although he's tense. His emotions are unsteady and I consider him for a moment before speaking. I decide to let his anger from earlier go unchecked. After all, I've heard having a vampire drink from you can be quite an experience. She's his mate and he's made his boundaries clear. I'll respect that.

"Are you sparring today?"

He nods and elaborates, "Dom and Caleb are going to go at it. I have to be around to see that." He glances at his mate and smiles. "And I thought it would be fun for them to see what Veronica can do."

I nod in agreement. Natalia taught Veronica, so I have no

doubt she can handle herself just fine.

"I'll have to watch her at some point as well." First I'll speak with Alec. Too much right now is uncertain. Alec will tell me what I need to know, and then I'll be able to take action. I'm responsible for the pack and my mate needs safety above all else.

Chapter 4

Dom

Lizzie looks so fucking small on the sparring platform. My mate, my gorgeous mate. Last night was a damn dream come true. Holding her in my arms while I rutted into her tight pussy. I've waited all my life for her. She's mine now and she's eager to have me. A low, rumbling growl barrels through my chest at the memory of her soft whimpers and loud moans of pleasure. An asymmetric grin pulls at Caleb's chest when he hears the animalistic sound rip through me. She took us both just as she was made to.

"Fucking perfect." He mutters in my head so only I can hear him. *"You think this is going to work?"*

I shrug my shoulders.

"I have no idea, but it's worth a shot." We decided last night that teaching Lizzie to spar may help bring her wolf out again. She's only felt her the one time since the offering and although I'm happy her wolf returned, it's fucking tearing up my sweet little mate.

She's been traumatized and her wolf abandoning her is a reminder of that. No matter how much she smiles and pretends it doesn't get to her, she wants her wolf to come back and stay. She wants to shift so badly; I know she does. I have no idea if she'll ever be able to, but I'll do everything I can to help her.

"Well, even if it doesn't coax her wolf out to play, she'll at least learn how to fight," Caleb comments and his thoughts turn darker. It's a side of Caleb I'm not comfortable with even if Lizzie is.

"You better not fucking bruise her." My statement, whispered aloud, carries a thinly veiled threat.

Caleb's reaction is dismissive. *"Have you seen our mate? I'm not the only one who's fucked up in our pairing, and if it's what she craves—"*

"We should've taken it easier on her."

"You didn't exactly think that last night," he rebuts.

The low growl is repressed as I tear my gaze from his. Shuffling my feet and kicking the floor, I avoid the sight of Lizzie's neck as guilt washes over me. Her hips are covered in bruises from where we gripped her, and her neck is covered in bites and bruises. Both of our marks are an angry red color.

I confess to him, *"I wish her wolf would come heal her. I hate seeing her so fucking wounded."*

"It might happen. It might not ... but she fucking loved it."

His comment doesn't help loosen the growing knot in my chest. He continues, *"Did you see her looking at herself this morning? She was delighted to see our marks."* His shoulder bumps into mine as he speaks. *"She'll heal up nice and the only thing that'll be left are two silver claiming marks on her neck. Proof she's ours."*

Imagining her beautiful slender neck with our scars on her makes my chest puff out in pride with a warmth spreading through me.

"Damn right she's ours." At my inner words, Lizzie glances over to us and smiles while walking toward the edge of the platform. Her leggings are practically painted on and her sports bra leaves nothing to the imagination. I'm hard again just looking at her.

"So which one of you two is going to fight me?" Her tone is flirtatious and a blush creeps up her chest to her cheeks as her gaze slips from mine to Caleb's.

"Both of us." Caleb's answer doesn't lack an ounce of sex appeal and she bites into her bottom lip, rocking slightly on her feet.

The flirtation is ... well, it works her up. But he's out of his damn mind.

"She can't handle both of us," I tell him.

He chuckles at my words as he climbs into the ring and it takes me a moment to register why. When I do, I let out a huff of a laugh.

"She won't be able to fight either of us off right now, but she'll learn." He answers me loud enough for her to hear.

"All right." I concede and follow Caleb onto the platform just as I see Veronica and Vince heading our way. A prick of unease flows through me. Vince has been … off. He's bothered, and we can all feel it.

"Showtime isn't until later. We're training our baby girl first," Caleb calls out to them.

With the arrival of guests, Lizzie seems to second-guess our plans.

"Can I just watch?" Her tone makes it obvious she's a bit hesitant to get physical.

"Nope. You gotta learn a little something first." Caleb's answer is immediate and casual, but as I remind him, she's been through a lot. Anything could trigger a trauma response. I want to avoid that if possible.

"I'm scared," she barely whispers as Veronica and Vince come up to the platform.

"Nothing to be scared of, baby." He kisses her left cheek. It's only a peck, but it soothes her instantly. The bond between mates will do that and the anxiousness I feel also dissipates.

"Fine." She draws her shoulders back and raises her little

fists while backing up to the edge of the platform. "But I want a kiss for every punch I get in."

I chuckle at the sight of her. Our sweet mate has a lot to learn.

"First of all, don't back yourself into a corner. Never," I say.

Caleb nods his head in agreement with me and adds, "It's even worse when you're outnumbered. Now get your ass back here."

She immediately walks back to join us at the center of the ring. He moves her easily, so that she's facing away from us. "So I should just stand here and wait?" she asks.

Caleb eyes her ass as he answers and then slips his hands around her hips before kissing her neck once again. "If you can't run, yes. Wait for your opponent to attack and watch carefully so you can block. Take your attacker off guard. If you can get in the first hit, make sure you make contact and really hurt them. Make it worth the energy."

"So if I can't run, hit first—" She's paying attention, even if Caleb appears to be preoccupied with other thoughts.

"Only hit if you can get a good hit in. If not, then you wait so you can block." Caleb interrupts her and I nod at his words although she can't see.

"How will I know if it'll be a good hit?"

"If you have easy access to the eyes, nose, throat or groin, then take the shot."

"Turn around and watch," I command her and she obeys

instantly.

I put my hand up to Caleb's nose with my palm out and motion upward. "Like this, little one. That'll break the nose and push the bone into the brain."

Caleb turns sideways and elbows me in the gut. "Or shove your elbow right here. Clasp your hands and push with all your weight." The move knocks the wind out of me, but I only smile. "Cheap shot," I grunt.

"You want to try to land a hit instead of waiting for us to come from behind?"

She nods and says, "Yeah, let me try." Our little mate licks her lower lip, excitement running through her. It's a good sign.

"Any hint this has turned into anything ... alarming ... and I'm calling it off," I remind Caleb internally.

"Agreed," he answers back.

"All right," I offer to Lizzie, "I'm going to block it, but don't stop." She takes a deep breath and tries to palm strike my nose, but she's too damn slow and I'm able to snatch her wrist without much effort at all. "Faster, little one. Make it count."

She purses her lips when I release her hand, her eyes narrowing at the challenge. "But you know it's coming."

I nod my head at her deflated tone.

Caleb's arms are crossed over his chest as he tells her, "Your attackers may expect you to attack also. You have to be quick."

Appearing dejected, she rocks back and forth with her eyes on the ground. I part my lips and take a small step forward ready to comfort her, and that little hand of hers comes up from fucking nowhere and she actually lands the blow.

Square against my nose.

"Fuck!" My hands fly to my face. The stinging pain makes me wince and I think I'm bleeding.

Caleb's laughing his ass off and Vince is doing the same. I glance over to see Veronica full-on grinning, Vince's arm wrapped around her waist.

"Your girl got a hit on you, Dom. You a big softy now that you're mated?"

"Come on up here, Vince, and find out." That wipes the smile off his face; only for a second, though.

"Are you okay?" my mate questions softly. I don't miss the fact she's having second thoughts about this plan to coax out her wolf and her wide blue eyes are shining with vulnerability.

"Of course," I tell her and lean forward, giving her a peck on the right cheek, a twin kiss to match the one Caleb gave her earlier. Grinning down at her I add, "Now I know both you and Caleb take cheap shots."

That makes her genuinely smile and seeing her beautiful face light up fills my chest with warmth. The moment's interrupted, though ... by her other mate.

"Good job, baby girl." Caleb gives her another small kiss on her cheek before raising his arms and getting into a boxing stance. "Now come get me, baby."

He looks ridiculous.

Lizzie just stands there shyly looking between the two of us. "You sure it's okay, Dom?" she says.

I chuckle at her concern and wipe my nose. The pain's already gone and I can feel it's mostly healed. "Yeah, little one. You did good. Now give me a kiss and don't ask again." She walks easily to me and brushes those soft, sweet lips of hers against mine. A rumble of satisfaction settles in my chest. I take a step back. "I wasn't expecting that one. You did well to take advantage of the situation and catch me off guard."

"Now we're ready, baby. Come on. It's not going to be easy." Caleb motions her forward and she practically lunges at him, aiming for his nose again. Caleb's quick to wrap his arms around her shoulders in a bear hug and tries to pull her into his chest to capture her, she quickly spins around so her back is to him. Shifting her hips, she drives an elbow into his side putting all her weight behind it. She moves fast. Faster than a human.

Caleb grunts and drops to the floor while I let out a bark of a laugh. I feel myself smile. Her eyes catch mine as I laugh and she stands confidently over Caleb's balled-up form.

Fuck, why does that turn me on like it does?

"You have such a beautiful smile," she tells me. Her kind words stoke the fire in me. I want nothing more than to pull her onto the ground and devour her body.

"Not now, jackass." Caleb's words resonate inside my head and snap me out of it. I walk forward to reward my little mate

with a kiss.

"You're a natural," I say. She leans into my touch and then looks to Caleb for a kiss from him. The small act makes me chuckle.

"Okay, how do I hit the groin? You didn't show me."

Oh, fuck that.

"Vince, get up here," I yell out to the now pale fucker who only stops laughing once I call his name.

"Nah, I'm good, man." I look at Caleb and open my mouth, but he beats me to the punch.

"I got the last hit. You can take this one." He walks to our little mate and kisses her cheek. "Hit him hard, baby. If you can get a knee to his groin, you'll get him on the ground for sure."

Lizzie's hesitant to ask something but before I can tell her to say whatever's on her mind she asks, "Are you two letting me get these hits in?"

I shake my head adamantly, as does Caleb. "Not at all. I wasn't ready for that. You're much faster than I expected." His fingers brush the hair back away from her face while he leans forward and whispers to her, "You're as fast as a wolf. I didn't expect that." A blush creeps up her chest and into her cheeks.

"My turn," Veronica calls out from below. "You three obviously need a break before you start giving the two of us a different kind of show. Come, pup, I want to see what kind of damage you can do."

I take Lizzie's small hand in mine. "It will be good for

you to watch." My eyes find Vince's. "And I'll enjoy watching Vince's mate beat the shit out of him." Caleb laughs on the other side of Lizzie before he pulls her hand to his mouth for another kiss.

She loves it when we kiss her. It keeps her smiling, keeps her happy. I imagine it keeps her thoughts from going elsewhere.

"Can we do it again after them?" Lizzie asks as we climb down.

"Of course. Especially now that we know you have some natural ability. Let's just take a moment, all right?"

"I'm happy she took that as well as she did." I speak to Caleb in my head.

"Yeah, that's our mate, though. She's such a wild spitfire."

"Sometimes, but other times she's so shy."

"Well, she did just meet us, Dom. She's gotta have some time to open up." He has a good point. *"And I think she's doing wonderfully."* I nod at his silent words.

He drops her hand to wrap his arm around her waist, pulling her into him and slightly away from me. Her hand squeezes mine and it gives me enough satisfaction to not be jealous of his possessive move.

"You did great, baby. Next time we'll be ready for you, though." She blushes as he whispers into her ear. Settling down on the ground next to Lizzie, I look up to see Veronica and Vince circling each other. "This should be a good show." I pull Lizzie closer to me and Caleb grins as he sits on her other side, knowing exactly what I'm doing. He can deal with me pulling cheap shots too.

He leans back resting on his forearms and concentrates on the two sparring. "Vampires are faster than us. Much faster, but we have far more strength than they do," I say. Lizzie nods, acknowledging my words.

I watch her pale blue eyes widen as Veronica lands a blow to Vince's chest before dropping to the ground to avoid Vince's attempt to grab her. She slides easily between his wide-legged stance and stands behind him, landing a kick to his back before he's even registered what's happened. He lands on all fours but quickly recovers, leaping and spinning in midair to snatch her wrist as she strikes. She's completely unaffected by his hold and lands a punch to his throat, right on his Adam's apple. The blow makes him loosen his grip on her enough for her to jump back to the other side of the ring as his hands fly to his throat. Vince growls his frustration and the two circle each other again.

The first round goes to Veronica. By a long shot.

"Holy shit, it's like a blur," Lizzie breathes out the words, clearly in awe.

"Yeah," I answer, equally impressed although I expected this. Still, it's something else to watch a vampire move and fight. The unease from earlier returns.

"Do you see how she kept fighting without hesitation? He had a grip on her, but she didn't let that stop her attack." I speak quietly into Lizzie's ear while she continues to watch. "You need to have that same tenacity. Never stop fighting." I notice movement from the corner of my eye and I glance at Caleb as he nods his head and smiles.

"Never stop fighting, baby."

She smiles at his words, but immediately winces as Veronica kicks Vince hard in the chest. The telltale crunch of broken ribs resonates in the air.

Vince is knocked off-balance from the hit. Dropping to one knee, he's able to grab her ankle. She brings her other leg back and nearly lands another vicious kick to his face, but Vince tackles her to the platform with her beneath him. His crushing weight pins her in place. He releases her leg and reaches for her waist as she wriggles under him in an effort to get free. They wrestle for a moment and he pulls her hips toward his with a strong grip. Just as he smiles, thinking he's won, she throws her elbow back and it lands hard on his nose.

"Oh fuck," Caleb comments, his hand moving to his nose in empathy.

She's ruthless, and her skills are designed to take advantage of the natural instinct to protect the sensitive areas she targets.

"Oh!" Lizzie's hands flies to her nose too as she grimaces. Yeah, I know that fucking hurt. Vince doesn't release Veronica, though, which is obviously what she was counting on. Instead he drops all his weight onto her and his head lays against her back, caging her in. She struggles beneath him for a moment before realizing he's got her pinned. Despite her formidable fighting ability, she's physically outclassed in such a vulnerable position by his massive strength.

I barely hear Vince say "Gotcha" in a playful tone and then he kisses the crook of her neck. Veronica continues to struggle, though. Her breathing picks up until it's nearly panicked. Looking at Caleb, both confusion and concern are apparent on his face. Lizzie's shoulders hunch and she stirs uncomfortably between us.

"Get off of me!" Veronica shouts and pushes forcefully against Vince's massive frame. He props himself up on his knees, lifting his chest off of her back. In a blur of motion almost too quick to follow, she moves to stand on the other side of the ring.

Vince holds both his hands up while he stays still on his knees. "It's just me." Her shoulders rise and fall as her breathing slowly evens out. Slowly, he gets off the ground and walks calmly to her as if she's a cornered animal.

She swallows and shakes out her hair. "I know. I know." He takes her hand and leads her to the stairs.

"What the hell was that about?" I ask Vince in my head.

"Don't worry about it. I'll take care of her." I nod my head slightly as they walk past us. Lizzie looks to Veronica with concern in her eyes, but the vampire stares straight ahead, obviously still shaken and embarrassed by her reaction.

"She'll be all right, little one." I kiss her soft lips as Caleb rises.

"Come on, baby girl. We're going to show you how to block like Vince should've done." I snort at his words and help our little mate up, who's still watching Veronica leave.

CHAPTER 5

VINCE

Veronica scowls when she sees the bed, her spine stiffening and she says, "You think you can chain me, pup?" There's humor in her voice and a little smirk on those beautiful full lips.

I love that nickname she's given me. *Pup.* The way the word spills from her lips makes my own lift in an asymmetric grin.

With every heavy step I take toward the pair of handcuffs dangling from the headboard, she follows behind me. I push aside the black velvet covering the cuffs so she can see the metal underneath. "They're silver. You won't be able to break out of these, babe." A thump in my chest makes me second-guess what I'm doing as she gasps and then goes still. It's hard to swallow with the flash of betrayal that lights across her eyes. Only for a moment, though. She needs this. She needs me to be a worthy mate. One who will heal her as much as she's already healed me.

With her gaze focused on the bright metal, she noticeably swallows. Her dark eyes find mine while she shakes her head slightly.

My tone is soothing and I add a hint of playfulness although that thump in my chest happens again. "Don't you trust me, baby?"

She hesitates, merely staring at the cuffs in my hand. Eventually she settles on a muttered truth spoken just beneath her breath. "I don't want to do this."

I know she doesn't, but after seeing her triggered and scared again today, I'm not going to wait to show my mate she can trust me.

"How about if I promise to give you the key and do everything you command me to do?" I offer her. Her lips purse and she narrows her eyes. I need to sweeten the deal. "It's just me, baby. Just me and only for an hour." Her posture shifts slightly, but she keeps her arms crossed tight over her chest. "Just one hour," I say softly, taking a step closer to her. My hand rests on her shoulder, but only for a moment before she leaves me.

Her dark eyes find mine again before she clicks her tongue and walks over to trail her fingers along the velvet covering the silver cuffs.

"I tied it up here too, in case you want to grip it. There's no way it'll touch your skin, baby." Her fingers slip inside the cuff. They're quality, the best I could find, and nicely padded. They won't hurt her at all.

"Why?" she questions.

"You're afraid of giving up control ... even when it comes to your mate."

Swallowing thickly, she stares back at me, the truth of my words sinking deep into her.

"I only exist for you. I would die for you. And you don't trust me." It fucking kills me to say it out loud. "I have to do something, Veronica."

"Fine," she states with an elegance and finality only a woman like her can deliver. "Do it quickly before I change my mind."

I smirk at her response, even as I see her shoulders rise and fall with her deep intake of breath, the deep red silk shining in the dim light as she does. She doesn't wait for me to undress her as she sits at the foot of the bed and lies back with her wrists lifted above her head. The thin straps of her nightgown slide down her shoulders and she doesn't bother to pull them back into place.

She'll have plenty of slack until I get to her legs.

Any bit of heated excitement turns bitterly cold as I watch her hold her breath and close her eyes when the cuffs snap in place around her dainty wrists. With a heaviness I never imagined I'd feel when it came to my mate, I tug the handcuffs to ensure they're snug and secure before moving to the cuffs at the foot of the bed.

The room is quiet. So quiet, the click of the last shackle locking around her ankle sounds impossibly loud. A shudder runs through her body as I take her in.

A gorgeous vampire, laid out on my bed clad in only a thin whisper of silk that hides next to nothing from me. My hand gentles on her calf as I prepare to test her restraints, but she beats me to it, yanking against the restraints.

"Key." She says the single word with authority although a hint of panic lingers.

I give her a tight smile and prepare myself for her wrath with gritted teeth as I slip the key in between her lips. Instantly her eyes widen as she spits the key out. "Give me the key!" Heated anger I've never felt from her before radiates off her. So much so, my wolf retreats.

She yells again, the pain and desperation she's feeling coming through clearly as I pick the key up off the floor and move closer to place it back in her mouth.

Her gorgeous frame struggles against the chains, but her arms don't move far enough to reach me. Even if she had the key in her hands, she'd be unable to unlock the cuffs. She's utterly at my mercy and I can see the moment she realizes she needs me to free herself. Sadness and betrayal flash across her face; in that instant I nearly regret my decision.

"You fucking dog!"

"It's just for one hour." My voice is soft, but stern. She needs this. She hisses at my simple statement. "I'm still yours, Veronica. I'll do whatever you say."

"Untie me!"

"Anything but that." Her nostrils flare and her face reddens with rage. Her wrists pull against the restraints to no avail.

"If you come near me to do anything else ... anything but untie me ..." she trails off as I take a deep breath and lean close to kiss her cheek. Close enough for her to strike me with her fist across my jaw, which she does. I pull back, but I'm not far enough away to miss the second swing. The sharp, metallic tang of blood coats my mouth.

Fuck, my mate knows how to fight and make every blow count. The burning heat from her punches jolts me backward. I nearly fall off the bed, but I steady myself. "Babe, that hurt." I pinch my nose to stop the bleeding and straighten it before it heals crooked. Drops of blood fall to the comforter. As I feel my nose mending, I hear her sobs.

"Vince." She whimpers my name in between gasps. "Vince, I'm so sorry. Vincent."

Still hunched over, I wait until the pain of the blows has passed, until physically it no longer exists. It's only a memory.

I wipe my nose with the back of my hand and lean forward to kiss her on her tearstained cheek.

"Please forgive me. Forgive me, Vince, please. I'm so sorry. I—"

I cut her off, pressing her plump lips to mine and caress her face. "It's all right, baby. I knew you wouldn't like this. I knew ..."

She shakes her head with her eyes shut tight and her lips pressed together, muting her panicked cries.

"It's not okay. It's not okay." Her words are rushed, a new panic taking over. "Vince, I'm sorry. I'm so sorry. I'm not okay."

I stroke her cheek until she opens her eyes and finds my silver gaze. "I forgive you, baby."

"I'm scared." She whispers the words before another tortured sobs erupts from her throat and she pulls against the chains again.

"It's all right, my love. I'm going to take care of you. I'm going to prove to you that you can trust me." Leaning in close, I kiss her again. Her mouth parts to grant me entry and I suckle her top lip before running my tongue along her sharp fangs.

"Please, Vince, I can't." She shakes her head and her deep brown eyes, rimmed in red, plead with me.

"I'm sorry, I can't. Not yet." Her head drops in defeat as she slowly nods and the sobs subside. "Give me a command, Veronica. I'm still yours."

Her dark eyes filled with red tears find mine and she says, "Hold me."

I lie down and settle my chest into her side before wrapping my powerful arms around her curves. I've never imagined her as this delicate before. I could easily crush her. She struggles against the shackles as another crying jag passes through her body; she trembles under my touch. A small part of me urges me to cave, not liking her reaction. My grip on her tightens. She needs this. She needs to learn to trust me. In time, I know she will.

"What do you want from me, Mistress?" I use her pet name, hoping that will calm her.

"I'm cold." Her softly uttered words contain a plea, not a command. Swallowing the lump in my throat, I pull the covers over our bodies and kiss the small dip in her throat.

"What else?" I need her to command me. I need her to find her strength.

"Just hold me." She sobs again and pulls against her chains as I lie back and gently place her head on my chest.

She cries silently. "I got you, babe. I promise." I barely speak the words, but my vow resonates through her, calming her. It hits me hard that she's not herself. She's not the strong, confident woman I know. She's so damn wounded. "I got you." I kiss her shiny black hair and let her cry.

Next time will be better. Next time I'll push her a little more. Until there is nothing between us but trust. Until she doesn't fear a damn thing in this world. Until she knows I will love her in her worst moments and through it all.

PART II

BLINDED OBSESSION

CHAPTER 6

DEVIN

E very wall of Alec's office is lined with shelves that run from floor to ceiling. They hold a priceless collection of ancient books that no doubt contain information lost to civilization over time. The dark wood of antique furniture polished to a high shine, yet bearing the marks of history, adorns the office. In the very center of the three-story room sits a heavy desk with books stacked high upon its glossy surface. Two leather wingback chairs have been placed across from it. The pendant lamp above Alec's desk encompasses an open flame, matching the torches placed in sconces around the room.

If I wasn't aware that magic protects this space, I'd worry the texts would be in danger of being lost forever in a fire.

It is common knowledge, though, that this room is heavily guarded by powerful wards.

I take a seat across from him and the old leather groans in protest. We're nearly matched in our attire: dark slacks and simple button-down shirts. Although my clothes are custom tailored to fit my body perfectly. A pair of wire-rimmed glasses peek out from his shirt pocket and today he's opted for a navy blue tie.

It's not the first time I've come to visit him here, but this is the first time it's been to deliver bad news.

"I'd almost forgotten how comfortable these chairs are," I say as I sit back. Alec's emotions are easily read. He allows his aura to coat the air around him. He's peaceful and the comfort of his office makes it simple to follow his lead and adopt a relaxed nature. Vaguely I wonder if he already knows why I'm here.

With a grin that emphasizes the wrinkles around his eyes, he nods agreeably. "I prefer for my guests to feel at ease. Although, you don't seem as comfortable as I'd like."

"It would help if I was here for a different reason." His small smile slips a bit and the air turns cold, but only for a moment. He parts his lips, but a quiet knock at the door stops him from speaking.

A petite blond woman with an upturned nose pushes through the door using her backside as she carefully handles a silver tray loaded with teacups and a teapot. She turns and gracefully strides to the desk.

She sets the tray down gently, jostling the cups only the faintest bit. With a deep breath, she offers Alec a bright smile. Her dark brown eyes seek Alec's approval, shining with obvious affection. A humorous smirk plays at his lips and his light blue eyes find hers.

There's unmistakable romantic tension between them. So much so that I'm given the impression I'm intruding and I readjust in my seat.

"Thank you, dear."

Dear. My brow lifts, although I attempt to hide my reason.

Her gorgeous smile widens further as she leans across the desk to give him a peck on the cheek. I hurriedly avert my eyes as her blouse slips, revealing a bit more than I think she realized. All the sight of the two of them does, is remind me of my own mate. I already long for her.

It's not until I hear the click of the door closing that I'm brought back to the present.

Back to Alec and the matters at hand.

"She seems very nice." Alec grunts a response and lifts the teapot.

"Just sugar? Is my memory correct?" I nod and eye the old sorcerer in front of me. With a heavy sigh, he finally acknowledges the obvious. "She's quite nice. I enjoy her company."

"I think she enjoys yours as well." His eyes dart to the

door with longing before he clears his throat and passes me a teacup with its accompanying saucer.

The porcelain clinks and it doesn't escape me that the dainty dishes look completely out of place in my callused hands.

"Your message was very vague. What is it that you need, old friend?"

His blunt response and dismissal of the conversation regarding the woman seems forced. I'm not sure why he seems so touchy about discussing her further. He's the leader of the Authority. The most powerful man I know, human or otherwise. Not because his magic is so much greater than that of the others, but because of his connections.

If he wants something, he's given it without question. I consider asking about the girl, but instead I move on to business. If he wanted to confide in me, he would. Besides, I hate to interfere. Still, the agreeable air seems dampened since she left and I don't care for the change.

"I wish you wouldn't call me that. I'm not nearly as old as you." He chuckles, knowing it's all in good humor. I almost smile at the sorcerer, but with the heavy situation weighing down on my shoulders, my body stays stiff. "Do you have somewhere more private we could speak?" He tilts his head and opens a drawer to pull out a notepad. A pen flies from the drawer and into his open hand before he scribbles something on a sheet of paper.

Away from meddling ears?

I nod my head once, maintaining eye contact while I set the teacup down on the desk.

"Of course. Let's head to the woods, shall we?" He snaps his fingers and the world blurs for only a moment before I'm sitting in the same comfortable chair, my hands still wrapped around the armrests, but in front of me is a babbling creek.

The morning light filters through the leaves onto the damp ground as a gentle wind passes. The shade of a large oak tree grants us privacy. It's a calm place that brings back memories.

I knew he'd bring us here. It's where we used to meet when I was younger. Back when I relied on him to get my footing as Alpha of my territory. Back when I struggled and worried I had made too many mistakes, and that I would fail my pack.

As I swallow down the recollections, a branch crunches under Alec's tread. "You didn't bring your chair," I comment. My head whirls for the span of a slow blink and then I feel settled once again. As if the world hadn't vanished and reappeared with the snap of his fingers.

"I have a feeling I'll be needing to stand." I get up from my seat to join him. We stand side by side watching the water flow over the small rocks. "Which one is it?"

"Which one?" I know what he's hinting at, but I'd rather he say it.

"Which one didn't you want to hear?" His hands are fisted and the balmy air around us stirs with irritation.

"Natalia." I answer honestly.

"Why is that?" His eyes darken, as does the sky. His anger isn't directed at me but I have to remind myself of that as I continue. I'm aware I'm one of a handful whom Alec shows this side to. The emotional, the part of him not ruled by logic. He doesn't need to hide in a cloud of comfort around me. He knows that. The sunless sky and chilled breeze are oddly comforting.

He echoes what stirs inside of me.

"What do you know about the blood you sell to the covens?" I'm relying on the last words of a dead man, but I have no doubt there's truth in what he said. And I trust Veronica's word.

"What blood?" Genuine confusion laces his question.

My fists clench at his ignorance. How the hell could they be conducting business right under his nose without him knowing? A tic in my jaw spasms with anger.

"The blood she's pushing on the covens." My hard words come out low, reflecting my disappointment with him. The clouds turn dark gray and thunder rumbles in the distance.

"She isn't—"

"She is," I say, cutting him off, and the seriousness of the accusation stretches between us.

He scowls and cracks his neck. The wind picks up and the water of the creek seems to heat, the steam rising.

"How did she get that by you?" I stare at him with disbelief. Alec is not a force to be taunted and that's exactly what Natalia's doing. It's not wise of her, yet she's getting away with it.

"Things have been distracting me lately." He slowly regains his composure as he closes his eyes and controls his breathing. His fingers flex, the clouds slowly parting to reveal the sun again and the simmering water cools.

"Things? What kind of *things*?" He glances at me before settling his eyes back upon the free-flowing water. Whatever is bothering him needs to be taken care of immediately. His position as head of the Authority is one that many covet, and they would all kill to have his place. He's all too aware of that fact, as many have tried before.

"Another time for that tale, old friend." He's never hesitated before to confide in me. I square my shoulders as I face him and wait for his eyes to meet mine. A different anxiousness settles through me as doubt creeps into my thoughts.

"We are friends, aren't we, Alec?"

"We are." He smiles warmly at me. It eases my discomfort. "Friends and allies."

"You have many friends."

"No, I have few friends and many allies. They're quite different. You are a friend who happens to be my ally. I have few allies who happen to be my friends."

"That doesn't sound reassuring." He grunts a laugh before sitting on the grass, fiddling with his tie as he stares across the creek. I follow suit.

"It's not. Allies will only stand by you while you have something for them. While you hunger for the same."

"Out with it, Alec. I don't speak in code."

He smiles at my impatience. "Another time. Now, back to Natalia. You're sure of this?"

"I am. She seems to have the backing of the vampires in the Authority."

He nods in understanding.

"I figured; they all work together. It's no matter. They'll face the same consequence." Absently, he plucks two blades of grass and twirls them between his forefinger and thumb. I watch as they lengthen in his grasp, their pale green hue turning more vibrant as they grow.

"They're tainting the blood. I'm thinking they're behind the abduction of the vampires who have gone missing recently. I'm sure they need test subjects."

His breathing stills and another round of thunder booms through the air. He crumples the grass in his fist and the stalks wither, turning brown, dying before my eyes. "Tainting it with what?"

"According to the shifter from Sarin's pack, Natalia made a deal with them. Drugs in exchange for control of Shadow Falls. She wants the blood bank so she can taint the blood she's forcing other vampires to drink. It's a new drug that voids their immortality."

Alec stares at me with disbelief evident in his expression.

"I knew she was overstepping her boundaries with the vampires. But I had no idea she'd take it that far." His pale blue eyes search mine as he questions with a single breath, "Are you sure of this?"

"The shifter had nothing to gain and everything to lose by telling me this."

"We need to be certain, Devin. I can't get the backing of the rest of the Authority without irrefutable proof. This needs to be done quietly. No one can know. Not shifters, or vampires. And absolutely not the humans. There would be widespread panic." I already knew that would be his decision, but his sense of urgency regarding the matter is reassuring.

"I came prepared with a plan. Veronica's coven wants the blood bank, so we'll give it to them."

"And then?" His quizzical gaze meets mine.

"Then we'll have the ability to keep tabs on every move that is made."

Alec shakes his head. "This needs to happen quickly and quietly."

"I'll send her to her coven and gain permission for her to observe another town's bank. It'll be under the guise of seeing how things are done. A town where vampires have gone missing. Vince will go with her. Maybe he'll be able to tail them and sniff them out."

Alec nods once. "Do you need anything from me?"

"Not now, but when we're ready I'll need men to take

them down."

"You won't have to worry about that. Keep me informed. When we have proof, you'll have the rest of the Authority on your side. It will be more than enough." His light blue eyes find mine and he smiles faintly before telling me, "She will pay greatly for this; I promise you that."

CHAPTER 7

VERONICA

The kitchen appears to be the meeting place for the dogs. It seems they prefer this room to the others.

I glance at Dom and Caleb before quickly averting my eyes. My chest thumps and I struggle to restrain my heart from beating faster.

Embarrassment floods through me still.

I know they saw evidence that I'm not well. If I could go back to yesterday and hide it, I would. Instead I'm trapped here, on an estate run by werewolves who are more than aware of my weakness.

Vince slips a hand down my arm, his thumb rubbing soothing circles as if he knows exactly what I'm thinking. I offer him my hand over his, all the while pretending to listen to whatever joke Caleb is making.

I laugh when appropriate and do everything I can to avoid asking Vince what they're thinking. I already know; the sympathy is there every time Lizzie's eyes meet mine.

Focusing on keeping my breathing even, I slowly flex my hands under the table. My breath threatens to hitch and I start to slouch at the betrayal, but I keep my spine stiff and shoulders squared.

I wish he hadn't pinned me like that in front of them. I wish he wouldn't push me in private, let alone in front of them. I massage my wrists in my lap as anger consumes me. He fucking chained me.

The conversation continues without me. Devin needs to tell us what happened so I can get out of here. Back to the coven and back to safety.

Vince's large hand splays on my thigh; it's rough with calluses. My pup, my mate. My heart weakens at his touch.

The thought of leaving him behind has drifted to the forefront of my mind.

I know he only means to help me, but it's not working. It makes me feel weak and helpless to be anywhere near him. I refuse to be either.

I've worked too damn hard for nearly two centuries to be made so vulnerable. He hasn't lived my life and he'll never know what I've endured. There's no fix or cure.

His simple mind thinks love alone will fix this. I pull away from him, but he grips me harder and turns his head to face me. His silver stare bores into me, but I refuse to look back. My fingers tingle with the itch to touch him; my body wants me to crawl into his lap, but I won't. I shift in my seat so I'm sitting sideways. The move breaks the contact his hand had on my thigh and settles my back to him.

I look toward Devin, defying my mate and my own needs. His exhale is long and slightly shaken. My heart sinks knowing I've hurt him. I don't care, though. He knows what he did. He can deal with the consequences. He knows the immense pain he caused me. What happened in the room was too fucking much for me to give him my love right now. There's nothing but silence and damage between us now. I should have known this would happen.

The last of the wolves, Jude, filters in and the atmosphere changes instantly.

"I want to make this fast and simple." Devin takes a long breath, both of his hands resting on the edge of the counter. His shoulders flex and Caleb stops mid-conversation. "Save your questions until the end." He looks pointedly at his mate and she huffs, not quite in annoyance, but then gives a short nod. She's quite brazen for a little human. I rub my wrists again and look down remembering yesterday morning. Remembering how weak I was yet again for sharing something so personal, too personal, with her. I have no idea what made me want to talk to her. I wish I hadn't. They know too much and I don't like it.

The name *Natalia* catches my attention and my eyes fly to meet Devin's as he speaks. "It appears Natalia and several of the vampires from the Authority are on a mission to eliminate any vampires opposing them."

A chill flows through me. I've suspected that for decades. I've felt she wished to reign over our species, to become the one true holder of authority. To have it spoken by someone else sparks a slight fear that my dreaded thoughts could become reality.

"What's the endgame there?" Dom asks.

"From what we've been told, Natalia wants to destroy their immortality," Devin replies.

A crease forms between my brow. *Destroy their immortality?* How is that even possible?

As if answering my unspoken question, Devin continues. "They're poisoning the blood from the donation centers and most likely the blood being sold to the covens." A mixture of fear and shock widens my eyes as I stare back at Devin's serious expression. His mate glances up at him, looking very much out of place.

It takes great effort to keep my lips shut tight although I want to bombard him with questions of how these allegations came to be. My gaze falls to Grace's laced fingers she's struggling to keep still as Devin delivers exactly what I want to know.

Her heart races and it doesn't escape me that she may feel what I feel in this moment.

"The shifter that attempted to take our mates told us they made a deal with a vampire. That they were going to cede control of Shadow Falls in exchange for a steady drug supply. Sarin's pack will deal with the consequences of their actions. But for now, Alec has asked for our help in proving the dead shifter's allegations are true.

"Veronica's coven wanted to make a deal with us to have a blood bank built in Shadow Falls." Devin's gaze settles on me and everyone else follows suit. "You'll go to your queen and let her know that we're willing to grant that request. No one will mention anything about what we've learned."

My lips part to object. I can't allow my coven to continue drinking tainted blood. Devin speaks before I can, though.

"No one, Veronica. Not one fucking word."

Vince stiffens beside me, but Devin doesn't hesitate to add, "If Natalia or any of the other vampires who are in on this find out that we know what they're up to, we'll be in danger. They will come to kill us and attack the allies we have within the Authority, or they will run. This is the best chance we have at stopping them."

Pressing my lips tightly together, I nod. I don't fucking like it, but I understand and I will obey because without his help, I have no way of knowing what is true and who to trust. Most don't adhere to the law anyway. I cling to that knowledge.

"What about Sarin's pack? Days have passed since the offering and we haven't heard anything," Caleb says.

"You'd think they'd give a shit that we killed four of their members." Jude's response to Caleb earns a nod from Dom.

Lev huffs and snorts before saying, "Yeah, right. Like they care."

"How are we going deal with them?" Dom's voice comes out hard.

"I should've ended him rather than let him run," Devin says, his brows pinching together as he drums his fingers along the table.

"What do we know of their pack?" I ask as I realize I don't know a single thing about the rival pack.

"They fled to a stronghold they have in the mountains. Maybe ten men remain; a few women too, I think," Devin tells us.

"They're weak now. We could easily take them," Caleb says.

Devin's fist slams on the granite countertops, forcing his mate to take a step back. "I will not risk our pack." He calms, softening his voice to add, "We cannot take on too much at once. Understood?"

The pack answers in unison, all but his mate, who peers up at him with uncertainty. Not weeks ago, this human had nothing to fear beyond mortal concerns. And now she's found herself on the brink of war, her fate tied to a mate who will lead us to it. Without looking back at her, Devin's hand reaches out for her and she takes his hand with both of hers.

"Jude, you'll scout out his pack. We don't know enough to go on the offensive. I want to know everything. Come back with intel and a plan of attack. We won't give them any mercy this time."

Jude acknowledges the command with "Yes, Alpha," and the attention turns to us.

"Vince and Veronica will go to her coven. Tell them I want to know how the blood banks are run and go to Still Waters. Three vampires have been abducted. Find them. I want to know everything that's going on. You have four days. No more than that. I also want you to take your fucking cell phone this time, Vince."

"You got it, Alpha," my mate says.

"What drug could possibly make us mortals?" I'm still reeling over this revelation. With all my thoughts running wild, I simply can't imagine it. In centuries there's never even been a whisper of magic or otherwise that could reverse our immortality.

"We don't know. The drug in the shifter we captured is an amphetamine called Captagon. It's highly addictive, plus it keeps them awake and energized." Devin's gaze finds Jude's as he adds, "That could be a problem for you. I expect to hear back from both you and Vince, every hour on the hour. Call Lev. If Lev doesn't hear from you, we'll come immediately. Is that clear?"

They answer in unison, but my question is still left unanswered. "What about the blood, what's the poison?" I can't imagine this drug actually existing.

"We don't know, Veronica. Keep her safe, Vincent."

"That goes without saying," Vince responds, his arm wrapping around my waist protectively. Although there's a warmth to his words and touch, I can't help the irritation. As if I can't keep myself safe. I'm one of the elites of the immortals. Shaking off the disagreeable thoughts I ponder the idea of this rumored drug's existence.

Something I could take that would rid me of this immortality; the thought lights a need deep within me I didn't know I had.

I could be a mortal again. I could be mortal like my mate.

A chill stiffens my bones. I used to dream of what my life would have been like if that day in the rainforest almost two hundred years ago had played out differently. With the knowledge I have now, I'm certain it would've been fucking awful. Still, I've often found myself envious of humans. A small curl to my lips reveals a single fang and I graze the tip of my tongue across the sharp point. If I drank this tainted blood, would I still have my fangs? How long would I live? Long enough to grow old with my mate? A comforting warmth surges through my body at the thought.

I turn slowly in my seat in his direction. He immediately

grabs my chair to pull me closer to him. My stomach churns at how cold I was to him just moments ago and so many times in the past few days. He doesn't deserve how harsh I am toward him. I'm certain of this truth, yet I can't help my reaction when he pushes me like he has. I know he means well, but I don't care for it. If I were mortal, though ... everything could change. This weight and burden could drift away.

I would give anything to grow old with him. Could I bear children for him? There's no doubt in my mind that I would trade my immortality to have a child. I've lived long enough and experienced more than most would ever dream of. But the pull between Vince and me ... this desire to carry a child, perhaps a wolf like him ... I would give anything, drink anything. The temptation weighs heavy on my heart. I need to learn more of this drug. If it's true, if I could be mortal again, I would sacrifice everything to have it.

CHAPTER 8

GRACE

"How do you know you're pregnant? It's way too early to tell, isn't it?" I still can't wrap my head around the idea that Lizzie could be pregnant. That she even said it.

There's just no way to know that so quickly. It's not possible.

"Dom and Caleb are convinced. They said they can smell it."

"They can smell it?" My nose wrinkles slightly and I take in the sight of my best friend sitting at the end of the counter. In gray sweats and an oversized white T-shirt that I think is Caleb's, she's relaxed as can be as she drops this bombshell.

"They're sure?"

"It's too early for it to be certain, but that's what they said." Pulling the sleeves of my cream sweater over my hands,

I keep my fingers tucked inside so I stop picking at the small tear in my jeans. Is she really pregnant? Everything has been too much too fast. I don't understand why she isn't freaking out right now.

"I don't feel any different. I'm just telling you what they said." She shrugs.

Lizzie pops a spoonful of yogurt into her mouth and closes her eyes before she tells me, "I fucking love strawberry yogurt. How come we never bought this before?"

I smile at her goofiness, although it's subdued. Seriously, it's just yogurt. "Didn't know you liked it." Shifting slightly on the barstool, I debate on getting into such a heavy topic, but it's too important not to. "Are you happy?"

Her bright eyes soften as she readjusts her stool and the legs drag on the floor. She puts her hand out on the table, palm up. I put my hand in hers and she squeezes in response. "Happier than I've ever been." Her reassuring words make my whole body relax.

"Are you really pregnant?" I can't fathom that in only days she knows she's pregnant. She shrugs her shoulders and goes back to scraping the plastic cup with her spoon, trying to get out as much as possible.

"They said between the two of them, there's no way they weren't going to knock me up during this last heat." She giggles into her cup, now licking the sides of it since the spoon isn't effective enough. I shake my head and hop off my perch to grab her another from the fridge.

"You're ready to be a mom?"

She smiles as she catches the new cup I toss at her. "I can't fucking wait, Grace. Can you just imagine it? A little baby, cooing at us, snuggling into my arms."

"They scream too, you know? And poop a lot." She laughs at my blunt statement and nods her head.

"Yeah, I know. They have their moments. But it's all worth it. All the late nights of them wanting to be held. When they're gone, I'll miss them. I may be irritated when they cry every time I put them down, but when they're older, I'll wish they'd let me hold them again."

I vaguely wonder if focusing on a baby is a way for her to cope with how different our lives are now. I wonder if it's all moving too fast. I worry for her, but I bite my tongue.

It's not my place and I'll stand with her through anything.

"It's not abnormal, Grace," Lizzie says softly, as if she knows exactly what I'm thinking. "When mates meet and the heat happens ... this is what is expected."

She offers me a small smile as she pats my hand. "I've always wanted to be a mom, and I love my mates, truly. Both of them. Even if it's all too fast and there's so much to learn. When I was little, this was my happily ever after. Before ... everything else. This was all I wanted."

Her doe eyes brim with tears and I wrap my arms around her in concern. "Fuck, I'm so damn hormonal, Grace." She lets out a sad laugh while tears slip down her cheeks. Wiping them away, she pulls back to tell me, "I don't just want a little baby; I want a family." She leans back farther, dropping her spoon and unopened yogurt into her lap. "I *have* a family."

"You do," I whisper, only just now realizing what she must be feeling. Reconciling her past and present, accepting love, and finally knowing she's safe. They'll protect her from everything.

"They love me so much and I love them too."

"Damn, girl," I joke to lighten the mood as she attempts to gather her composure, "you're definitely pregnant. All emotional." She laughs and pulls her legs into her chest, wiping her eyes.

"I hope I am." Her happiness makes me question my decision to wait. The way she's come round to them makes me wonder if I should do the same with Devin.

The thought of Lizzie holding a baby suddenly sends all sorts of emotions shooting through me, jealousy being the most prominent. It catches me off guard. I'm not a jealous person, and especially not of Lizzie. I want her to have happiness. It's quiet for a moment as I stand up, wanting to shake all of this off.

I shuffle to the fridge to find something to eat while I question my feelings. "What do you think it'll be like?"

"Having a baby?" Her eyes catch mine briefly before I look into the freezer.

"Yeah."

"Heaven. Well, sometimes heaven, sometimes hell. But it's all a phase and it will be worth the hard times."

"It's so much responsibility, so life changing." I snort at my own words. Everything has been so fucking life changing. It seems like every day there's something new, yet Devin is unaffected. Is this world of chaos and danger my normal now?

"It is, but I've always wanted a big family."

"Really?" Surprise coats the single word. "I never knew that."

She nods as I shut the fridge, a package of yogurt in my hand. She says, "I never really talked about it. It's not like I'd ever let a guy near me so ..." She breathes deep before tossing the cup at the trash can and missing. "Crap." Getting up, she walks over to clean up her mess.

"Is that why?" I question as I lean against the counter.

"Why what?"

"Why you never dated anyone?" I feel like a shit friend for not knowing any of this before. She's always been flirtatious but that's as far as things went. To be honest, none of the guys we would hang around with ever seemed like they were good enough for her, so I never questioned her not getting serious with anyone.

"I don't know. I just buried it all and tried not to think about it." She's pitching the cup in the trash; this time it makes it. "You know, I never thought I'd have kids. Since I'm latent, I didn't know if I could risk trying to have a family. What if

I settled for some guy back in Shadow Falls? Obviously he would've been human. I peel back the lid slowly, taking my time and letting Lizzie say whatever's on her mind.

"If I settled down with some guy, I never could've told him about what I am. Heck … I couldn't even tell you. And then if we had a baby, and that baby was a werewolf …" She shakes her head as she trails off, the rose gold and moonstone earrings I gifted her gently chiming. Lizzie retakes her seat and spins on her stool. She bites her lip, obviously thinking about something. Finally she stops and looks at me as I take the seat next to her. "I always wanted to tell you, but I just couldn't. I didn't want to believe it was true. Some days I'd actually convince myself it was just a nightmare. It was so much easier living like that." She leans in and lays her head on my shoulder. "You're not mad at me, are you?"

Resting my head on top of hers, I answer honestly, "I could never be mad at you, babe. Besides, I knew you went through something and when you were ready, you'd tell me."

"I didn't think I would have ever been ready, though. I never wanted to deal with it, you know?" She leans back to look me in the eyes while I swirl the spoon in yogurt I don't even want to eat.

Setting it down on the counter with finality I nod slightly and tell her, "I know. I really do get it. You don't have to be worried about me. You know I still love you."

"I love you too." She kisses my cheek before going back to

spinning on her seat.

All this heavy talk is making a lump form in my throat. My whole world is nothing like it was before. It's as if I'm living in a completely different reality and so much is out of my control.

I decide to change the subject to something I've been wondering about and something I'm certain Lizzie will want to hash out. "Are werewolf babies born human, or like ..." I trail off as I think about getting pregnant with Devin's *pups*.

"Do you remember in biology when we talked about the difference between altricial and whatever the fuck the other word is?"

I just blink at her before stating flatly, "I fucking hated bio." My comment grants me a belly laugh from Lizzie that lights up her face and I'm forced to smile in return.

When she recovers, she starts one of her little tidbit tangents she's known for.

"Some babies are born and they're completely dependent on their mother, like humans and dogs, whereas other species give birth and the babies go on their merry way, fully independent, like"—she scrunches her nose in thought—"like sharks, I think."

"You're such a dork." My cheeks hurt from grinning at her. My best friend appears to be back to her usual happy-go-lucky self. For a moment, it all feels normal. For a moment, the smallest moment, I forget everything has changed.

"The first one is called altricial and that's what werewolves are."

"That doesn't really answer my question."

She stares blankly at me. How does she not get this?

"So your baby may be a werewolf, or definitely will be? And ... importantly, do they look like human when they're born or ..." I let the question hang between us, not wanting to imagine the alternative.

Her sarcastic smirk tells me she pities me for my complete lack of knowledge. "This form, as humans, is how they're delivered." I let out a deep breath at that statement. Her next, though, has me tensing right back up. "They'll be werewolf. So will yours, by the way." Lizzie raises her eyebrows at me before continuing. "I just don't know if they'll be latent like me or if they'll be normal."

Latent. My heart sinks as I watch her shoulders hunch. I don't fucking like her getting down on herself. "But you said you felt her, right? Your wolf?"

"Just the once since we've been here. I don't know why she left me." Her somber statement dampens her mood as she spins slowly on the stool.

"What brought her back?" Lizzie blushes at my question, which makes me really want to know what happened. Yes! This is a much better conversation to have. My cheeks burn and I lean in to whisper, "Was it the sex?"

She bites her lip again, looking shy. It's an odd look for

her to give me when she tells me, "We didn't have sex, just did other stuff." She shakes her head and composes herself. "But we've had sex since then and she didn't come back. Unless—" Her eyes brighten and she takes a quick inhale.

"What? What was it that brought her back?" I love the hopeful light in her blue eyes.

"Caleb punished me with a belt—"

"What the fuck!" I jump out of my seat, causing it to fly backward and crash on the tile floor. *Punished?* My head spins as the word registers.

Every hair on my body stands on end as adrenaline has me seeing nearly red.

I practically scream as my body burns with anger. "I'll fucking kill him. Where the fuck is Dom?" My heart races as my hands ball into tight fists at my sides. *How the fuck could he hit her?*

"Knock it off, Grace!" Lizzie's quick to tug at my arm while scowling. "And shut your mouth about Dom." She hushes me with a tone I'm not used to and a hurt in her doe eyes that I don't understand. "He didn't do a damn thing to me." I step back, the wind taken out of my sails by her offended reaction.

"He hit you." Staring at her wide eyed with disbelief, I don't understand how she could possibly be defending him.

"First of all, Dom has never laid a finger on me." Her voice cracks as she speaks. "Dom loves me and so does Caleb. Caleb's the one who used a belt to get me to open up to him. And I fucking loved it." She points her finger at me and pushes out each choked-up word with a tone that brooks no disagreement. "You better not fucking judge me for it, Grace."

"I—" I don't know what to say. A numbness of regret runs through me. "I had no right to react that way. I'm sorry. I'm sorry, Lizzie." Putting my hands up in surrender, I walk toward her. My best friend is practically shaking with emotion. "I'm so sorry, babe, it was wrong of me to jump to conclusions." She leans into me for a hug.

"Please don't think badly of me. Don't hold it against him," she says softly. Lizzie pulls back with her hands on my shoulders and says, "Tell me you won't think badly of him. Please." My lips part, although I'm somehow able to hold my tongue. He hit her. He punished her.

"You liked it?" She nods her head and brushes the tears away with the back of her hand. "A belt?" She blushes again, bright red this time.

"I swear, Grace. It was … kinky and I loved it."

"Okay." I try to imagine it and then regret it. "If you're happy, then I'm happy." Taking a deep breath, I look right into those baby blue eyes of hers when I tell her, "But if either of them hurts you, you know you can tell me, right?"

"It's a good hurt." Her cheeks flush beet red before she gives me a hug as if to end the conversation there. "I love them so damn much. I'm so fucking happy."

To each their own, I suppose. I don't know if I'll ever look at Caleb the same again. Between the pair of her mates there's no way I'd have guessed it was Caleb who'd be into that. An odd feeling comes over me as a weight seems to lift off my chest. I glance at my best friend, so happy and at peace with everything. I feel like I can let go, like for the first time in our lives, she doesn't need me. She has her mates now. Walking past her to pick up my fallen stool, Lizzie gasps and touches her chest.

"Lizzie?" The chair drops back to the floor at the sight of her shocked expression and her hand clutching her shirt.

"I feel my wolf, Grace. I feel her!" Staring at Lizzie, I'm frozen in place.

"What should I do?" I'd do anything for her, but I have no idea how to help her or what to do.

"I don't know. I don't know. I'm so scared she's going to leave me." Tears well in her eyes again. She rubs her chest before whispering, "Please don't leave me."

CHAPTER 9

VINCE

I've never been afraid of vampires. Never in my whole life have I even bothered with the thought of fearing bloodsuckers.

But holy fuck. Walking into the den of Veronica's coven, surrounded by vampires on all sides, I'd be lying if I said there wasn't a cold prick traveling down my spine and eliciting a hint of fear.

Veronica is the first vampire I've met who I've seen as more than an enemy. She's the first I've been able to interact with beyond strategizing about defense and offense. I've seen them before, of course, from the Authority, whenever Devin invited them into our estate, onto our territory. I've killed them when necessary. I've never had to question what would happen if they attacked. Our pack would have demolished them.

There is no pack with me now, though. On their turf and highly outnumbered, I'm not naive enough to think I stand a chance against them. If they decided I was their prey tonight, there isn't a thing I could do to win a fight against the coven.

Acutely aware of such facts, I wrap my arm casually around Veronica's waist. I may be humbled by the terrifying thought, but I'm sure as shit not going to let them know. In my periphery, I keep tabs on them watching me.

Swallowing thickly, I keep my pace even with Veronica's. The click of her heels is muted as she walks, the sound absorbed by the hardened earth.

Why the fuck do they live underground? They're wealthy beyond belief.

They've had hundreds of years to acquire riches and properties. It's known as fact among supernaturals that vampires are stacked with cash. They could afford to build mansions above ground where no sunlight would ever touch them. Yet they live in a fucking cave.

As I lick my lips, the salty air from the damp walls settles on the tip of my tongue. It's a refreshing taste. If I closed my eyes I could almost picture myself on a beach, but it's far too cold.

Again, I'm not a bitch, but why live like this when you could live anywhere? Fucking stupid, if you ask me. Of course, if they're going for intimidating, then they hit that nail on the fucking head. With only torches lining the pitch-black passageway, secured in sconces placed every few feet along the rock walls, it's dark for those whose sight is weak. Realizing I can see better than any of them puts a smirk on my lips.

A relatively large form passes in front of us down another dreary, fire-lit hall; he's a few inches shorter than me and only wearing a pair of white linen pants. His bare feet and chest reflect the light off his pale skin. I catch his scent and the sight of him clearly: human.

My forehead pinches in confusion for only a moment before I see the small scars along his neck. They form an interesting overlapping pattern, like the scales of a dragon. It must've taken hundreds of bites over a long period of time to make that kind of rough scar on the thin skin of his neck. They're only in a small patch on the right side. I lose sight of him as he walks farther through the passage and we continue straight ahead. With a glance down, I note that Veronica doesn't react.

The tunnel appears to end in front of us. No fire on the walls is present to light the path. It only takes a moment to spot the thick, dark red curtains pulled shut that are blocking our way. Veronica reaches forward, drawing one curtain aside. I take the other heavy panel and pull it back much farther than she can, then gesture for her to take the lead. She tries to hide it, but I see her small, satisfied smirk she immediately represses.

My chest constricts. I don't know whether we're okay or not. She's barely spoken to me since I let her off the bed. She's been glacial to me, icing me out. She hasn't tried to boss me around or even called me pup. Nothing. She's given me very little of her attention. She shies away from any physical contact between us. At least she's accepting my touch now that we're in her territory.

What worries me is that I don't know how I'll react if she continues to ignore me while we're here. Where I have no one but her. There's only so much I can hide and my wolf yearns for her touch and acceptance. Brushing off the unwanted feelings, I remind myself she's been more receptive since we left the estate. She's not giving me her full attention, but she's not ignoring me either.

At the thought, her hand briefly brushes against mine. As if she can perceive I need the reassurance. Veronica makes me weak. I would drop to my knees, begging for her to command me if that would ease the tension between us. If she told me to submit to her this very moment, I wouldn't hesitate.

She hasn't told me shit, though. Not a single word.

I'm not sure if she'll ever trust me. What little trust she had in me seems to have been diminished by me chaining her to the bed. It was only meant to help; to show her she didn't have any reason to fear me or my touch. That I would always be hers even if she had no physical control of me. It didn't work. I fucking failed her.

Again.

My chest constricts and my heart skips a beat momentarily. Nearly forgetting where we are, I remind myself to be more mindful of their hearing. Fuck.

After a minute, I shake it off. I *will* heal her. I will help my mate learn to trust me. It's going to take time and I need to accept that. Exhaling a long breath causes Veronica to take a peek at me. Her gorgeous dark eyes pierce through me, not hiding her concern.

Even if she hates herself for it, she cares for me. I know she does.

I smile down at her. Everything in me yearns to kiss her, but I hold myself back. I won't be able to contain myself if she rejects me. And we're in her territory, not mine. I repress the low growl from my wolf. He wants her. I haven't had her since the claiming and that didn't go well. I need to feel her body against mine. I need to give her pleasure and hear her moans of approval. Tightening my arm around her waist brings her closer to me. She stiffens slightly at first, which puts my wolf on high alert, but then she relaxes against me. He's still not happy. He paces restlessly inside me, knowing something's wrong, just not knowing what.

My focus leaves me as I sense a flood of warmth in front of me. Again the tunnel seems to end, but as I expect, thick curtains cut off the passage. I pull at the dark fabric to reveal a brightly lit room. Veronica doesn't hesitate to walk into the luxurious space and I follow her lead. She leaves my hold, but I'm quick to pull her ass back to me. She's mine. And all these fuckers are going to see that.

Apart from a raised brow, she doesn't object to my touch. *Good girl.*

The vast room is more of what I expected to see from her queen and ancient coven. The walls and ceiling are covered in ornate designs. Breathing in deep, I take in the scent of minerals. Gold. It's painted in gold. A closer look at the rough rock walls reveals luxury and decadence beyond belief. The masterful artistry on display must have taken decades to create. I have to squint to make out the hundreds of small fires blending together across the expansive space to make a literal wall of fire. The tone-on-tone metallic paint reflects the flames to the point where it nearly pains my eyes to stare straight ahead. Most of the furniture in the room appears ancient; the seats are intricately carved pieces lined with bloodred velvet fabric. It's completely at odds with the modern, clear acrylic table in the very center of the room.

The seat at the head of the table is taken by a tall, pale woman with smooth skin and black silky hair down to her small waist. Her sharp red nail pierces into her lip as her dark eyes find us. She rises in a blur of motion but then takes a small, slow step forward, making the black jewels adorning her dress clink together as she walks. She reeks of wealth and power. Her nearly black eyes have a youthful shine although I know better.

The other vampires in the room hardly take notice of our entry. But the humans, all wearing the same pants or halter dresses of white linen, take an obvious interest in our presence. All look to us but a single woman lying still on a plush white hide off to the right side of the room. For a moment I tense, thinking the human is dead. But the air carries no scent of decay. I watch her chest gently rise and fall. Fresh, open wounds on her neck indicate someone drank from her recently, but she's alone on the floor. My gut twists with the thought that the humans are here against their will, present only to satisfy the thirst of the vamps. The delight evident in the sets of eyes following our movement begs to differ with my assumption. I would quietly ask Veronica for confirmation, but vampires are known for their ability to hear at great distances.

My curiosity will have to wait.

The seductive voice of the black-eyed queen echoes gently off of the walls. "Veronica, my darling. You've brought a guest?"

A devious smile brightens Veronica's crimson lips. The firelight illuminates her tan skin. She's breathtaking in this lighting, glowing with a golden sheen. My pulse races and desire threatens to consume me. My gorgeous mate is in her element and she thrives here. I can feel her strength through our bond; I practically see her transform into the fierce warrior I met in the alley.

Before I claimed her.

Before I broke her. I shake off the thought. No, I'm *healing* her. She's hurting. Her ability to hide her pain is extraordinary. My eyes travel along her beautiful face, alight with mischief and seduction.

"A guest, or a snack?" a pale man with the same dark eyes says. In less time than it takes to blink, he makes his way across the room to stand in front of me. I swallow thickly, not letting their speed and number cause any more alarm than the initial shock. His clothes and the way his short blond hair is styled nearly make him look human. But his eyes give away his dependency on consuming blood.

"Braeden, you know I don't share." Veronica's voice is playful as she turns her back on her coven to pat the center of my chest. Her head tilts up at me and I don't waste a second to bend down and give her a small kiss on the lips. I keep my eyes closed longer than necessary, sending a clear sign to them that I don't fear their presence. They're no threat to me. At least that's what my actions suggest.

She waits until I open my eyes and I'm caught in her gaze for only a moment as she peers back up at me. There's something there, something between us, but it's quickly forgotten.

Veronica spins to face them, causing her leather skirt to

flare around her. "I've found a mate, Adreana. I'll be staying with him for a while." A tic in my jaw spasms and my eyes harden on her back. *A while?* My stomach sinks as I realize the full weight of her words. My life span will be a blip in her existence.

"Of course, darling. Of course." The queen's eyes travel down my body with appreciation. I don't care for it. "So he's yours alone?"

Veronica nods her head slightly before walking past the table to a chaise longue in the corner of the room, extremely close to the wall of fire. "Funny that fate should give me a mate. Don't you think so, my queen?"

"It's odd. It's not completely unheard of, although I thought they were just rumors before."

Braeden appears by Veronica's side, but sits on the ground and stares at the fire with his knees pulled into his chest. He's so motionless he looks like he's made of stone. Veronica shifts her long legs onto the sofa in a very seductive move and pats the seat between her legs. I move deliberately with a casual pace and take my seat, a smirk begging to form on my lips. Her right calf rests on my thigh as her queen stalks toward us.

"What are the rumors, Adreana? I've no memory of a pairing like ours." My thumb rubs small circles on the inside of my mate's knee. She's relaxed and at peace, although it seems false. My eyes linger on her face, her expression one of disinterest; however, she's obviously curious. Her queen sits to my left and I lean back to give the two women an easy view of each other. I feel very much out of place in the quiet room, but I continue to follow Veronica's lead. I'd much rather have her queen's approval as quickly as possible to go to Still Waters and stake out the blood bank, but Veronica doesn't appear to be in any rush.

"I couldn't tell you, my dear. There was word that a vampire had mated with a wolf, and that was all to be said. I'm not sure he ever returned." Adreana's eyes focus on my fingers stroking the inside of Veronica's knee before traveling to her neck. "And you let him claim you, I see. Rather barbaric, wouldn't you agree." I don't let her words affect me in the least as I hold the queen's gaze. Veronica lets out a huff of a small laugh.

"It was quite primitive, but it suited my taste."

"If you say so. And what of the Alpha, is he willing to negotiate? I'm hoping this mating benefited us." Her voice rises toward the end.

"It did, my queen. Devin is willing to give us the bank and allow our control without any interference."

The queen laughs in obvious amusement, then says, "You toy with me, darling?"

Veronica's eyes spark with delight at her queen's approval. "I'd never. He of course desires a plan and would like my mate to receive information from a successful territory. He chose Still Waters. We're planning on taking our leave this evening, I believe."

"I see." The queen sighs and leans deep into the chaise, beckoning an onlooking human to come to her. The man smiles and rises slowly, kneeling in front of her, waiting for her next command. She gently runs her fingers through his thick brown hair.

We sit in silence for a moment. Braeden seems to grow bored and stands, walking to the young woman lying on the plush rug. He squats in front of her and runs his fingers down her chin. "Come, pet."

"I'm tired ... You drank so much." She barely breathes the words as she leans into his touch. He chuckles deep and low.

"You need to sleep; would you prefer the floor to my bed?" His voice is full of humor.

"Your bed, please."

He lifts her in his arms as though she weighs nothing and saunters easily out of the room.

"And what do the Alpha and his pack think of the law? Are you expected to only drink from your mate?" The queen's alluring voice brings my eyes to hers, although she's not looking in our direction whatsoever. Her focus is on the man waiting patiently on his knees in front of her.

Veronica smiles easily and says, "He holds the same opinion as I." Her hand finds mine and she brings my fingers to her mouth to suck. My dick instantly hardens. With a quick inhale, I suppress my groan and the need to let my head fall back. The room's sweet smell and the heat of the fire add to the seductive quality of the unnaturally beautiful vampires. "My mate enjoys my touch and I continue to drink from him."

Although her voice is even, the queen's next statement holds a viciousness that's unexpected. "Do you think of me as a hypocritical bitch? Or a coward for bowing to Natalia's demand?"

Veronica sits up abruptly, her speed shocking me for a moment. She bows her head slightly with her lips grazing my knee. "Neither, my queen," she says and her softly spoken words tickle my knee.

"Up." Adreana rests her hand on Veronica's shoulder, and in turn my mate's dark eyes find her queen's. "I'm itching for a war, darling."

"We would stand at your side, if you so desired." My spine stiffens at the turn of the conversation.

This will all be taken care of shortly. The coven would only interfere. I keep my lips pressed tight and rest my hand lightly on Veronica's back, rubbing soothing circles. Her eyes close briefly at my touch, making my wolf pant with longing.

"For now, we'll build the bank. Her presence here will not be tolerated. Not after what she did to Stephan."

For the first time, I turn and look the queen in the eyes. "My Alpha was not pleased to hear what Natalia has done. He sends his sincere condolences."

Her dark eyes search mine for a long moment before she

finally speaks. "Well thank you, my dearest wolf. Please send him my regards." Her hand stops in the human's hair and the lack of her touch has him seeking out her gaze. "Would you like me to drink from you, Jaret?"

"Please, my queen." His tone is deferential, but his green eyes practically beg her.

"Come." In a blur that leaves a gentle breeze in her wake, suddenly the queen is standing by the entrance. She passes through the heavy velvet curtains without a single glance over her shoulder as the human quickly follows her path. It's an abrupt end to the conversation to say the least.

"I need to pack, pup." The use of Veronica's pet name for me stirs my dick. My lips lift into a grin as she leans in for a kiss.

"Yes, Mistress." I feel her smile against my lips. Something deep inside me twists, knowing I'm playing into her hand. I'll give her this for now. A give-and-take of sorts. "When we get home, I want you chained again." My words turn the quiet room silent and I feel several pairs of dark eyes boring into me. My mate stiffens, but only for a moment. She leans back and stands.

"When we get back. Until then ..." Her words are left hanging in the air as she walks toward the exit. The blazing heat from the fire quickly fades, leaving me cold in its absence. I pull her frame into my chest and kiss the crook of her neck.

"I love you." Those eyes bore into me again as she turns in my embrace. Her hand rests on the center of my chest. Her lips part and close before her dark eyes find mine.

"I love you too, Vince," she says, barely speaking the words loud enough for me to hear. Her soft, plump lips press against mine in a chaste kiss. She hums her appreciation and turns, straightening her back and lifting her chin. Her strong voice returns. "Now come, pup; we're going to be late." My lips curl in a grin as I follow my mate down the dark, damp hall.

CHAPTER 10

VINCE

It's easy enough to catch the scent of the vampires among the humans. Special contacts disguise their eyes and they're dressed in the latest fashion trends unlike Veronica's coven, allowing them to blend into their surroundings. Even so, there are two I spot immediately. One near the entrance, appearing preoccupied at a desk as his fingers click along a keyboard. He pauses momentarily when we enter, but doesn't seem to care enough to fully stop his work. The other I scent is somewhere down the hall.

The building on the whole is small and sterile.

As we enter, I calculate every escape route available should we need one. In front of us are several couches and a small TV on the wall, playing some sort of animated comedy. There are three humans seated in the waiting room and I can smell blood being drawn from at least one more somewhere. I whisper softly to Veronica at the shell of her ear, "I thought the Authority only allowed humans to work the building and deliver the blood?" From what I know of their laws, there shouldn't be any vampires here at all.

"That was before vampires started going missing. They used to come alone once a day to pick up the blood and that was all. Now they have two in place at all times, although they aren't to present themselves as anything other than human." I grunt, taking in her words. A little warning would have been nice.

"Do you two have an appointment or are you walk-ins?" a peppy blond woman asks from the front desk. Her eyes drift down my body slowly as she licks her lower lip and clenches her thighs far too noticeably. Veronica surprises me by gripping my hand in a possessive response.

I must admit, her claiming me in such a subtle and human way is more than attractive. I squeeze her hand in return, reveling in the contact.

"Neither. We're here to take a look around, thanks." Her short dismissal nearly makes me laugh as she tugs me along.

"You're here for the tour?" The first vampire I made out rises and strides over, extending his hand for me to shake. Making eye contact, I grip him firmly. His gaze darts to

Veronica's. Not that his coworker notices, but subtle clues indicate he's surprised; I'm guessing he didn't realize I was a werewolf. I grin at him before releasing his hand.

"Are you going to show us around or what?" I comment casually, still grinning.

He recovers quickly and says, "Right this way, miss …?"

"Mrs." Veronica's response makes me snort a laugh. "Please call me by my first name, Veronica. I believe Melinda arranged the appointment." There's slight tension between the two but it's quickly eased.

He gives her a small smile while leading us through the hall. His demeanor turns professional as a short woman leaves the small room to our right with an adhesive bandage on her arm, obviously having just given blood. "Have a wonderful day," he tells her.

"You too," she replies. The woman leaves without even glancing in our direction.

The vampire's fangs aren't visible at all. He's obviously practiced a smile that hides them. I wonder how long he's hidden here among them and what he's heard. Humans have always left me curious. With my new mate, however, vampires may just become my new obsession.

"After you." He motions us into a small room, his button-down shirt shifting slightly as he does and the scent of vampire permeates the air. There's a simple desk with a computer that looks old as shit sitting in the corner. Behind it are a swivel chair and a cabinet housing a variety of equipment. A medical waste bin sits in one corner. Overall, everything looks very simple and not nearly as high tech as I was expecting.

"It's a bit outdated, isn't it?" I quirk a brow at the vampire and he smiles, revealing a bit of his fangs. With no humans around, he freely drops the act.

"Humans get suspicious of wealth."

I nod at his admission. "Makes sense."

Veronica takes the lead, asking him, "What changes have been made since the abductions? We want to know the ins and outs of operations. If you could also explain how vampires managed to disappear in human territory, I would appreciate that information as well."

Her nose wrinkles at the modest surroundings as she paces to the chair with her arms crossed listening to the vampire's response.

"Melinda said a member of Adreana's coven would be here. She didn't say anything about a wolf."

In a blur, she's beside me. "He's with me." With a smirk, she trails her nails along my arm. The move elicits a low growl of approval for the public display of affection.

"Is your Alpha open to relations with other covens?" His question is directed at me, although he noticeably swallows and doesn't make eye contact.

"No. We are willing to appease my mate's queen. That is all."

"I see. How … unusual." The vampire eyes Veronica's

neck, lingering on my mark.

"I asked about the changes to protocol?" Veronica says coolly.

"As you can see, we have two of us on guard now. At all times. The three who were abducted were alone when it happened. Since then, we haven't allowed the rogue vampires a chance to take anyone else."

"Rogue vampires?" My hackles raise.

"It had to be other vampires." There's a pause and Veronica's gaze narrows. "There's no way it could've been anyone else. Humans wouldn't dare even if they had the ability to kidnap vampires. The wolves here in Still Waters respect our treaties. Our coven showed the security footage to the Authority. They haven't found anything yet."

"Who was it from the Authority that you spoke with?" My voice comes out hard and his gaze shifts from Veronica to me, back to her and then settles on me once again.

"I'm not sure. It was between them and my queen." He clasps his hands in front of him, not hiding his unease at my presence.

"It's no matter. Do you know why your queen is convinced it was vampires?"

He nods his head at Veronica's question, much more comfortable addressing her. It's probably better that way. Vampires naturally fear my kind and it should stay that way. "We could clearly see the vision of a running vampire. But only for a moment on the screen before Joshua left the property."

"So he was lured away by a vampire?"

"We have no doubt." With a curt nod, his voice is firm. "However, you have nothing to worry about. Although the Authority hasn't made any arrests, we haven't seen any strange activity since we've placed two of us on the property at all times. It is safe and operations have gone seamlessly since then."

"So you simply collect the blood and bring it back to your coven?"

"Yes. Nothing less and nothing more. I'm certain you won't encounter any problems." My eyes search the room for anything amiss. Devin's convinced they're poisoning the blood somehow. My eyes narrow as they zero in on the boxes behind the door.

"Where do you get your equipment?" I ask.

"The Authority sets you up with everything you need to start. It's cheaper than buying everything separately from the humans. And this way we avoid doing any more activity with them than we have to."

"Well, that's very convenient." Veronica voices my own thoughts. If I had to guess, I'd say the blood bags used to collect donations are what's poisoned; maybe they lace the plastic lining.

But what the hell do I know? We're going to have to test the materials after we place an order.

"Do you drink it?" I can't help but to ask if for no other reason than curiosity. A part of me feels complicit for knowing these vampires could be consuming drugs without knowing. It's obvious that Veronica's coven isn't adhering to the law, but how many other covens are as lenient as hers?

His eyes dart between the two of us before he replies, "Of course I do. It's law."

Veronica laughs a sweet, low seductive sound while trailing her fingers down my neck and resting them in the dip of my collarbone. "I prefer sweeter tastes."

"Wolves are sweeter?" His brows raise as he regards my wrists and neck curiously. The way his gaze lingers makes me think he must be hungry. Maybe they are only drinking what's been donated. When his eyes reach my hard stare, he flinches.

"I think we're good here," I state bluntly. I don't appreciate being looked at like I'm a fucking meal. Not by him anyway.

With a soft hum of agreement, Veronica laces her fingers between mine, peering up at me. The male vampire is quick to look away.

I lead Veronica out, loving that she holds on to my hand without hesitation.

Still, I can't help feeling a twisting knot deep in my gut. I just don't feel right. We haven't been intimate since the offering. My wolf isn't happy. My balls aren't either. Every few hours I'm rock hard for her and I'm going to need a release soon. Preferably before I lose my damn mind.

As we walk down the narrow hall, the scents mingle and that unsettled feeling turns into something else. "Let me do a lap and try to catch the scent."

Veronica pauses in the middle of the hall with me, the vampire to our backs. "Do you think you'll find anything?"

I shrug and tell her, "Possibly. A vampire's scent is much different from a human's."

"Oh," she says and purses her lips, "and what is it that we smell like?"

"More metallic and salty." That's the best response I can come up with. It's hard to describe their smell.

She huffs in distaste and says, "So you're saying I smell like a rock."

"No, you smell like honey and jasmine." I lean in close to her ear, backing her body against the handrail, then tell her, "You taste like them too." Heat dances between us instantly and she sucks in a breath, taken aback and very much weak for me. She lets her head fall back, which gives me a clear view of my mark on her. I bend down to kiss it, but she seems to realize my intention and pushes away from me. That twisting sickness in my stomach roils.

"Do a lap and see if you can smell anything." She maneuvers her way out of my hold and it takes everything in me not to react. Not to hold her still, press her against the wall and take her lips with mine. I watch her walk away from me, staying as still as I can.

Taking one deep breath and then another, my tense muscles relax. At least she's found her strength and is giving me orders again.

I follow her out of the blood bank walking a step or two behind. When she stops at the car and turns to face me, I step into her space. It fucking kills me when she stiffens as I cage her body in. Her eyes flash with fear, and then defiance as they narrow at me. She has no reason for either reaction.

I lean down and breathe in her sweet honey scent before kissing her neck. If I want to kiss my mark on her, I'm going to fucking kiss it. I leave an openmouthed kiss exactly where I want it and breathe into her neck, "My Mistress."

As I pull back, she doesn't react. There's a sadness in her eyes, followed by nothing. In a blink, nothing. It guts me.

How have we taken such a huge step back in our relationship? It was so fucking easy, so damn good before. My fists clench as I leave her and head for the back of the building, the thin skin over my knuckles going taut and turning white. My jog turns into a sprint. How the hell did I mess this up so fucking bad?

No. My fist pounds against the dumpster as I near the back exit, leaving a massive dent in the side. I look around and release the breath I was holding when I see that no one saw my outburst. I need to check my anger before it creates more trouble.

I didn't mess this up. I'm fixing it. I only have to think

back to her lying on the ground in fear of me after claiming her. That's enough to solidify my decision to keep pushing her. She will learn to trust me again. The fucked-up part is that I think she's really pissed that now I know she can be shaken. Like it somehow makes her weak. That's a load of shit. My mate is anything but weak.

The building is small and it's easy enough to encircle it, drawing in air as I go.

I pause as I scent the air, detecting a number of vampires in the tall grass by the fence. It's easy to catch the trail. I move to follow it through the field but stop short, thinking I shouldn't leave my mate for too long. It's only a moment for me, only seconds until she's back in my sight. I can smell her and feel her even. The thought of leaving her alone, though, even if only for a moment? I don't fucking like it. That tightness in my chest eases as I see my mate's fingers on her neck, running along the little indents of the scar I gave her.

Knowing she very much feels me as I do her, I stride to the passenger side and open the door for her.

"I'll drive," she demands as she walks to the driver's side, ignoring my attempt to reconcile.

Just as she opens the door, I tell her, "It would be better if I drive. After all, I'll be trying to scent our way." She purses her lips and clicks her tongue against the roof of her mouth before striding toward me, her heels tapping out a staccato rhythm on the pavement. "Fine, pup."

Before she can slip into the seat, I wrap my hand around her waist, holding her there. Tension crackles between us as her chest rises and falls. My gaze is locked with hers.

"I want us to be okay," I admit to her in a whisper. Her fingers wrap around mine, releasing my grip as she swallows and says, "Me too."

That's all I get. But it's better than nothing.

It's silent in the car as I pick out the way to go. Veronica's still and quiet.

There's an out-of-sync energy that surrounds us and I despise it. The atmosphere is so different between us. It's as though we're at war, but neither of us wants to be fighting. It takes less than half an hour until I find a gravel road. It reeks of vampires. Far more than what I smelled back at the donation center. Braking, I stop the car. I squint down the road, but it's too difficult to make out what it leads to.

I look to my mate and tell her, "We should continue from here on foot." Watching her hand open the door, suddenly I'm not liking that she's with me. I'm slow. They could outrun me, but they could also grab her. They could take her and do to her whatever the hell they're doing to the other vampires. And what could I do? If they stay to fight, I'll win. My strength is unmatched. But their speed is superior. They could easily outrun me. They could take my mate captive and leave me nothing but a trail to follow.

"Wait." My voice is far too loud, considering vampires are

close. She leans into the car with her hands braced on the doorframe.

"What the hell, Vince," she hisses. "You need to be quieter."

"Get in the car." Her eyes narrow at me, not liking my tone. "Baby, there are too many vamps. I don't trust it."

"We'll be fine, Vince."

"I won't be able to live with myself if something happens to you."

"I'll be fine; stop worrying. I can handle myself." She stresses the last part, shifting her stance and the gravel crunches beneath her heels.

"No, I can't live if something were to happen to you." Sadness flashes across her eyes and I don't understand it.

"You'll be just fine if I die. You'll have to learn to live with it." Her hard words seem out of place with the sorrow reflected in her dark eyes. It takes a moment for me to grasp what the hell's going on. My hand slams against the wheel in anger as it hits me. She's going to have to keep living after I die because she's a vampire, not a wolf. I'm such an insensitive asshole. She jolts at my harsh movement.

"I'm sorry. I wish things could be different." I barely get the words through my gritted teeth. I haven't really thought about the fact that my mate is immortal. What the hell is wrong with me? "Get in the car."

"I'll be fine, Vince."

"Get in the damn car right now, Veronica. I'm not going

to risk losing you. I will *never* risk you." She fidgets outside the car, her feet gently moving the rocks beneath her again, and for a moment I think she's going to ignore me and walk down the path without me. Instead, she quietly gets in the car and shuts the door with a faint click, staring straight ahead while I gaze at her.

"You'll be fine if I die, Vince. You'll have to be fine and just keep living." Her head turns to face me and her cold dark eyes are devoid of emotion when she tells me, "You can't keep me by your side forever." Her words cut deep into me.

"I'll keep you safe for as long as I live, I promise you." I move to grasp her hand and she lets me. Even as the cords in her neck tighten with a swallow, she lets me hold her hand in mine. I brush my lips against her knuckles and turn her hand over to kiss her palm. "You're mine to keep by my side if I wish."

Her sigh is one that will stay with me. One of stubbornness, hardness, and a somber note of regret. It fucking kills me. She rests her hand in her lap while I start the car and leave the trail. I'll call Devin and tell him what we've discovered as soon as I swallow this lump climbing up my throat. There's no need for us to go down that path into God knows what by ourselves, most likely outnumbered. We're a pack for a reason.

"Do you want to talk about it?" I murmur the words while I drive us toward home. "We should make it there in a few hours. Plenty of time to talk." Before she can answer, my phone's timer goes off, indicating it's time to call Lev. I wait a moment and Veronica only shrugs, her gaze focused on the phone. Reluctantly, I put it on speaker and the other end rings once before Lev picks up.

"Yo, you good?"

Clearing my throat, I tell him, "Yeah, heading back now."

"No leads?" Lev's disappointment is obvious.

"We got something. We're going to need backup, though." I can practically feel his grin through the sounds of his howling laughter. My first thought is new to me: he doesn't have a mate to protect. There's not an ounce of worry for him. "We'll be back soon."

"Still, check in with me again in an hour. I don't need Devin up my ass."

"You got it." I end the conversation and glance at my mate. "Baby, talk to me."

"What do you want me to say?" she's quick to respond, but doesn't look back at me.

"Are we all right?" Her dark eyes find mine and I decide to pull over to have this conversation. There's a hint of worry laying heavy on my shoulders and I can't fucking stand it. Putting the car in park, I push the seat as far back as I can so I can pull my mate into my lap. She gasps as I lift her up and settle her right where I want her.

Both of her palms brace against my chest. Her eyes are wide and the vulnerability she tries to hide shines back at me. I'm gentle as I brush her hair back from her face with my knuckles. Her skin is smooth and that simple touch forces her to close her eyes.

"I need to know we're okay, baby. I know I pushed you. I was just trying to help and I'm worried I did the opposite of what I wanted."

"I know you were. It's fine." She shrugs off my concerns, the cords in her neck tensing as she swallows. My entire body bristles at how she tries to play it off. Her tone is glib, but her body language isn't.

"It's obviously not fine," I answer, my voice louder than I wish it was. She tenses but I don't stop, telling her, "You aren't the same. I'm sorry, baby." Taking her chin in my hand, I force her to look at me. "I love you and I'm sorry."

"I know, and I love you too. I do." Her words act as a balm, easing the tension and numbing the burning concern that's had me twisted up all day long. Her hand rests on mine and she waits a moment before admitting, "I'm trying to be okay with being scared."

"You don't have anything to be scared of."

A soft smile that's far too sad pulls up her lips and she says, "I'm already scared of what I'm going to do when you're gone ... and how that's going to feel."

"Baby," I breathe and my fingers spear through her hair. "Don't think about that."

All she does is huff and then her eyes drop to my lips. "I

love you. You know that, don't you?"

My lips crash against hers instantly. Parting her lips with mine, I suckle her top lip. "I know," I groan. "I love you too." Her fangs gently graze my lips, making me moan into her mouth. She rocks her body against my hardening length.

"This. This is something I never dared to want or dream," she tells me as her back straightens and she spreads her legs wider.

My head is instantly cloudy with lust. Her lips drop to my neck and her fangs slip down my tender skin. I let my head fall back, giving her more room. "Don't tease me, baby. I need you so fucking bad."

"Aww, is my pup hurting?" A smile creeps onto my lips at her teasing. *That's my mate.*

"You know I am. I've been wanting inside you all damn day." She climbs off of me and my wolf growls at the loss of her touch, making my eyes instantly widen. I force my wolf to stay back, knowing she's not going to tease me. Not too much, at least.

She settles in her seat, making me think maybe she is just fucking with me. *Shit.* I can't take being teased like this. Not with this tension between us. Her hands slip up her skirt and she slides her lace panties down her slender, long legs. Over one heel and then the other until they're off. *Fuck yes.* My hands fly to my zipper so I can unleash my cock, precum already beading at my slit. I need to be inside of her as soon as fucking possible. I lift my ass up so I can pull down my jeans and stroke myself a few times, waiting for her to climb on top.

She gracefully straddles me more quickly than should be possible, and easily slides down my length before I can do anything to help her. *Fuck*, she's so damn wet and hot. And fucking tight. I moan as she pushes herself all the way onto my dick.

"Fuck, baby. You feel so fucking good." My hands rest on her hips and she stills for a moment. I close my eyes and hold my breath, hoping I haven't scared her off. I only dare to breathe again once she starts moving up and down, stroking my dick with her hot pussy. My hands remain on her hips and my fingertips dig into her flesh, but I don't dare take control. She'll give it to me when she's ready, but for now I'll be patient.

"You want me to let you go?" I offer and she only shakes her head, her eyes closed as she practically fucks herself on my cock.

I nip her neck. As I do, her dark nipples harden and I'm tempted to rip her clothes from her. To tear them off and take her how the beast inside me wants to.

It's what the beast inside me wants, but there's not an ounce of me that would dare. That would risk frightening or triggering her in the least. I tilt my hips up so the angle lets me fill her deeper, lets me hit the back of her cunt and her bottom lip drops down with the faintest mewl of pleasure. Giving her this is all I want.

"Tell me what to do, baby."

Her head falls forward to rest on my shoulder as her pace picks up and I have to let go of her to grab the wheel behind her. If my hands stay on her, I'm going to take control. I'm barely able to keep myself from bucking into her and pounding into that sweet heat of hers. The smell of her arousal and the little moans pouring from those dark red lips have me on edge. Sensing my growing need, Veronica stops and puts her hands on my shoulders.

"Take me, Vince." My eyes shoot to hers, finding her nothing but serious. "Take me again. I want you to claim me again."

I don't hesitate to take control. "Turn around." She quickly spins around and positions my cock at her hot entrance. Gripping her hips, I pound her wet hole as my heels dig into the floor of the car. I piston into her tight pussy and nip at her shoulder. She moans in pleasure at the feel of my teeth grazing her neck. I refuse to lose focus. I need to pay attention to her reaction and make sure I don't cross the line.

I concentrate on the sound of her soft whimpers as her pussy pulses around my dick with the need to come. My hand reaches around to her front and I rub ruthless circles against her clit. She writhes beautifully, the pleasure taking over. She throws her head back and it lands on my shoulder, exposing her neck to me and making it that much easier to put my teeth right where her claiming mark is. The time has passed to truly claim her, but I'll give her exactly what she wants. And at the next full moon, I'll sink my teeth into her neck and claim her as my mate once again.

It's not a normal thing, to claim a mate twice. But we both need this. And I'm sure as fuck not going to deny her. Her pussy spasms on my dick and nearly has me finding my release as I slam into her to the hilt, but my eyes are centered on her expression, making sure it's only pleasure that has her trembling in my arms.

"Vince," she says, moaning my name. I lick her neck and watch as her body jolts from my touch. It makes me smile. As aftershocks pulse through her body, I ease my still-hard dick out of her and push the head against her ass. Her eyes pop open at the foreign touch. "Vince." This time my name on her lips is a warning. I'm ready to push her a little. Now that she's sated and has more control than she did when she was chained, I think she'll give it to me.

Moving her arousal to her puckered hole, I press a finger in and then another, making sure there's enough to lubricate her.

"Grab the wheel, baby, and don't you dare let go." She hesitates to obey, but her delicate hands grip the wheel as I ease into her. Her sharp fangs sink into her bottom lip and the sight alone has me leaking more and more into her. I watch closely as inch by inch of my cock slowly disappears into her ass. *Fuck me.* I press in deeper and don't stop, burying myself to the hilt as she squirms on top of me.

"You are so fucking sexy, so damn strong and fierce," I tell her as I move in and out of her slowly. "And you know what I'm going to do with you? With my powerful mate?" I nip her earlobe as she moans in ecstasy. "I'm going to come in your ass."

Fuck, just saying the words almost has me losing it. Thrusting harder into her, I pick up my pace. Her arousal leaks out of her pussy, dripping between us and down my thighs. Veronica's moans match my groans and I kiss her neck frantically. My eyes don't leave her face, though.

I need to make sure she enjoys this. I'm going to push her and take from her, and make her fucking love it. I buck into her over and over again until I feel my balls tighten and lift, and that familiar tingle pricks at my spine. "I'm going to come in your tight ass and you better fucking come with me."

The rough pad of my thumb strokes her clit again and again, demanding another orgasm from her. My fangs dig into her neck; the move makes her body tremble as she screams out with another release. I dig my teeth further into her soft flesh as I pound into her ass four more times until I shoot wave after wave of cum into her. I don't let up on her clit or release her neck until I've drained every bit of her climax from her.

She lays limp in my arms as she comes down from the high. I smile in satisfaction, knowing I've taken her and she enjoyed me being in control. I lick away the bit of blood on her neck and kiss the new mark. A satisfied rumble barrels through my chest; my wolf is finally settling.

Nuzzling into the crook of her neck, I ask her, "Did you enjoy that, my mate?"

She softly murmurs, "I love you so much." Her heavy head drifts to the side as her lips find mine. Finally, I feel like everything is going to be all right. I nip her top lip, which makes her smile and my wolf howls with pride.

"Vince?"

"Yeah, baby?"

"I'm thirsty." Her dark eyes focus on my neck as she licks her lips. *Fuck, yeah.* My dick twitches, still inside her.

"Go ahead, baby," I tell her and arch my neck so she can dig in.

Her small laugh draws my attention back to her. "Can I take my hands off the wheel?" My smart-ass mate. I give her a kiss on her cheek.

"Yeah, baby, let go. I've got you."

PART III

IMMORTAL LOVE

CHAPTER 11

DEVIN

"Come on, sweetheart, don't look at me like that." I don't even recognize my own voice as I plead with my mate to be reasonable. Yet again.

"Like what?"

"Like you're pissed at me and ready to fight." Steam is still drifting from the bathroom door I just walked out of and I can tell she's ready to lay into me again. I fucking love her fire, but damn, what the hell did I do now?

"I don't want to fight and I'm not mad." Grace crosses her legs in the center of the bed and lowers her head. I watch as she bunches the covers around her naked waist and pulls at the threads on the comforter.

"Then why are you pouting?" I don't understand my mate and her emotions. Humans should come with a fucking handbook.

"I don't want you to go. I'm nervous something bad is going to happen." Her raw confession is laced with vulnerability as she looks up at me through her thick lashes. Her hazel eyes are brimming with unwarranted hope that I'll stay with her rather than head out to Still Waters.

Fuck.

Striding over to the bed, I run the towel over my face and hair once more before dropping it to the floor. The chill on my damp skin does nothing to calm my growing erection. Seeing her naked on a bed, how could I not be hard? Even if she is mad at me. Shit, her anger only fuels my fire. It only makes me want to tame her that much more.

"I won't be gone long." I pick her up easily and settle her ass in my lap where she fits just perfectly. She nestles her head into my chest and runs her fingers through that bit of hair above my belly button that trails down to something else I'd rather she play with. I shut down those thoughts and concentrate on my mate. I need to distract her and get her preoccupied with something before I go. "Have you decided what you want to do?" She surprises me when she nods into my chest. She lifts her chin and meets my eyes for the first time since I came into the room.

"I want to start a charity with Lizzie. For abused children."

"Humans?"

"Yes, of course." *Of course.* I resist the urge to tell her no. I can give this to her. It'll be a pain in the ass and she'll fight me with all the restrictions I'll have to put on her, but if she really wants it, I'll bend over backward to give it to her.

I'm not sure what part she doesn't understand, but that life and her are over. Or at least they're supposed to be. Those are the laws set forth. If a human is taken, they are dead to that world. If not, then the well-protected secrets of our lives can bleed into the human realm. We can't allow that to happen.

"It will have to be done under a false name. Also, you won't be able to make public appearances or be seen at all."

She readjusts in my lap before going back to picking at nothing on the blanket. "But I'll be able to see what they do, right? And set up events and monitor how they help the kids?"

A million questions filter through my mind in response. I shut them down one by one, reminding myself that she'll learn. She'll be happy here one day. I should count myself lucky, after all. She has no family to crave to return to. Lizzie is here with her and she's adjusted quickly given she didn't know a damn thing about us prior to being taken.

With that in mind, I concede.

"You can do it the same way I run the banks. Have cameras everywhere. Hire a dedicated go-between who acts on your behalf and relays everything. You can be involved as little or as much as you'd like. I prefer being a silent partner. If you'd rather be more involved, then you can. You have to set up a business plan and a budget while we're gone. When I get back I'll set up a meeting with my consultant to get a timeline established. He'll prepare everything you need to get started." It'll be easy enough and if it makes her happy, then I'm happy to give her whatever it'll cost.

Her smile presses against my chest. She tilts her head to nuzzle her nose across the base of my throat with her eyes closed. She's so damn beautiful when she's content. I wish I could make her this happy all the time.

"I thought of something for you to do while I'm away."

She sighs sleepily and stretches, apparently ready to start the day now that she's gotten the green light for her charity with Lizzie. "What's that, *Alpha*?" My dick twitches at her use of the word Alpha.

I groan and lean my head back. "Say it again."

She smirks knowingly and says, "What's that?"

"Don't toy with me, Grace," I scold her smart ass. I'm even more determined to hear it on her lips as I realize it's the first time she's called me Alpha.

Heat races through me as she rises on her knees and straddles my thighs, bringing her eyes level with my mouth. She lifts that defiant little chin up and I swear to God if she picks a fight, I'm going to flip her ass over and fuck her into the mattress. She lets her voice come out soft and seductive when she says, "Me?" Her hand trails over my shoulders, sending a shiver through my body. I resist the urge to shudder as her nails gently run down my back. She keeps my gaze as she bites her lower lip before saying, "I would never toy with you." She parts her lips and I can practically feel the word begging to come out of her mouth. I wait with bated breath as she whispers the word, "Alpha."

My palms grip that lush ass of hers and I pull her lips to mine, my fingers digging into her flesh. I moan into her mouth, ready to push her down and rut into her. I've been taking it easy on her since the claiming, but she's healing nicely and isn't sore. Besides, she'll have a few days to recover while I'm gone and I want her to feel me every time she moves for as long as I'm gone. I smile against her lips and flip her ass over. She gasps, taking in a sudden breath as she lands on her hands and I steady her hips until her knees find purchase on the bed.

I don't miss how she smiles and that her thighs clench. She knows what's coming.

"That's my good girl."

I run my fingers through her heat, finding her slick and ready for me. I groan in satisfaction and my wolf claws at me to fuck her. As I prod her with my fingers to test her readiness to take me, she pulls away, catching me off guard.

My first thought is that I hurt her, but she's not red or swollen. "You okay?"

She turns her head, looking away and giving a short,

muffled response. My forehead pinches in confusion as I bring my hands up in defense. A tic in my jaw pulses at my eagerness to be inside my mate. I must've missed something. My dick protests my hesitation. I put both of my hands back on her hips and ask, "Sweetheart, what's wrong?"

"I don't know." I still behind my mate. I just want to fuck her, but I hold back, knowing there's something off.

Grace rolls onto her back; I withstand the need to keep her where I want her and fuck away whatever thought is bothering her. I keep my expression straight as she looks up at me while on her back. My hands instantly go to the curve of her waist, my eyes traveling to her breasts.

"What don't you know, sweetheart?" Goosebumps appear on her body as I gently trail my fingers down her sensitive skin. She squirms under my touch.

"I don't know if I'm ready."

"Wait as long as you want to start it, my love. There's no rush and I'm sure Lizzie will understand."

"For a baby." I freeze at her confession. This is the one fight I've lost between us.

"I don't know if I'm ready." She picks at the blanket again and the loss of her eyes on me makes me want to rip the damn thing off the bed and rip it to fucking shreds. "Did you know Lizzie's pregnant?"

I grunt at the thought and tell her, "It's way too early to tell." Licking my lips, I bend down to take her nipple in my mouth. She doesn't protest. In fact, she runs her fingers through the back of my hair. Her nails gently scratch my scalp, urging me to do as I'd like. I pull away releasing my tight hold on her with a *pop*. Grace slaps my arm as I admire the bright pink mark on her breast.

"Dom and Caleb are convinced," she says. A low growl vibrates up my chest and out of my throat. I'm happy for them, if she really is pregnant, but I don't really give a shit about that right now. I'm far more concerned with the fact that my own mate is taking active steps to avoid getting pregnant. And she's currently avoiding getting fucked. Another low growl leaves me.

"I'm sure they both think the baby is theirs too." My head shakes of its own accord at their arrogance. "They can't know yet. It's too early to scent it."

Grace's face falls. "Oh. If she's not, she's going to be really upset."

"Don't worry about her, sweetheart. Her heat will come again and then Dom and Caleb will be fighting each other to be inside her." The more I think about it, the more I'm worried about her delivering pups. I don't think either of them will be truly content if they don't father the first pup. I keep my mouth shut, though. Grace tends to worry and intervene, and none of that is something she should be concerning herself with.

Running a hand down my face, I wish we were talking about us rather than them.

"She's so ready to be a mother. We've never talked about it, but she's sure she's ready." Her head falls to the side and she sighs while her eyes meet my gaze. "How can you know for sure that you're ready?"

I don't understand her question, either because I've always known I'd have pups or because all the blood in my body is currently pounding in my throbbing dick. "What do you need to be ready?" If she'll just tell me, I'll fucking give it to her.

"To feel ready. Once we have a baby, we can't go back and we've just met each other."

"What the fuck does just meeting each other have to do with anything?" A hint of my anger comes out in my words and Grace narrows her eyes at me.

"We haven't had time with just the two of us. If I start popping out babies, then we really won't get any time for just the two of us."

"We'll have plenty of time while you're pregnant. Once the pups come, we'll hire help if you'd like time alone. That's an easy fix."

"I just don't *know* that I'm ready." I resist the urge to sigh in exasperation. She's fucking killing me here.

"It'll drive me crazy every heat, to know you're actively working against getting pregnant. Everything in me wants to breed you." My wolf howls in agreement. "Do you think you'll ever know that you're ready?" I pinch her chin between my forefinger and thumb, then ask her, "What are you afraid of?" Her hazel eyes widen at my question and she whips her head out of my grasp in anger.

"I'm not afraid! I just don't know." Her anger catches me off guard. We already covered this. I fucking caved already. I gave her what she wanted, but she's still fucking fighting with me.

"You told me that you weren't ready, so we're waiting. There's no reason to fight. Why are you yelling at me?"

"I'm not yelling!" She practically screams the words and I just stare back at her unreasonable ass.

After a moment, a heavy sigh leaves me and I climb off the bed. My hard dick protests the movement, bobbing up and down with every movement. I rake my fingers through my hair.

"Where are you going?" she asks and I respond by grabbing her angry ass by the ankles, then dragging her to the edge of the bed.

"Nowhere, sweetheart." I flip her over and prop her ass up for me.

"Devin!" She scolds me but with my hand against her shoulders, her back bows perfectly. I half expect her to protest, to do anything other than close her eyes and moan.

"You worry too much," I tell her and then give her cunt a languid lick. "Right now I need you to do anything but that."

She writhes slightly, a sight to behold. The second I slip two of my fingers into her greedy pussy, she melts against my touch. Her back arches and she rests her head on the bed as I curve my fingers and stroke her sweet spot. I push my thumb against her clit without any mercy.

"You've got to come, sweetheart. You're too wound up." She moans something incoherent into the mattress and I smirk at the sight of my gorgeous mate letting her arousal get the best of her. She's not in heat anymore. This is just her, loving my touch and letting it soothe her.

I kiss the small of her back as her skin heats and she pulls slightly away from the sensation. Her pussy tightens on my fingers as a bit of her honey drips down my hand. Picking up my pace, I fuck her ruthlessly with my fingers. All her small whimpers fuel me and I can't help but think this is perfect. Pregnancy or not, we have time. So long as she's mine, it doesn't matter.

I lean my chest against her back and lick my mark before growling the command, "Give it to me," at the shell of her ear, letting the heat of my breath tickle her neck. She obeys like the perfect fucking mate she is and comes on my fingers. "Good girl."

Her body is still shaking with aftershocks as I thrust my dick in to the hilt. *Fucking perfect.* Her pulsing heat feels so damn good, trying to milk my cock. Her pussy knows exactly what she wants; at least I can satisfy part of her. Rocking into her slowly at first, I take my time enjoying the feel of her warmth. But I know my mate likes it rough.

I pull her closer to the edge and piston into her without

any warning. She screams into the mattress as her little hands fist the blanket and her hips buck against mine. Her small body thrashes against my hold, but I don't let up. Instead I reach around her hips and start circling her throbbing clit.

"Fuck!" She lifts her head to scream and I know everyone in this damn estate is going to hear my mate come. And I fucking love it. Let them hear how I please her. How she submits to me. I slam into her wanting more of her cries of pleasure. My hips rock against hers as I pound into her tight sheath. My dick hits her cervix and I fucking love the feel of it.

She moans out my name as I push myself inside her deeper and hold it there. She claws at the sheets to get away from the pain of me stretching her and pushing her to her limit, but I know she fucking loves every second of it. "I want a baby." She barely says the words through her panted breaths.

My eyes widen at the admission. *Fuck!* Now that her heat's gone, now she wants a baby. I slam into her, punishing that sweet pussy as I lose myself in her. I'll fill her with my cum and do my damnedest to knock her up even though the odds are not at all in our favor.

As my cock pulses inside of her, I lean down and groan in the crook of her neck, "You want my cum? Your greedy pussy wants my cum, doesn't it?" I smack her ass so hard my palm stings and watch a red mark form on her flesh. I spank her ass again and again until she finally answers.

"Yes!" She moans out as another wave of arousal makes

fucking her that much easier. Gripping her hips, I angle her to take the punishing fuck as deep as possible. I slam into her over and over again. Even as I feel her pulse around my dick and coat it with her cum, I don't stop.

I push deep into her as she thrashes on the bed beneath me. The sight and feel of her like this has my balls drawing up and a cold sweat breaks out over my skin. It takes four long, deep strokes to have her screaming in ecstasy. Her pussy tries to milk my cock and when I feel the tight walls squeeze and flutter around me, it's enough to set me off. I come hard and I stay deep inside her even when I know I'm spent. I pick her ass up and leave her like that.

"Don't move." I slip out of her only to get a cloth from the bathroom. My dick is at half-mast but when I come back to the room it springs to life at the sight of my mate, head down and ass up. Her hazel eyes watch me closely as I stride back to her. I smirk at my feisty mate, subdued from her orgasm. Her chest and cheeks are flushed, and her breathing is still ragged. "I prefer you much more when you're sated."

"Mmm." She murmurs a sound of agreement although I imagine she'll give me hell for it when she's more coherent. "I prefer you fucking me to telling me no," she manages. Her voice is coated in sarcasm but her smile is genuine. A deep, low chuckle rolls through me at her barely spoken words.

CHAPTER 12

DOM

"**Y**ou still feel her, baby?"

My apprehensive mate nods her head with a weak smile playing at her lips. She's barely moved from the position she's in. She's so damn worried her wolf's going to leave her. It fucking kills me to see her like this, as a nervous wreck.

Sitting cross-legged in the field with the sun setting behind her, Lizzie looks just as apprehensive as she does wildly beautiful.

"Smile, baby. It's a good thing that she hasn't left." Lizzie's hand rubs against her chest like she's petting her wolf. Like the kids at my old pack used to do. I chuckle at her. If it wasn't heartbreaking, she'd be adorable right now.

"Do you think she'll stay this time?" Her question is whispered, like she'll scare her wolf off if she speaks any louder. The half smirk on my lips vanishes when she peers up at me with tears brimming. My poor mate.

I shrug, trying to make light of the situation. I've noticed she mirrors what I'm feeling. If I'm serious, so is she; if I'm not, she's not either. "Sometimes my wolf goes on hiatus. It happens to all of us, and it's okay when it does."

"That's right, baby girl," Caleb says from behind me as he pulls his shirt over his head. He strips in the field, getting ready to shift. "My wolf loves going for a run, though." He smiles at our mate, eating up the distance between the two of them to help her up. It works. She stands easily enough although her hand stays on her chest. "He's especially excited that you're going to ride him, baby."

She smacks his arm and takes two small steps away from him before she says in a sultry voice, "Don't make it sound so dirty." He grabs her small hips and pulls her body into him to kiss his mark on her neck.

"You know you want to ride me." She blushes at his teasing words and I can't help loving that warmth of happiness that flows through me. I kick off my boots and watch the two of them. The sight of her smile makes me radiate with pride. We've come such a long way. I know she's always going to want her wolf to show herself. Being latent will only make it worse, but I'll do everything in my power to help her and her wolf.

"You want to get naked too, little one?" My dick hardens at the thought of our mate exposed and bared to us. "Your wolf may want to come out more if she feels the wind on your skin." I have no fucking clue if that's really true, but I don't mind telling a little fib so I can feel her bare pussy on my back. Caleb glances at me for a second like I'm a fucking liar and I don't give a shit. Then he smiles at my deviousness and plays along.

"Strip, baby girl." He gives her neck a hard open-mouthed kiss before releasing her. She bites her lip, but nods her head and starts undressing. I stroke my dick at the sight of her curves. Her full breasts bounce as she pulls the little dress over her head. There's a bit of a chill in the air, but the temperature's nice enough. She should enjoy the feel of the sun kissing her skin. She bends over to put her clothes in a neat pile and I groan at the sight of her. My wolf wants me to push her down and take her. Caleb's palming his dick and I can see he wants the same thing. A low, possessive growl rips through me. The sound makes Lizzie jump a bit.

In the blink of an eye, Caleb shifts easily.

His black wolf trots to our mate and lowers his head. She's so small next to his beast. He licks her cheek, making her grin and she pushes his snout away letting out a peal of feminine laughter as she does. He whuffs and I shift as she spears her fingers through his thick fur.

The familiar crack of my bones is comforting and feels natural as I change form. My vision is heightened and my control waning but present. My wolf trots to her with ease and pride. He's a bit smug that he's larger than Caleb's wolf.

I shuffle back as Caleb lowers himself flat to the ground and she straddles him. My wolf whimpers with desire to see her wolf. He can smell her and he wants her more than anything. I huff at his impatience and rein him in. He may never get to see his mate, but at least he can smell her now.

Caleb takes off without warning, making Lizzie cry out and then laugh as she clings to his fur. He heads straight to the forest and I know he must want to take her to the clearing where we claimed her. I round the bend and sprint, pushing my limbs and straining my muscles to get there first. I hurl my body over the boulders in my path and duck under a fallen tree. The wind rustles through my fur as my wolf strains and I push him to run faster. I hope she sees me. The bark of passing trees barely grazes my fur as I spring forward. I don't stop running even as my breathing quickens and my muscles tighten; I want her to see my wolf at his best. He huffs in agreement and leaps through the trees.

I slow my sprint as I round the bend and come to the clearing. Panting but proud. I trot toward the entrance and wait for them to come through the path. My wolf starts pacing and I give him control. He doesn't like that we let her out of our sight; he doesn't want to share our mate right now. I shake my body, ridding myself of the leaves and debris that cling to me from my run. I calm my breath and wait impatiently. After a moment I close my eyes and try to hear where they could be. I hear a laugh to my left and my wolf snorts at me, wasting no time to head to the stream. Damn, I thought he'd take her here.

"You fucker." I hear Caleb laugh in my head at my words as I sprint to get to the stream. I'm faster in my wolf form so it doesn't take long to catch sight of them. My wolf growls low at the sight of Caleb pounding into Lizzie from behind. His fingers dig into her hips and each thrust makes her breasts bounce.

"I couldn't help it," he groans out in my head as I shift and make my way toward them.

"Selfish prick." He laughs at my admonishment.

"Admit it, you would've done the same thing." I nod at his words as he continues thrusting into her. Lizzie moans in pleasure as her knees scrape against the ground and her palms dig into the dirt. Her long blond hair flows over her shoulder as she takes every one of Caleb's thrusts. Her head arches back with her eyes closed and her full lips parted while she whimpers for more.

Walking confidently up to my mate, I put my hand on her throat and drag it up to her chin. Her soft blue eyes slowly open and stare right into mine. She peeks at my erection and then looks back up to meet my gaze. Her mouth is agape with pleasure while Caleb continues thrusting into her. I stroke my dick a few times, watching how her body jolts with each of his powerful strokes. The remnant of a faint bruise on her neck can be made out and part of me wishes Caleb would go easy on her, knowing her pussy must be aching still too. But her loud moans and her body pushing back against his hips, keep my mouth shut.

I slip the tip of my cock between her lips and she shifts forward to take more of me into her mouth. My head falls back and I let out a groan as her warm mouth sucks down my dick. Her tongue massages the underside and makes me leak down her throat. She moans as I pulse in her mouth and the vibrations make my legs tremble with the heated anticipation and need to release. I gather her long hair in my hands and wrap it around my wrist. Gripping the hair at the nape of her head, I push myself into her mouth until I feel her throat give and constrict around my length. Fuck, she feels so fucking good. I pull out and give her a moment to catch her breath before sliding my dick to the back of her throat again.

Out of fucking nowhere, Caleb's fist comes down on my arm, making me drop my hand from her hair. She whimpers from the slight pain and I shoot fucking daggers at Caleb. My wolf rears back and snarls at him.

"I can't fucking see when you do that." He doesn't slow his rhythm as he voices his concern in my head. It takes me a moment to register his words as Lizzie diligently takes my

dick back into her mouth, oblivious to the fact that I'm two seconds away from ripping her other mate's head off.

"What?" My wolf snarls again, not liking that my attention is being pulled away from our mate's touch.

He shoves himself deep into Lizzie and holds her there, making her moan around my dick and try to push away from the intensity of his shallow movement.

"Don't fucking think of coming in her. I'm up next." I pull my dick out of Lizzie's mouth and push it back in slowly as he withdraws and strokes himself, aiming his dick at the small of her back. With his right hand wrapped tightly around his dick, his left moves between her legs making her writhe beneath him.

"Hold still, baby girl." He watches as I fuck her mouth, just waiting for the chance to get into her pussy.

"Switch with me." I hear his voice in my head, but I don't register his meaning until he's pushing me out of his way to shove his dick into her mouth. My anger is barely contained. *"You better come in her pussy. If not, I'm going again."* I'm tired of him being in my head when all I want to do is give and take pleasure from our mate.

I grunt at him as I push my length into her heat. "Fuck, you feel so good." I start out nice and slow and within seconds she pushes against me, wanting more. I can't deny my mate. I rut into her with a primal need. I don't even realize Caleb's found his release until he commands her, "Swallow every drop."

I glance up from where my dick's ruthlessly pounding into her pussy to see her lick her lips and shudder with her impending orgasm. Caleb reaches down and pinches her nipples while biting her throat. She arches her neck and the sight of my mark on her has me coming in waves in her pussy. I reach around and pinch her clit to make sure she gets off and she does. *Holy fuck.* Waves of heat crash through me and make me dig my heels into the dirt. Pushing myself deeper into her, I wait for the aftershocks we're both feeling to subside before pulling out.

When I finally catch my breath and open my eyes, I see Caleb squatting in front of our mate, kissing her and nibbling her lip. She's still panting and struggling to stay up on all fours. Her skin's flushed and her legs are still quivering from the intensity of her release. I take her small body in my arms and roll us to the ground, cradling her with her back to my chest. I lift her body on top of mine and run my hands over her trembling limbs, comforting her as best as I can.

"Don't be selfish." I ignore Caleb's scolding. I just want to fucking hold my mate.

"You had her first and I didn't give you shit about it, did I?"

"I didn't get to come in her. I count that as you giving me shit."

"Stop it!" Lizzie shouts and lifts her head from my chest to glare at the two of us. I blink at her pissed-off expression.

"How the fuck did she hear us?"

"Lizzie, can you hear us, little one?" I question her

telepathically and wait for her response. I get nothing, not a damn thing.

"I'm sorry, baby girl." The fuckface decides he's going to scoop her off my chest to cuddle her and I grit my teeth to keep Lizzie from sensing how pissed I am. I don't want her getting upset again.

"Knock it the fuck off, asshole." I fucking hate that he's taking her from me. I only just lay down with her.

"You knock it off! You can keep petting her, but I get to hold her now."

"I told you two to stop it!" Lizzie pushes off of Caleb and makes to stand with her back toward us.

"You can hear us?" I'm overwhelmed with happiness, but as I search for her wolf, I can't feel her or hear her.

"Talk to us." Caleb pleads with her in my head, but she doesn't respond. Instead her shoulders start shaking and that gets both of us up on our feet.

"Don't cry, little one. We won't fight. I promise." I still don't know how the fuck she knew we were fighting. Rubbing her shoulders I try to console her, but she only sobs harder.

"You can't hear me!"

Caleb looks to me before answering her, "We heard you, baby. We'll stop fighting. Dom's just a little moody today."

"No, you can't hear me! I keep talking to you. I can hear you, but you can't hear me." Her voice cracks and the realization breaks my fucking heart.

"Your wolf can hear us?" My wolf paces inside of me at the mention of his mate.

Lizzie nods and buries her head into Caleb's chest while reaching for my hand. I take her little hand in mine and squeeze it while gently rubbing her back.

"Try again." My softly spoken words are meant to offer her comfort, but her head rears back and she practically spits at me.

"I am! I'm screaming in my head and you can't hear me!" Tears spill down her reddened cheeks as she shudders from the chill of the air.

"Let's go home," Caleb speaks into Lizzie's hair, but he glances at me with a pained look. I'm sure I share his expression. We don't know how to help our mate. I don't like feeling helpless but that's exactly the situation I'm in right now.

"It's all right, little one. She isn't ready for us to hear her, that's all."

"We'll keep on loving you and one day she'll learn to trust us and let us in."

"You can't know that," Lizzie says. Her words are hard, but then she softens her tone to add, "What if she never does?" She sobs into Caleb's chest. My poor mate.

Caleb pulls away so she has to look at him when he answers, "Then she never does and life will go on. Everything will still be perfect. It might even be a good thing. When we have pups, you'll be able to listen in and they won't hear you."

I chuckle at Caleb's reasoning and add, "Our pups won't be able to get away with shit." Lizzie looks between the two of us as a small smile plays at her lips.

"You two won't be able to get away with anything either." She wipes under her eyes and rubs her hands against her thighs, pulling herself together. "I really don't like it when you fight."

"I'm sorry, baby, I was just fucking with Dom. I'll stop." Fucking Caleb, why's he gotta be the hero?

"I'll stop too. I don't want you to get upset." She cuddles into my chest and I kiss her hair. Her warmth and touch are everything. I can't imagine hearing but not being heard. My poor mate.

"I love you two," she whispers and molds her body to mine. Caleb and I both murmur our love for her and as unfortunate as it is, there's a bond that's unbreakable. It's stronger with every small step. Forward or backward.

"Time to go home, baby. They'll be heading out soon and I'm sure Grace is going to be lonely with Devin leaving her behind. You want to ride one of us, or do you just want to walk?" Caleb runs his hand up and down her back while he talks and I can tell she's losing her energy.

"My feet are going to hurt if we walk."

"Piggyback ride?" he suggests. A grin covers his face and I snort a laugh at his words.

Her head turns to face Caleb and she smiles as she says, "You're going to make such a good father." She leans away from him and gives me a kiss on the lips before looking into my eyes. "You too, Dom. You're going to make a great dad too." My chest fills with a sense of pride that spreads warmth through my entire body. "I got to ride you up here, so I'll ride Dom back." She pats Caleb's chest and gives him a quick kiss on the lips.

"We're going to be just fine, little one." I say the words in my head and she meets my eyes, acknowledging that she heard me. I reward her with a quick kiss.

"We love you, baby." Caleb kisses his mark before he shifts. I follow his lead and shift in front of our mate. She runs her hands through my hair before settling on top of me and gripping onto my fur.

"I love you too. Both of you."

Chapter 13

Devin

With my car parked behind Vince and Veronica, I kill the ignition. The rumble fades as he does the same and all that's left is the quiet, dark night.

Neither of us gets out just yet ... there's a third party we're waiting on. I check the clock and he should be here soon. It only took a few hours to get here, but I'm already missing my mate. Lev was pissed he had to stay behind, but I wanted him and the Betas to keep our human mates safe.

Vince is attached to the coven and I'm Alpha; this task falls squarely on our shoulders.

I glance in the rearview to see Alec park behind me. There's a man seated on the passenger side I don't recognize. I've never met him before and I'm not sure I like the fact that he's here. A heads-up would have been nice. It takes me a second to register that he's a vampire and there's another vamp in the back of Alec's car. I'm not sure why Alec thinks he can trust them and I'm real fucking reluctant to let my guard down.

This surprise isn't something I would ever expect from Alec. Bristling and already irritated, I message Vince that it's time.

I shut the door as quietly as I can and wait for him to walk with me to the edge of the gravel path. It'd be far too noisy to drive up the path. It would give our arrival away as well. They'd have plenty of time to bolt, so we'll be taking it by foot.

Veronica leans against their car, eyeing the fuck out of the two vampires Alec brought. She isn't subtle and I'm guessing she's not too keen on the fact they're here either.

"How many do you think?" I question Vince.

"No clue." He takes a whiff of the air and adds, "It's stronger than yesterday."

"Just the three of you?" Alec's steps are so quiet I didn't notice he'd come up behind me. I don't give that shit away, though. I continue looking down the gravel road and nod before turning to face him.

"I didn't want our mates to be left alone."

Alec nods and says, "Makes sense." He takes a deep breath and motions the two vampires to come over to us.

"I want to introduce you to my allies, Devin." He stares

hard at me while he speaks. *Allies?* My spine stiffens and my wolf raises his hackles. I suppress his growl. These are not friends. Alec's lip rises in an asymmetrical grin as my stern response registers with him that I've understood his meaning.

"They're enemies, Vince." I speak the words calmly to Vince so he can pick up what Alec has insinuated. The fact that Alec confirmed my gut feeling heightens the anticipation for a fight. Vince makes no outward sign that he's heard me, but I can feel his anger and readiness to rip them apart. He calls Veronica over and wraps a possessive arm around her before murmuring something in her ear. I can't hear what it is, but the two vampires huff humorously with thinly veiled judgement at Vince's display of affection.

My eyes stay on Veronica, watching her as she takes in the knowledge Vince is giving her. She narrows her eyes at Vince and takes in a heavy inhale before nodding in understanding. He responds with a kiss in her hair.

"Nice to meet you two," I begin and wait for Alec to give me any more clues or signals. The plan was easy enough before, but this adds a speed bump I wasn't expecting and now I second-guess if the plans we had are realistic at all. Has our cover been blown and this is nothing more than a setup? We could be walking into a giant trap for all I know.

"This is Marcus and Theo," Alec says, pointing to his left and then right. The vampires nod respectively. "Meet Devin, the Alpha of the Shadows Fall pack. This is Vince, and his mate."

"So you're the vampire who aligned with the werewolves?" Vampire Prick Number One speaks over Alec to Veronica. "I didn't realize wolves even mated vampires."

Vince appears calm and easygoing on the outside, like he always does, but I know inwardly he's fuming. He looks to his mate with a smirk and rubs her back. She leans into his embrace before engaging with the vampire who spoke. "It's rare. I got lucky, I guess," she tells him. One of the two snorts at her response and her calm smile turns to ice.

"She's going to fuck them up. I can feel it." Vince smiles at his mate like everything's fine while his irate voice echoes in my head.

"Did you tell her what's going on?"

"Can't. They would hear. But she'll pick it up fast."

"Devin, your guns are in the trunk. Marcus and Theo, I brought guns for you too." Alec pops his trunk with a click of his key fob and the vampires and I head to the car trailing behind him. I have no fucking clue what guns he's talking about, but I'm happy to accept whatever gifts he's decided to lend me. Adrenaline courses through me, every muscle tense as I round the car on high alert. I grin at the sight, not at all disappointed.

There are three semiautomatic pistols and an assault rifle.

"Fuck yeah." Vince's voice booms with excitement. "The rifle's mine, right, Alpha?"

I see Alec nod from the corner of my eye as he hands two

of the pistols to Marcus and Theo, then stuffs the third into a holster at his hip.

"I don't think so, Vince." I pull the strap over my body and secure the weapon.

"Careful. It's all silver," Alec says.

"Silver?" Theo looks to Alec for confirmation while examining the bullets.

"I took the liberty of preloading everything." He meets the vampires' curious expressions and adds, "Aim to wound, but if you have to, killing is acceptable." The vampires exchange a glance, then nod and mutter that they understand, seemingly content with the orders.

"What's the plan?" I speak aloud, waiting for more direction and any information Alec can give me.

"Friends will be on the left," he says and turns to face the vampires. "That's where the exit is, correct?"

"No, the exit is on the right side. They're coming through there," one of them replies although neither look at him. The vampires are still examining the bullets rather than giving us their full attention. *Friends on the left.*

"Ah, got it." He looks me in the eyes and there's a beat that's serious and prolonged before he tells me, The Authority will get them from the right."

"Vince, you got that?" I start a silent dialogue with him.

"Yeah, stay to the left. Is it just the vamps we're ambushing?"

"No idea. You sure you want to bring Veronica in on this?"

"They fucked with her coven. There's no way she's not getting in on the action."

"You have to keep her safe." I know he already knows, but I can't help giving the command regardless. My mate is human, but even if Grace wasn't as vulnerable as she is, even if she was a vampire like Veronica, I still wouldn't want her here.

"I told her to stay with me. She'll listen." I hope Vince's right.

"You expect them to be waiting for us?" Marcus asks Alec.

"Absolutely." He doesn't hesitate to answer. "If they're still monitoring the blood banks, they know we're onto them. If they planted a spy in the system, they know. I think it's fair to assume they know we're coming for them. They may already know we're here now."

"So we're walking into an ambush?" I question as though I have no idea what Alec is really orchestrating.

"We're going to ambush the ambush." His silver eyes flicker with anger, but he keeps it contained and flashes a wide smile, radiating a false sense of trust and calm.

My blood heats as I draw in a single deep breath. There won't be time for hesitation. Masses have been slaughtered in seconds. We'll be in and it will be over in minutes at most.

Gripping the handle of the gun, I nod. "After you," I say and motion for Alec to lead the way, the two vampires following close behind him.

I'm locked and loaded and ready to get this shit over and done with so I can get back to Grace. My pulse races as we stalk down the grass that surrounds the gravel road. Each step quiet and in line with that of the others. I'd be quieter in wolf form, nearly silent as the vampires are now, but that would render my gun useless. And surely Alec gave it to me for a specific purpose.

Veronica hisses to reprimand her mate as Vince steps on a twig, breaking it and disrupting the quiet trail to our target. I doubt the vampires can hear us this far out, but it's best to keep perfect form until we're there.

I'm not sure if this is going to be a bloodbath, or if Alec has a plan to capture the vampires and force them to face a trial. With every silent step, my heart races faster, prepared for what may come. It's slow and steady, and every second tense and wound tight. We're only about halfway there when a loud bang shocks the quiet night. It came from the warehouse a mile or two in front of us.

The vampires take off almost too fast to register, forming a blur in front of us. I push my limbs as fast as they can go, but it doesn't even come close in comparison. Veronica's form rushes past me and the gust of wind from her speed comes a second later.

"Stop." Vince forces the word out as he gains momentum and nearly passes me. Veronica halts just outside the stairs to the warehouse. She's fuming with rage and her chest is frantically heaving in air as her fists shake at her sides. Her dark eyes follow us as we get closer to her.

"Stay behind me." Veronica doesn't respond aloud to Vince's command, but she doesn't go in without him either.

The tension between those two is thick. It's an unwanted distraction at this moment. If they can't do this, if my attention is spent on the two of them being safe, this could all go to shit.

"I've got her," he reassures me and I keep moving, passing her, following Alec as he sprints toward the double doors. All I can do is trust that he's right, that she'll catch on and that she'll listen to him.

As I rush to come up behind Alec, keeping to his left, he lifts his hands and gestures in the air. The doors are torn off their hinges and crash hard on the cement as he nears them. It's eerily quiet. Not at all what I expected. There's a noticeable lack of gunshots or screaming. *Nothing.* I don't trust it. My heart hammers in my chest. I slow my pace, planting one foot in front of the other and stand to the right of the opening as Vince and Veronica come up from behind me.

"I'll go in first, follow behind. Don't get blocked in, Vince. If I go down, run. Don't look back."

"Fuck off, Dev. That shit's not happening." I growl at his response, but quietly make my way through the doors. I sweep the room, aiming my gun to the right and left, quickly taking in my surroundings.

There are too many people in this space for me to feel anything close to comfortable. On the left half of the room are two witches, both female and both with pissed-off expressions and clearly irritated. I don't recognize either of them, but their green eyes and wild red hair suggest they're related.

In the center of the room are three humans bound and gagged, tied to chairs with silver rope. The acrid smell of their urine makes me cringe as they audibly struggle, their eyes wide with fear.

I walk in a slow line across the room, keeping my left shoulder pointed at the witches and my gun trained on the center of the room. Alec stands before the humans, but his eyes are on the eleven vampires off to the right. Behind them are two more sorcerers and a shifter, that fucker, Remy. Carol is also among them. If my math's right, that makes eleven vampires and one shifter against three sorcerers, three witches, and the three of us. The numbers aren't in our favor. But with our strength and the magic on our side, we should come out the victors, with little to no casualties. If they're smart, they'll surrender. But then again, if they were smart, they wouldn't have crossed Alec.

Natalia stands in front of Alec, waiting for him to speak. She appears confident and strong before him, but the miasma of fear surrounds her. "We got here just before you. Luckily they were easy to round up."

"Humans?" His question is laced with disbelief.

"We found two dead vampires in a silver cage in the back." She gestures at them, then faces Alec and stares into his eyes as she faintly laughs. "These humans tried to outrun us."

Heat engulfs me as the tension swells.

"Humans!" The room shakes with his anger as he roars the word. The witches to my left spread their arms wide as thunder explodes above us; the doors and windows of the warehouse suddenly close in on themselves, crumpling the steel and brick in an unnatural way, caging all of us in and cutting out all light save for the three large dome lights above us.

Fuck. My pulse hammers and I stay steady, prepared but on edge. Waiting and praying I don't react too slowly.

Natalia shudders at the witches' display of power. The vampires behind her shift slightly on their feet. Marcus and Theo slip their pointer fingers onto the trigger of the guns Alec gave them. They may be fast, but with nowhere to run, their speed will be irrelevant. Adrenaline spikes through me. A sweat breaks out along my skin and I welcome it. I crave to let my beast out, but I wait. Alec will give me a sign when it's time. My body begs to shift, I remember the gun and fight the need to shift even harder.

"Stay behind me." I hear Vince's command come from my right, but my eyes stay forward, focused on the scene in front of me.

"You thought I'd fall for this?" Alec sneers at Natalia.

"Fall for what? You think I'd betray you?" Her eyes flash with anxiety, but her voice is level.

"I know you would." Alec speaks his words slowly as

Natalia's anger gets the best of her. Waves of fear drift from the line of vampires. I watch Remy as he slowly retreats from the crowd. He has no escape now that the witches have closed everything off.

Natalia's shoulders rise and fall as she slowly backs away from Alec. Her gaze stays glued to him as she nears the line of vampires behind her. She's a caged animal with wild, desperate eyes. The realization that she's trapped and Alec knows what she's done hits both her and the rogue vampires in unison.

I steady my breathing and concentrate on the location of each vampire. Remy is the only other enemy to watch for. But he'll be slow enough to see coming. Just as I clench my fist, all hell breaks loose. The quiet is shattered with shrieks of pain and growls of rage.

I'm not sure who to take down first, but as I block a vicious attack from one vampire, I witness Theo and Marcus aim their guns at Alec and pull the trigger. In a split second, everything seems to slow. A shock of white shoots through both Theo and Marcus, forcing them to the ground as their bodies shake uncontrollably. Their limbs continue to twitch, rendering them useless.

Gritting my teeth, I keep an internal count. Two down, ten to go. Alec was smart enough to level the playing field immediately by sabotaging their weapons. I growl in triumph that we were the first to take the numbers down.

The vampires spread out in a blur behind them and attack in pairs. The two sorcerers and Carol are instantly surrounded. A beam of blue sends two vampires flying in the air and slamming against the wall behind me; it won't kill them, but at least it gives us time to get to the other side.

With every muscle wound tight, I run forward trying to reach Carol as two vampires attack her in unison. One behind her and one in front. Both of them bite into her neck and pin her to the ground. Witches have power, but their strength and speed are poor. She's knocked down to the ground as they drain her of her blood, weakening her. As soon as I reach her petite body, I jerk the nearest vampire off of her. His fangs rip her flesh, spraying blood in front of me as I grab his chin in my right hand and hold his body still with my left arm. He frantically pulls against me, trying to gain freedom, but I strain my muscles against his struggle and twist his neck, shattering his spine. His bones crack and I drop his limp body, knowing that's another one gone.

I lunge for the other vampire, prepared to fight him off of Carol, but he's convulsing on the ground with blood that's nearly black spewing from his mouth. My eyes find Carol on the ground, barely moving. Her wounds are seeping and I bend to cover them with my hand and stop the flow until she can heal herself. She coughs blood from her cherry lips and smiles at me.

"Silver doesn't hurt us, even in our blood." Her eyes

twinkle with trickery as she pushes my hands away. They're soaked with her blood and I realize she knew about Alec's plan. Who else knew?

Adopting a protective stance over her weak body, I take in what remains of the chaos as she hums and slowly heals her wounds. It's taking far too long, but I can't leave her alone and vulnerable. I stand guard and scan the room, searching out Vince and Veronica. Veronica's going head to head with Natalia, and Vince is fighting off Remy. He's not fully committed to this battle, his gaze darting to his mate with distress far too often. A snarl rips up my throat from my chest. Alec is fighting off two vampires at once, and the other two sorcerers and two witches are facing off with a vampire each. We're on the verge of losing this battle. My blood heats and pumps through me, urging me to fight.

A roar leaves me as I allow the anger to take over. The pure rage and animosity. The need to return to my mate and end this battle just as quickly as it began.

Carol slowly rises to her feet. She's still weak and in no condition to be left alone, though. If a vampire attacks her, she won't make it. Even so, I can't just stand back and watch them die; Alec is being slashed repeatedly as the vampires break through his defense and get in small hits each time. Blood sprays from his wounds as knives slit his flesh.

"Go." Her weakly spoken word is all I need to run to Alec. I push my back against his, giving him support as I wait for the inevitable blows. With our backs protected, the vampires can only attack us head-on, giving us a better chance at defending ourselves. In a blink, a gash is slashed across my face. Another blur and a gush of wind whip in front of my face. My arm reaches in front of me, but I catch nothing. The fucker is too fast. My wolf roars in anger.

Thump, *thump*, my blood pounds.

"Your gun!" Alec reminds me of the weapon strapped to my body. My fingers reach for the trigger at the same time that the vampire attacking me tears it from my body. The instant the trigger is pulled, there's a loud bang and a blinding flash of white. Instinctively I reach up to shield my eyes from the bright light. As I drop my hand and open my eyes, I gaze in wonder. Everything has slowed before me. The once loud surroundings are now a haze of white noise.

The gun is slowly being turned to face me as the pale vampire points it in my direction. I'm able to easily snatch the gun from the vampire's grasp and smash it across his face as his body seemingly continues to defy time and gravity.

Cold drifts around me as I move, seamlessly and easily while others are trapped for only a moment in this warped field.

I watch in awe as time speeds once again and the sound of screams ring in my ears, seeming louder than before. The vampire crashes on the ground and time returns to normal. My finger pulls the trigger and I welcome the flash of white as I barrel toward the still vampire and rip his throat out with my fangs. The magic relents quicker than before and time ceases to still for me as I watch Alec take the strike of a blade across his throat. I pull the trigger a third time and don't wait for the flash of light. I ram my body into the vampire, whose fangs are bared, prepared to feast on Alec's weakened body. I smash his head into the cement floor over and over without mercy. Even as time resumes, I continue bashing him into the hard, unforgiving ground until his skull breaks and his struggle becomes nothing.

Alec's body falls to the ground and he reaches for his throat. I crawl on the floor to reach him, but his eyes find mine before darting behind me in warning. I turn prepared for an attack, adrenaline spiking through my veins, but instead I see both Veronica and Vince losing their respective battles. Fear crushes down on me. Natalia and Veronica are each armed with blades, and they both have several pierced into their bodies. Veronica is much worse off, though, with a glaring gash down the front of her chest. Her body heaves, but her eyes are focused on vengeance.

Vince is struggling beneath Remy, both with their fangs out and snarling as they attempt to reach each other's throats. I quickly pull the trigger waiting for time to stop, for the moment to easily rip Remy into two, but time no longer obeys. I pull the trigger over and over as I run toward the two werewolves, wrapped around each other in a fight to the death. I toss the gun aside in a fit of anger as the magic no longer grants me an advantage and barrel into Remy's body, forcing him off of Vince. The second I have him pinned under me, Vince rises and quickly wraps his hands around Remy's throat, pulling with all his weight. I push my body on top of Remy's and wrench against Vince's strength. Remy screams in terror and pain as his neck snaps from the strain and his body goes limp.

I rise quickly, preparing for more, only to find myself surrounded by bloodshed. Carol hovers over Alec. Two sorcerers are surrounding the witches with white light. The vampires all lay dead, scattered in pieces across the large room.

The only noise is a violent hiss as Natalia and Veronica circle each other in the center of the room. Their dark, distorted dance of death has them weaving in and out among the humans who are still tied to the chairs, which have toppled over. Vince races to the center of the room, ready to help his mate.

"Behind me!" The bellowed command and the blur of Veronica's vision comes to form, her back to his. Natalia's body whips in front of Veronica's as Vince bends forward and Veronica leans her back against his as she wraps her legs around Natalia's neck, forcing the vampire to claw and slash at her legs. Vince moves as fast as he can, pushing the two vampires to the ground before grabbing Natalia's arms and pinning them behind her back. Veronica's legs bear several wounds. A deep gash in her upper thigh seeps blood as she squeezes her thighs around Natalia's neck, cutting off her oxygen.

Natalia struggles violently as she's forcefully contained between the two members of my pack. Veronica reaches forward and grips both sides of Natalia's mouth as she screams; she pulls with all her force against the vampire's jaws until they finally snap and separate. A shattered scream ricochets against the hard walls as Natalia's life is ended.

Vince releases the dead vampire, but Veronica's dark eyes are fixated on Natalia's tormented face. Her body is covered in blood and still badly wounded, but she disregards Vince as he tries to take her in his arms. Her fingers wrap around one of Natalia's fangs and she rips out the pair in turn before smiling in triumph at her dreadful victory. Vince raises his brows in question at his mate when she finally looks at him.

"For my queen." Her softly spoken words offer an explanation that Vince accepts as she heaves in a steadying breath. He opens his arms to her and she immediately goes to him, finally resting in his embrace.

They're safe. My pack is safe. Even that knowledge doesn't grant me reprieve, though. I need my mate. With my shoulders heaving as I attempt to calm, all I know is that I need my mate.

"I'm glad they used the guns I gave them." Alec's voice resonates in the quiet warehouse as he walks slowly to where Theo's and Marcus's bodies lay, still trembling in shock. "They'll talk if they want to live. All we need is one to tell us what we want to know."

"Is it over?" I question, eager to leave and return to Grace.

Alec glances around the room before settling his kind eyes on me. His large hand raises and slaps against my shoulder.

"It's never over, my dear friend. But this battle has come to an end." He gives me a weak smile before walking to join Carol. No one has escaped unscathed, but we'll all heal. Except for the vampires who dared to betray the Authority. Two will live to give answers, but they won't live long after.

I will get back to my mate. I will love her and she will love me.

Heaving in a breath, I know that's all that matters. With death surrounding us and corruption in every corner of our world, our pack is safe and that's all that matters.

GRACE

Devin hasn't taken his hands off of me. A warmth swept over me the second he stepped foot on the estate, and it hasn't left. With every soft hum that vibrates up his strong chest, it only intensifies. It's not the heat, it's something else that sparks between us. With his back braced against the threshold to the kitchen, he holds me close to him, his hand running soothing strokes up and down my back. His chin rests on the top of my head and every so often, he kisses my crown.

Each time he does, a smile is pulled to my lips.

Even if he was broken and bruised when he arrived, the shower seems to have cleansed all of that away. For each of them, every member of my pack.

The night has set and the sun will no doubt be rising soon, but the adrenaline hasn't left the room.

I shift against Devin to peek at Veronica and Vince in the corner nook of the room. Something's changed between them, something possessive and raw. Something that's dropped her guard and that's not the only noticeable change between them but it's so hard to place what's changed.

"Did something happen?" I whisper the question to Devin, peeking up at him through my thick lashes, exhaustion beginning to weigh my eyes down.

"Nothing that didn't have to happen. It all happened as it should." He kisses my temple and the warmth spreads throughout me once again as I close my eyes, feeling a familiar comfort I associate solely with my mate wash over me. "Fate conspired in our favor."

I can't help but whisper back, "Something's changed," and when I open my eyes, Veronica's sharp gaze meets mine. There's only a knowing look that she gives me before Vince cups her chin in his large hand and kisses her. He takes her lips with his and the gentleness between them is genuine and it shouldn't surprise me so, but it does. It's not unlike Caleb, Dom and Lizzie.

"A lot has changed very quickly, sweetheart," Devin murmurs into my hair and I shake my head, refusing to let the shift go.

"Something … something in the air is different," I say and the moment the thought leaves me, a chill runs down my shoulders. Devin's hand soothes the goosebumps that appear on my arm, running down my arm in the chill's wake.

In only his shirt and a baggy pair of gray sweats, I know I don't look glamourous, but I wanted to smell him. I wanted to feel him here when he was away. It helped, but not much. The lonesomeness that came over me … Lizzie felt it too. As if she heard her name in my thoughts, she glances over to me with a gentle simper. But my friend doesn't give me too much attention for too long. How could she, with both beasts on either side of her? Just as Devin hasn't stopped touching me, they haven't stopped touching Lizzie. The atmosphere is far more joyous between them, and I do feel the same relief, the same contentedness. I can't deny I feel whole in his arms.

I thought it would go away, though, this uncanny sensation, when Devin and the pack came back an hour ago, but it didn't. I repeat, more sternly, "Something's changed."

"The new moon is coming," Devin responds as if it's an obvious answer.

"What does that mean?"

"It just brings a different energy, different powers."

"Powers?" I question and he only smiles down at me, his dark and hungry gaze flashing with desire. Sucking in a breath, I try to steady my racing heart as he tucks a lock of hair behind my ear.

"You have so much to learn, Grace."

That I can't deny.

I can't help but feel like this is only the end of a chapter for a story that hasn't finished yet. It's an eerie feeling that washes over me, and one that's only dimmed when Devin kisses me.

"I love you," Devin whispers at the shell of my ear and the warmth of his breath against the crook of my neck does more to me than any other feeling could. When he holds me like this and kisses me, it's as if the entire world can wait. It could stop, it could vanish, and I wouldn't even notice.

"I love you too," I whisper, my eyes closed as he takes my lips with his and deepens it.

Chapter 14

Vince

Three Days Later

I know something's off as I walk to our room. A metallic tinge of blood coats the air. It smells god awful and reminds me of death. It's been quiet for days since we've been back and there's no reason to fear an attack, but that fucking smell makes my skin crawl and my body shake with anxiousness. The scent gets stronger and I find myself picking up my pace as a sick churning stirs in my stomach. *My mate.*

I grip the doorknob so tightly it nearly breaks off in my grasp as the door bashes violently against the wall. Veronica's form is a blur as she spins to face me. Seeing she's safe calms the beast clawing inside me. My frantic breathing eases as I walk to her. The sense of peace is fleeting as I study her face.

With wide eyes so black they match the silk negligee she wears, my mate looks as though she's been caught with her hand in the cookie jar. I grin and look past her to the large walnut desk. My smile falls instantly. My mate swallows and opens her mouth, but I silence her with a glare.

At least a dozen blood bags line its polished surface. They've been opened and drained, and it looks like she's been scraping the insides of the bag with a razor. There's a small pile of white powder in the center of the desk. The poison. She's collecting the poison designed to corrupt her immortality.

Unable to breathe, I stare into her eyes and search for an answer.

This isn't real. It can't be true. Disbelief comes in waves. What the hell is she doing with this shit? My blood runs cold as all manner of possibilities race through me.

"Did you drink the blood?" That's the first concern on my mind. I don't think my mate would hurt herself by drinking this shit. She can't. She wouldn't. She drinks from me daily. I can give her everything she needs.

"No." Her voice is small and her eyes are brimming with bloodied tears.

I nod my head and back away from the desk, walking to the bed with my back to her. If she's collecting this drug, it can't be for anything good. I think of any enemy she could have that's vampire, but I come up with nothing. I haven't the faintest clue why she would be harvesting this weapon. And it's one fucked-up weapon. They found four vampires at the warehouse; their fangs were barely visible and their immortality gone. Two were already dead and the other two were no stronger than humans. They needed a complete blood transfusion and to be bitten and turned again. They're still weak, though, nowhere near the vampires they used to be. There's no reason Veronica should have this shit here.

What the fuck is she doing? Did her queen give her orders without me knowing?

"Explain." The single word falls hard between us. I hope she can sense my disappointment and the agony at being kept in the dark. She's up to something, something of grave proportions. If she's hurting and planning revenge, she should've told me. Why wouldn't my own mate confide in me?

"I don't want this anymore." Her chest rises and falls with the admission, pain laced in her tone.

What the fuck? My heart sinks at her words. A spiked lump forms in my throat. She doesn't want me anymore? If she thinks she can run from me, she's dead fucking wrong. I'll always find her and bring her back to me.

"What have I done that makes you want to leave me?" Her head tilts and confusion is easily read on her face.

A beat passes and a hard lump grows in my throat.

"Why would I want to leave you?" Her softly spoken question instantly eases my body and I struggle to hide the fact that I'm fucking crumbling on the inside.

"You said you don't want this anymore?" I need her to clarify her words, and I fucking hope it's something I can handle. Because this shit is fucked beyond recognition and I'm failing to see what the hell is going on.

"I—" Her eyes look around the room as if searching for an answer I'll find acceptable.

I move into her space and growl out the words, "Answer me."

She stares straight into my eyes as she speaks, "I don't want to be immortal. I can't live when you die. I don't want to. I don't want this. A life without you isn't one worth living."

I stare into her dark eyes as my heart clenches in agony. My poor mate. Taking her head in my hands, I kiss her plump lips and lick across the seam for her to part for me. My tongue rubs along her bottom lip and caresses hers, while I allow the pain to subside and find the words to give her peace.

What do I know of immortality and how she's feeling? I know I would want to die if she was taken from me. I wouldn't want to go on without her. But my mate is strong and is destined to live once I've been buried in the dirt. I would never wish her to be in pain, but to want her to give up her immortality? Never.

I part from her and miss the warmth immediately. "What about our children? You're blessed to be able to care for them and watch them grow once I'm gone. You'll have peace loving them when I can't."

Tears fall from her eyes. "I don't know that I can ever give you pups, Vince." She sniffs and turns her back to me to take a tissue from the package on the desk. How did I not know this? How have I let myself be so blind to the cost of her immortality.

"You think this poison will give you that ability?"

"I don't know, but it's worth it to try if it can."

My head spins. How could she be so reckless? "But we haven't even tried without resorting to something like this. Something that could destroy you!"

She lifts her chin and defiantly tells me, "I will give it all up to be the mate you deserve!"

"You are the mate I deserve, Veronica. You're more than that." I push her against the wall and cage her in with my body. She moves easily, not resisting in the least. "Tell me you haven't taken the drug. Please tell me you haven't."

Her shoulders shake with her sobs and then she says, "Only a little." I feel my heart fall and the crushing weight of guilt push through my limbs.

"Veronica." I place a hand on her neck and kiss my mark on the other side. "Don't. Don't do this. I love you just the way you are. I don't want this. I just want you."

"But I want to give you more. I want to be more for you." My head shakes at her words.

"How can you think so little of yourself? You're perfect in every way." I kiss her forehead as tears slip down my cheeks. "I've failed you as a mate." Her hands shove against my chest.

"Don't you dare say that; you've shown me glimpses of the kind of life that is possible without the burden of immortality. You've given me hope and desire for more. How could you think you've failed me?"

"You're drugging yourself to be something you're not!" She cowers from my words and the sinking feeling of defeat races through me. "Promise me you won't take any more." She refuses to look at me and sobs harder. "Promise me, Veronica." She slowly shakes her head, but I'm not going to accept that. There has to be another way.

"Just wait for me, then." Her eyes finally find mine at my desperate words. "We can try without it. We can wait until the Authority is done with their testing." I pull her into my arms and let her head rest against my shoulder. I stroke her back and settle some as her breathing relaxes. "We can try without it." I kiss her hair, inhaling the sweet floral scent of jasmine and add, "We have time to wait."

"I'll wait." She whispers the words.

"Promise me. Promise me you'll tell me if you think about it again."

"I will, I promise."

I kiss her hair again. "We can try without it. I will give you everything you need. I promise you, my love." She sniffles and kisses the crook of my neck. The feel of her soft lips against my skin brings a warmth to my chilled blood. "I love you, Veronica."

"I will love you forever, Vince."

About the Author

Thank you so much for reading my romances. I'm just a stay at home Mom and an avid reader turned Author and I couldn't be happier.

I hope you love my books as much as I do!

More by Willow Winters
www.willowwinterswrites.com/books

This is the Discreet Edition so no-one knows what you are reading.

You can find each edition at

Milton Keynes UK
Ingram Content Group UK Ltd.
UKHW011958190124
436321UK00004B/192

CHESHAM SHUTTLE

Chesham
Buckinghamshire

CHESHAM SHUTTLE

THE STORY OF
A METROPOLITAN BRANCHLINE

Dr Clive Foxell CBE FEng

First Published 1996

Clive Foxell
4, Meades Lane
CHESHAM
Buckinghamshire
HP5 1ND

ISBN 0 9529184 0 4

Produced by

Axxent Ltd
The Old Council Offices,
The Green, DATCHET
Berkshire, SL3 9EH

Front cover illustration

The classic image of the 'Shuttle' that plied the Metropolitan branch from Chalfont & Latimer – Here in October 1955 an ex-LNER class C13 tank engine no. 67420 waits at Chesham Station for the return journey. The 'Ashbury' auto-coaches added an extra period flavour with their narrow compartments, dusty upholstery and distinctive smell of leather and smoke.

(Keith Bannister/Colour-Rail – BRE1344)

Rear cover illustration (Upper)

In October 1958 the 'Shuttle' climbs from the Chess Valley, past Raan's Farm and begins the approach to Chalfont & Latimer parallel to the main line. The 4-4-2 tank engine no. 67420 was built by the GCR around 1904, whilst the 'Ashbury' coaches date from 1899. These had a long and varied life for, after later modification into multiple-electric stock, they were converted back for steam operation with the 'shuttle' in 1940-1 and travelled over 800,000 miles before withdrawal in 1960.

(L V Reason/Colour-Rail – BRE1125)

Rear cover illustration (Lower)

In the period immediately before electrification the 'Shuttle' was hauled by BR Ivatt 2MT 2-6-2 tank engines, and in March 1959 an infrequent visitor – no. 41329 – waits at Chesham Station. In the background to the north the extensive goods sidings indicate the direction in which the Metropolitan Railway originally intended to extend the branch to link-up with the LNWR at Tring.

(G H Hunt/Colour-Rail – BRE1364)

CONTENTS

PREFACE

Although at first sight the Metropolitan branch from Chalfont & Latimer to Chesham might appear to be just a typical railway by-way, nevertheless it reflects not only its convoluted origins but also the evolving mixed role of serving both a country town and a growing commuter population. Compared with most similar towns, Chesham had to wait over 50 years until 1899 for its railway, but the eventual arrival of the branch was over the next century to dramatically change the nature of Chesham. Hard fought for by the townspeople, they have had to continue to fight for its existence and no doubt will have go on doing so in the teeth of a pervasive indifference to the advantages of a proper transport infrastructure.

My interest in the 'MET' was first aroused when, in the 1940's as a schoolboy cycling home past Harrow on the Hill station, I would be able to watch the 4.45pm ex-Marylebone express draw in, hauled usually by a grimy, but magnificent, former GCR Robinson 4-4-0 Director class locomotive, which, somehow always seemed to be 'Ypres' or 'Jutland'. Apart from the atmosphere of smoke and steam I remember the vast number of mailbags, parcels and evil-smelling fish crates which were unloaded in double-quick time, whilst in the background a MET electric loco – it might be 'Sherlock Holmes' – would be taking a rake of 'Dreadnought' coaches through to the City complemented perhaps by a semi-fast to Watford of multiple-unit electric T stock. Later I remember there was a picnic trip with a friend to Chorleywood Common, which then sported very few trees and bushes and so provided an ideal vantage spot for us to watch the railway. What we were struck by was the amount of goods traffic on what we had assumed was a passenger line.

My next contact with the MET was towards the end of the war when, between leaving school and starting work, I went with the same friend to clean locomotives at the then LNER Neasden shed. These included engines used on the Chesham branch and I came to know some of them literally inside-out. I recall that I was issued with a bucketful of paraffin plus a bundle of cotton-waste and paid the equivalent of 25p a day.

When I embarked on my intended career at a research laboratory at Wembley, one of the other people who started with me was someone who I would now recognise as a true 'Cheshamite'. He travelled in each day on the 7.30 am 'through' train and regaled me with many stories about the line that I then found difficult to believe – until later when I came to travel on it myself! It was in 1956 as a married man, now moved to Chesham and commuting by train over the branch. The line was then seemingly little changed since the turn of the century. There were a few 'through' trains at peak periods but mostly the branch line train 'shuttled' to and from Chalfont & Latimer to connect with the Aylesbury and Baker Street or Marylebone lines. Its character then perhaps was best indicated by the fact that for the cost of about 10p it was still possible to have our luggage collected by a local carrier, taken to Chesham Station, sent on 'in advance' by train to await our arrival at the hotel and then returned after the holiday. However the following period was to witness the greatest changes since the opening of the line and the move from LNER to BR steam. For then came LT electrification, followed by the threat of potential closure. Even now the survival of the line is dogged by uncertainty.

In this booklet I have attempted to place the history of the Chalfont – Chesham branch in the wider perspective of transport evolution. I have tried to show how, in spite of being a virtual pawn in the larger machinations of the railway companies, the landowners and the politicians, the branch has been saved by initiatives of the local people at crucial times. I have made every effort to employ as many contemporary photographs as possible. Although I have been unable to resist including some of the classic pictures, I trust that some will be fresh to readers.

My sincere thanks go to those photographers who are credited in the text and particularly to Ray East who provided so many of the photographs. I am also grateful to the late Ernie Woodstock, who worked on the MET for many years and who allowed me to quote from his recollections. I must also thank among many others Tony Geary, John Gercken, Harry Norman, Colin Seabright, Mark Stephenson and Ron White. I have consulted many publications on the Metropolitan Railway and these are acknowledged in the Select Bibliography at the end of the book. My thanks are also due to the Buckinghamshire and the Hertfordshire Record Offices, the Aylesbury and Chesham Reference Libraries and the London Transport Museum together with their staffs for their kind assistance in allowing me to consult original sources. Needless to say I am responsible for any errors that appear in the text. Lastly I am indebted to my wife Shirley, both for getting me involved in a Exhibition on 'The Shuttle' in conjunction with the Chesham Town Museum Project which provided the impetus for this booklet , and for her advice and encouragement in bringing it to fruition.

Clive Foxell
Summer 1996, Chesham

1

INTRODUCTION

The topography of Bucks has been largely determined by the Chiltern Hills which bisect the county from south-west to north -east. This chalk scarp rises sharply and then drops gently to the east through a series of valleys, in one of which by the Chess, lies the town of Chesham. The Chiltern hills and valleys have been a source of both wind and water power, well drained slopes, plentiful supplies of wood and fertile land in the silt from past and present rivers, attracting agriculture and a host of local industries. However the hilly terrain made travelling difficult. Settlements tended to be modest and isolated and not many larger towns were to develop. This was to reflect in the lack of a larger pattern of trade and communications both for Bucks and, more especially, for the Chiltern Hundreds.

In prehistoric times the Icknield Way, along the scarp of the Chilterns, was a major communications route and most tracks ran either parallel or at right angles to it. Subsequently the Romans settled in the area and Verulanium became an important town, but there were smaller sites such as the villa at Latimer and access must have been created to these. However, the main Roman roads took easier routes either to the north-west from London via Verulanium (St Albans), or to the south-west through Staines, or by using the valley of the River Ver to reach Alchester. Later, during the medieval period, the road system grew in an ad hoc manner coping inadequately with the increasing amount of horse transport. By Tudor times it was the parishes who tended to be responsible for many of the roads. However, traffic continued to increase with wagons and carriages adding to the existing columns of packhorses and the herds of cattle being driven across Bucks to feed London. Even flocks of ducks were required to walk all the way to the London markets! Wagons grew heavier and the already inadequate roads were often impassible with ruts in dry weather and quagmires when it rained. Such was the state of the roads that parishioners were no longer able to afford the obligatory repairs for the benifit of what after all was often just through traffic. There was now pressure for the users to pay for the upkeep of the roads. This was to lead, in the early 18th century, to the establishment of local turnpike trusts which imposed a toll intended for maintenance. Gradually these turnpikes became interconnected and the semblance of a national network was formed. These supported numerous coaching services which offered a significantly faster mode of travel. Inevitably the turnpikes through the Chilterns took the easier routes of the river valleys through Amersham, along the Misbourne and through Berkhampsted via the Bulbourne, so that it was now feasible for local people to travel to London or Oxford in a day.

It seems characteristic that no sooner does one mode of tranport become feasible than the seeds of its successor germinate: and thus it was, that just when the new roads were now carrying the bulk of traffic, so the canals came onto the scene. From early times water had provided a convenient method of transporting bulky materials such as stone and grain. But inevitably these had to be restricted either to the coast or the navigable rivers. The only major waterway in South Bucks was the River Thames, but this was of little benifit to the Chilterns. However in the latter half of the 18th century the technology of waterways had developed to the point where creating new channels with locks was possible. It was obvious that a canal between the Midlands and London would be an attractive proposition and this led to the Grand Junction Canal (Grand Union) through Berkhampsted along the valley of the Bulbourne, completed in 1805. Again due to the practicalities of coping with water levels, gradients, and now locks, it was important that these should be minimized. Preferably, it was desirable to have a source of water nearby. Even so, massive earthworks could not be altogether avoided and these were tackled by contractors with large teams of labourers, or 'navvies' (an abbreviation of the form 'navigators'). Branches were excavated to Wendover and Aylesbury, and numerous wharves were built along the main canal to serve the Chiltern villages along the Tring Gap. Now coal was to become readily available locally togther with metalware from the industrial Midlands, whilst grain, hay and wood products could now be shipped out. A passenger sevice was now also provided by relatively fast 'fly' and 'packet' boats.

However, even whilst all over the country canals were being built, a new competitor powered by steam, was about to emerge. It is true to say that rail or plate-ways had existed since the early part of the 17th century, in which waggons loaded with coal and stone were man-handled or pulled by horses on crude tracks. It took the industrial revolution to create the ability to fabricate metals for iron rails and steam engines to provide a means of power.

James Watt's engine was to be a low-pressure design, ideal for slow speed applicatons such as pumping. Other pioneers such as Hackworth, Blenkinsop, Hedley all had a part in the invention of the steam locomotive. But the crucial step was the development by the great Cornishman Richard Trevithick around 1804, of the high pressure engine for locomotives. And it was George Stephenson who, in building the Stockton & Darlington Railway which opened in 1825 with the engine 'Locomotion', brought together all the elements into a recognisable railway. He went on to build the Liverpool & Manchester Railway, the first major line in the country, which held the famous Rainhill trials to select the most suitable locomotive power available from among the wide range of often eccentric inventions that were being offered. Robert Stephenson's 'Rocket' was a clear winner and it was he who went on to build many of the railways in Britain.

This was a time of enterprise and of relative prosperity for Britain and it provided finance for the rapid expansion of the railways, encouraged by a mixture of entrepeneurs, financiers, landowners and also local people who wanted to ensure that their own town or industry was not left behind. The contractors and their armies of navvies moved on from the task of building canals to this new and larger task. The southern Chilterns were to be crossed by two of the earliest main lines from London, but unfortunately not for any reason other than that they were on the route to somewhere else! Here was a compromise between the shortest route, coupled on the one hand with an acceptable gradient for the low-power engines of that time, and on the other, by minimizing the cost of the earthworks. So again, these followed in the way of the turnpikes and canals. One of these was Brunel's Great Western Railway built with broad gauge track from Paddington to Bristol which took the Thames Valley route and reached Maidenhead in June 1838. Meanwhile Robert Stephenson decided to construct his London & Birmingham Railway in standard gauge through the Tring Gap alongside the Grand Junction Canal, with Berkhampsted Station opening in July 1837.

It is interesting that an earlier route proposed by Rennie for the L&BR in 1825 would have taken the intermediate path along the Misbourne via Uxbridge, Amersham, Wendover, Aylesbury, Banbury and Oxford. If this had succeeded South Bucks would have gained its railway access over 50 years earlier, and the area would no doubt have developed in a completely different, and possibly less attractive manner. But this was not to be. Branch lines were soon to be built from the L&BR (Cheddington – Aylesbury 1839) and the GWR (Bourne End – High Wycombe 1859 – Princes Risborough 1862 – Aylesbury 1863) isolating South Bucks as an 'island' without railways. There is a final irony. Some of the original stone blocks used by the L&BR to support their rails through Berkhampsted have eventually ended up in Chesham's Lowndes Park as seats! How this came about is explained in the next chapter.

2

LONG LOOKED FOR

Whilst the area around Amersham and Chesham remained somewhat isolated, the arrival of first the canal and then the railway at Berkhampsted had improved matters to some extent. Traffic increased markedly to and from Chesham and the prosperity of the towns became closely linked to mutual benifit. Agricultural and wooden products were transported to the station whilst coal, building materials and foods were brought back into Chesham over the intervening hills by a growing number of carts, later supplemented by higher capacity steam waggons. The 1847 Kelly's Directory shows some 14 different local carriers serving the surrounding villages and towns such as Beaconsfield, Windsor and Aylesbury.

In the past passengers had been able to use the daily Chesham Accomodation Coach to journey to London but in 1845 this was discontinued in favour the LNWR coach (later 1/- inside and 3d outside) to Berkhampsted Station which had a service of about six trains to London on weekdays. However then, as now, there was a faster and more frequent train service at Watford and Barnes's Chesham & Rickmansworth Railway Coach left the George Hotel on weekdays to make a suitable connection.

Nevertheless the local people suffered significant inconvenience in not having their own railway line. Transhipment of goods from the LNWR line involved extra handling, delay and cost. For example it was stated that the same type of coal cost 8d per cwt in Berkhampsted compared with 1s 2d by the time it reached Chesham. Equally it took passengers by coach over 2½ hours to reach Watford for a train. Against this background the local people had a tantalising picture of what a railway of their own might do for the town in terms of business and communication and they lobbied ever harder to attract one.

Their feelings are well illustrated by a report in the Buckinghamshire Advertiser of a meeting held in Chesham Town Hall on the 19th January 1853 to consider a railway line proposed by such local gentry as Lord Chesham, Sir Harry Verney and 'Squire' Lowndes, to be built from the LNWR at Watford to Wendover via Rickmansworth , Chalfont St. Giles and Amersham. The meeting had been called "to take such measures as may be requisite for procuring for the town of Chesham reasonable and proper railway communication". The Hall was crammed full and many were turned away. Those present included B Fuller Esq, the Rev A S Aylward (Vicar of Chesham) Thomas Butcher Esq (banker), J Garrett, G Hepburn, W Faithorn (doctor), T Nash, J Field, J Judge, R Clare, W Payne, J&W Suthery, H Gurney and J D Francis Esqs. The towns of Chesham and Amersham were compared. Chesham had 6000 inhabitants: Amersham only 3000. Chesham was engaged mainly in wholesale and retail manufacture, while Amersham was engaged mainly in agriculture. As regards suffrage, in Chesham there were 132 voters with owners' qualifications whereas Amersham had only 30. Chesham had 3 flour mills, a silk mill, 2 paper mills, 2 small water sawmills and one run by horsepower. The town had 3 breweries , 2 using steam engines . Shoes and wooden ware were made and sold to the London markets. Chesham was a centre for straw and tuscan plait. Altogether there were 30 master manufacturers for the London markets, but in Amersham there was only one, and that a chair maker (loud laughter here). In Chesham 12 Butchers killed for the London market. The meeting was at pains to point out that Amersham would have little use for the railway and there were more hoots of mirth at the picture of the 2 passengers a day who would board the train there. But Chesham, on the other hand would have much more use for the service.

CHESHAM & RICKMANSWORTH RAILWAY COACH,

From the George Inn, Chesham, to the Watford Station, Daily, except Sunday.

Punctually Leaves

Chesham, ...	. 20m. before 8.
Chenies, ...	. 15m. past 8.
Chorley Wood, ...	half-past 8.
Rickmansworth, ...	. 15m. before 9.

Passengers arriving in London at a quarter-past 10 A. M.

Returns from Watford,

On the arrival of the 30 minutes past 5 P. M. Train from Euston Station ; arriving at Chesham at 8.

Every information can be obtained and Parcels booked, at the Spread Eagle, Gracechurch Street ; Swan - with - two - Necks, Gresham Street ; Golden Cross, Charing Cross ; George and Blue Boar, Holborn ; Bolt-in-Tun, Fleet Street ; Spread Eagle, Regent Circus ; and Griffin's Green-Man-and-Still, Oxford Street ; from whence also Omnibuses are in connection with each Train to and from Euston Station.

Coach from Wendover to London, through Amersham—8 in the Morning.—Down, 6 in the Afternoon, daily, except Sunday.

COACH TO ST. ALBANS—leaves WATFORD STATION every SUNDAY, at Quarter-past 9 A. M., and returns from ST. ALBANS at 5 P. M. in time for the UP-TRAIN TO LONDON, which leaves WATFORD at 6.

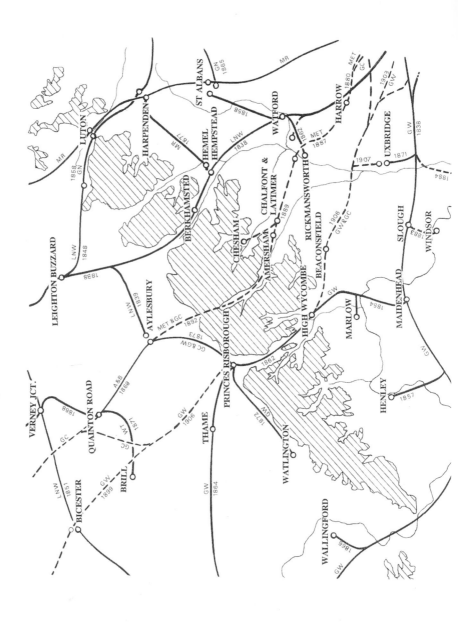

This map shows how for many years the spread of the railways was constrained by the terrain of the Chilterns. The first were built around 1837 and the 'full' lines represent those completed by 1880, showing how for over 50 years the central Chilterns were without easy access to a railway.

Whilst this particular project came to naught because the LNWR had other irons in the fire this episode reveals the old rivalry between the two towns, and also indicates the prosperity of Chesham and something of the local frustration at this time.

Meanwhile the first wave of railway development which created the GWR and L&BR had escalated into the 'Railway Mania' which swept the country. This was driven by unscrupulous promoters of whom the best known was George Hudson – the Railway King – and who before his crash controlled railways worth then over £30M. The momentum of the mania depended on attracting ever increasing investment for new schemes to fund dividend expectations. Charles Dickens well describes this chicanery in the character of Merdle in 'Little Dorrit'. Inevitably the bubble burst in around 1850 and many ordinary shareholders lost all their money.

However by then much of the basic railway network in Britain had been laid down and many of the lines now being built were to consolidate and extend the interests of existing railway companies, often poaching from each other. Over 400 railway companies came into being and the stronger ones under the control of determined managers were jostling for business by trying to form trunk routes or tap prosperous centres in their catchment area. They were often short of finance due to the crippling burden of the past construction costs and the expediency of paying attractive dividends, usually by means of manipulating their accounts. Thus the larger companies were content to let over-optimistic townspeople and landowners pay to establish their own local railway, only to kindly offer to take it over for virtually nothing when it failed. This not only avoided the building costs, but also the often abrasive negotiations involved in acquiring the necessary land and then the tortuous navigation of relevant authorising legislation through Parliament.

The reaction of local landowners varied in their extreme. There were those who encouraged railways on their property in order to develop their estates. One such was the Duke of Buckingham who actually built his own railway on his property at Wotton. Others had their price. But there were some as in South Bucks who believed that the coming of the railway would destroy their way of life. Indeed it was said when the L&BR was unable to build from London to Birmingham through Amersham, that "the only time the Tyrwhitt Drakes, Wellers and Earl Howe agreed was to keep the railway out"

During this period many railways were promoted in the vicinity, usually influenced by either the LNWR or the GWR as ploys in their bids to capture the traffic from the no man's land between their main lines to the north and west. Some promoters were naive and their enterprises foundered quickly. Sometimes enthusiastic local people promoting a railway would ultimately lack the finance to complete the task. Other promotions came from major railway companies seeking to enlarge their empires or endeavouring to keep the competitors out by means of a pre-emptive strike. Not all the proposals of the time are recorded since often the plans and surveys were kept secret in order not to alert landowners and other vested interests. Indeed the first mention of a local railway had occurred in Chesham's Almanack of 1845 and concerned a survey, undertaken around the 5th November for a line along the top of Town Field, past White Hill and along The Vale. But apparently no plans were laid before Parliament. The next Almanack of 1846 refers to an extension of the L&BR (soon to become the LNWR) from Aylesbury to Harrow and relates to a statement of the 26th August from the Directors to the effect that the line would not proceed.

Also in 1845 a peripheral railway line to avoid London had been mooted between Tring and Reigate. This received support from some quarters because it would enable trains to link the L&BR, the GWR at Slough, the South Western Railway at Weybridge and the Dover & Brighton Railway at Reigate. The route was designed to enter Chesham via The Vale and then pass west of Amersham and through Beaconsfield. Nothing had come of this, nor was anything to come from the proposal of 1853 which was the subject of the meeting in Chesham Town Hall described earlier, due to the shortage of capital.

Again in 1853 the West Midland Railway was to put forward a line from Oxford via Princes Risborough, High Wycombe and Beaconsfield with a view to reaching London, but their Bill was defeated.

Another orbital route was now championed by Lord Ebury who resided in what is now the club house of Moor Park Golf Club. He was an enthusiast for railways and proposed a number of railways in the vicinity. These culminated in a successful Bill in 1860 authorising the Watford & Rickmansworth Railway. There soon followed proposals for an extension on to Uxbridge and construction to Rickmansworth was completed in 1862. The line was operated by the LNWR who later in 1881 absorbed the bankrupt company. The original hope of connecting with the GWR at Uxbridge resulted in 11 unsuccessful attempts to get various Acts passed by Parliament. Lord Ebury also used this Rickmansworth branch to propose a Rickmansworth, Amersham & Chesham Railway bill in 1862, and again in 1880, which would have run via Chorleywood, Chenies, Amersham and into Chesham at Amy Lane. Later a branch was promoted from Chenies to Aylesbury in a vain attempt to attract funding for the whole scheme from the GWR.

The then independent Wycombe Railway operating to Bourne End was within GWR influence and in 1864 a Bill was drawn up seeking authority to build a line from their railway south of Loudwater to Uxbridge(GWR) via Beaconsfield, Chalfont St.Peter and Denham. However when the WR was formally absorbed by the GWR they dropped the proposition on financial grounds.

To the north the LNWR encouraged the so-called Bucks & Herts Union Railway to obtain acts in 1862 and 1866 to build a line from the Great Northern Railway between Luton and Dunstable to Hemel Hempstead and then linking with the LNWR at Boxmoor before terminating at Chesham (near the Three Tuns in White Hill). However the LNWR "hesitated to incur the expense of cutting through miles of irregular hills to reach a place ensconced in the deep valley of the Chess". Nevertheless the Midland Railway took up the northern part of this scheme opening a branch from Harpenden to Hemel Hempstead in 1877, but there was no physical connection with the LNWR mainline at Boxmoor – whose own passengers therefore still had to take a horse bus to the town. The MR was also behind an abortive schme of 1865 for a London, Buckingham & East Gloucester Junction Railway which would have run from Quainton Road via Aylesbury, Amersham and Rickmansworth to their main line at Hendon.

Then in 1887 and 1888 locally-inspired bills for a Chesham, Boxmoor & Hemel Hempstead Steam Tramway were brought forward to act as a feeder to the MR branch for the straw plait industry centred on Luton and Dunstable. Various routes for the light railway were proposed: one would have run from Boxmoor, via Bourne End and Nashleigh Hill to a site in North Chesham at Cameron Road. A steam-hauled tram running on track of 3' 6" gauge was proposed for cheapness and also because the track was expected to be extended to run along the road from New Town into the centre of Chesham at the Broadway. A second version was to have been constructed in standard gauge and terminating at Nashleigh Hill. In the town the supporters included 'Squire' Lowndes and some brewers, Messrs Burt and Nash, who sought to encourage the project by buying some of the redundant granite sleeper blocks from the L&BR at Berkhampsted. However once again it was abandoned, as well as a reincarnation of the plan in 1900 in the shape of an electric railway. Failure here was due to lack of funds and opposition by the Boxmoor Turnpike Trustees who still collected some tolls in the area. Some of those unused granite blocks were then used to support local cattle troughs and three of the stones now rest in Lowndes Park.

But in the event the fate of the tramway had already been sealed by the moves of a new major player in the railway chess game of the time.

A saviour for South Bucks was in sight.

3

METROPOLITAN MACHINATIONS

The railway to Chesham came about in an unlikely manner, in that it was built by a company that until then had been thought of as only serving central London. Indeed the very name, the Metropolitan Railway, epitomized its mission. The development of the Metropolitan was to be shaped by three strong, but very different, characters – Charles Pearson who conceived it – Edward Watkin who employed it as a springboard for his wider ambitions – and Robert Selbie who turned it into MetroLand.

The Charles Pearson Era

The history of the Metropolitan Railway has been well-covered in the works listed in the bibliography and therefore the period up to the arrival on the scene of the catalyst Edward Watkin is only mentioned here as a background to subsequent events and to demonstrate its London orientation.

The concept behind the Metropolitan arose in the 1840's as a possible solution to several of the problems besetting the City at that time. Congestion from horse and other traffic was reaching serious proportions in Central London and a by-pass was needed to the north. A start had been made several years before when the New Road (now the Marylebone, Euston and Pentonville Roads) had been constructed to avoid the need for cattle to be driven along Oxford Street to reach Smithfield Market, and the City Corporation were now considering extending this via the Clerkenwell Road and Faringdon Street in order to clear the slums along the River Fleet. Equally railways were now proven and tunnels not unusual and so Charles Pearson, a solicitor in the City, proposed that an underground railway could be built along the route of the New Road and extension, thus easing cross-London transport and also linking the various new mainline terminii now being erected in the vicinity. Using the line of the roads would also have the advantage in minimizing the costs of acquiring land, demolishing buildings and compensation.

Many schemes to this end were floated during the 1840's, but failed. Undeterred, Charles Pearson with his enthusiasm and persistence ensured that when the financial climate improved around the time of the Great Exhibition an Act embodying the foundations of the subsequent Metropolitan was incorporated in 1854. However again the lack of finance due to the uncertainties of the Crimean War and the practicalities of long underground railways delayed a start on building the line. Pearson kept doggedly to the task and by obtaining funding from the City Corporation(where he was now The Solicitor) and the GWR, enough capital was put in place for construction to start in 1859.

Using the roads as the route , deep trenches were dug for the railway and then the tracks covered by a roof which carried the new road surface. This created the first underground railway in London, running between Paddington and Farringdon and built with double tracks each suitable for both Standard and Broad Gauges. Apart from the general unease of the public about travelling underground there was particular concern over the effects of smoke and steam from the locomotives in such a confined space. In order to avoid this problem their Chief Engineer, John Fowler, designed an idiosyncratic locomotive that was supposed not to emit smoke between stations, but inevitably this was a failure and at short notice the GWR quickly built some condensing engines in time for the opening in 1863. Soon the uneasy relationship with the GWR broke down, not for the last time, and after having to borrow some engines in the emergency from the GNR, the Metropolitan ordered their own to be built. The new line was immediately popular with over 10M passengers travelling in the first year and this initiated the upsurge of underground railways in London, however the problem of sulphurous smoke combined with inadequate ventilation was to dog the Metropolitan for years until electrification.

The company extended its catchment area by encouraging the independent construction of the Hammersmith & City Railway in 1864 and in the same year the authorisation of the Metropolitan & St. Johns Wood Railway. The latter is of interest for what followed but at that time it was only a single track from East Baker Street into the country as far as Swiss Cottage. However their main concerns were in other directions with in-fighting over the potential Inner Circle and access by the mainline railways. During this time the financial affairs of the Company had declined to reach a parlous state due to a combination muddled accounts, excessive expenditure and the expediency of keeping shareholders sweet by paying excessive dividends out of capital. In consequence the Directors were taken to court, their actions decalared fraudulent and the angry shareholders pressed for a clean sweep of the Board. A group of the larger shareholders arranged for an experienced industrialist and railwayman, Sir Edward Watkin, to join the Board and rapidly he became Chairman in 1872.

Watkin's Hidden Agenda

The new Chairman was to exert a profound influence on the Metropolitan as it became an essential part of his greater scheme of things. As a result Watkin became one of the greatest railway magnates in late-Victorian times, seizing opportunities as they arose by dint of his forceful character. In view of what transpired, it is worthwhile looking at his career in order to try to understand his mercurial actions.

Born in 1819 as the son of a wealthy Manchester cotton merchant, training in the family concern developed his commercial acumen whilst his father's position in the town led him to be involved in many public works. These included founding the 'Manchester Examiner' and he was soon demonstrating his ability to manage several different enterprises at the same time. Striking out on his own he left the family business in 1845 and took the job of Secretary to the Trent Valley Railway and showing his characteristic shrewedness negotiated its sale for £480,000. Notwithstanding that, after a visit to America, he joined the LNWR to whom he had sold the TVR. Here he became personal assistant to Captain Mark Huish, who was the most ruthless railwayman of the day, and no doubt learned from him the agression and manipulation that was then the norm in this second generation of railway entrepreneurs.

Soon Huish appointed him as General Manager of the Manchester, Sheffield and Lincolnshire Railway but later Watkin showed what he had learned by converting the company into his own and becoming Chairman. This activity was interspersed by further visits to Canada, where for the Government he examined the Confederation, control of the Hudson Bay Territory and the planning of the railway system. The latter led to Watkin becomming President of the Grand Trunk Railway of Canada. On returning he also became Chairman of the South Eastern Railway, for brief periods a Director of the GWR and the Great Eastern Railway, promoted the Cheshire Lines Committee and also the Athens and Piraeus Railway together with a railway between Liverpool and Cardiff. He was at the same time involved in a number of major infrastructure projects such as the Mersey Tunnel, Connah's Quay swing Bridge, a new port at Dungeness, a Dublin-Galway Canal and a tunnel between Scotland and Ireland!

However in spite of this restless drive over such a wide front his main attention was devoted to the three railway companies that formed the heart of his empire: the MS&L, SER and the Metropolitan. Whether this grouping came by chance or deliberate planning is difficult to judge but he not only took every opportunity to expand each company but also to look for synergy between them. Watkin was diplomatic and concious of creating the right impression with bankers, shareholders, landowners and others he needed to acquiesce to his plans, but without revealing too much. In formulating and carrying out his plans he was forceful and autocratic, being extremely unwilling to reveal his intentions or delegate to his colleagues. Indeed his senior managers often admitted to being unaware of the reasons for particular decisions.

In retrospect it would seem that he was attracted to the 'grand design' in which trunk routes could be created to generate major trading opportunities. However he recognised that if they were put forward in specific detail this could be counter-productive in provoking shareholders, landowners and competitors, and thus he adopted a more pragmatic approach in gradually building up the necessary pieces of the jigsaw. In doing this he kept several options open at any given time, seizing chances where they arose to create incremental benefits to his existing operations and squeezing advantages from the whole of his empire. For example, when the Metropolitan was held up for lack of ballast for track laying, he ordered the SER to provide some from Dungeness.

Although never stated in explicit terms it appears that he was motivated to create a through rail connection from Manchester to Paris, two towns to which he was greatly attached, using his power as Chairman of the MS&L, Metropolitan, SER and the Submarine Continental Railway which was trying to build a Channel Tunnel to link up with the Chemin de Fer du Nord and Paris. To achieve this he turned the MS&L into a mainline as the Great Central Railway thereby extending it southwards towards London to join the Metropolitan, which in turn was linked via the ELR and the Thames Tunnel built by the Brunels, to the SER thus giving access to the south coast. This is now leaping ahead of the time of the railway to Chesham but it is of interest to note how far Watkin got in achieving his goal. The GCR was built to London, and as a Francophile he started to build an imitation of the Eiffel Tower, on what became the Wembley Exhibition site, but it did not attract the anticipated traffic and only reached the first level. Meanwhile the Channel Tunnel Company had started work in 1881 and dug a trial bore for over 1,900 yards under the Channel before being halted by Government concerns over invasion. Watkin tried every manouvre he knew to overcome this by means of private Bills 1888 and 1890 but shortly after marrying a lady of 81, who was the widow of the founder of 'The Illustrated London News', he suffered a stroke in 1894 which incapacited him to the extent that he took no furher executive role in the various enterprises, dying in 1901 without quite realising his dream.

The 'Extension'

Watkin had rapidly made himself felt at the Metropolitan by imposing stronger management and economies in all departments, whilst giving the Company a higher profile in the railway world. In his other role as Chairman of the SER he had been embroiled in a personal rivalry with John Forbes who was Chairman of the London, Chatham & Dover Railway, each vying over traffic to The Channel and this animosity escalated as the two were now competing through the Metropolitan and the Metropolitan & District railways which formed parts of an embryonic 'inner circle' for London. In this matter, as others, neither would give way for the common good and relations deteriorated to the ludicrious extent of chaining up the rivals locomotives and building a station by stealth! Indeed even after the formal completion of the Inner Circle route the parties remained in dispute.

However on another front Watkin was quick to see the potential of the single track spur to Swiss Cottage which had run out of money before reaching the objective of Finchley Road, and as a result the moribund company came increasingly under the control of the Metropolitan after 1874. He saw that completion could give useful connections here to both the MR and the LNWR. This was an example of Watkin's objective of extracting every possible benefit from a new line, often by effecting interchanges with larger railways which would generate transit traffic for the Metropolitan. In particular, he was concerned to attract freight workings to balance the inherent preponderance of passenger operation. This was part of his wider view that it was desirable to join the individual railways to form major trunk routes and thus obtain the economies of scale necessary for the efficient transport of goods and raw materials between the mines, factories and ports. He also had a stronger reason for developing the Finchley Road extension in that it would form a springboard to break out of London in a gap between the major players. To this end the erstwhile branch was extended to Finchley Road in 1879, then a twin tunnel added and the whole made compatible with the Metropolitan in 1882.

In true Watkin fashion he had several other irons in the fire. Of particular relevance was the relationship he had established with the Duke of Buckingham, who had become something of a freelance promoter of railways, in order to develop his extensive estates in the Vale of Aylesbury. Hoping to ensure an outlet for his farm products to large towns he proposed a number of grandiose schemes, one that came to partial fruition was the Aylesbury & Buckingham Railway which emerged as a light country line from an isolated Verney Junction(LNWR) via Quainton Road to Aylesbury(GWR) in 1868. Sensing the possibilities, Watkin encouraged him to promote an major extension in the shape of The London & Aylesbury Railway which would have helped his own plans – at the expense of others – although in the end authorisation was never given. Meanwhile he convinced the Metropolitan Board to build on from Finchley Road to Willesden Green in 1879 and on to Harrow on the Hill in 1880 on the basis of generating more business and attracting links from other railways. Now the Metropolitan had almost as much track outside as within London and new locomotive and maintenance facilities had to be created at Neasden, which being in the countryside meant that the Company had to build houses and shops for their employees. In doing all this Watkin had established a base that he could use to expand northwards or to tempt others to join him. Typically, whilst continuing to encourage the Duke of Buckingham and support his involvement in proposals for an Oxford & Aylesbury Tramway which had the potential of another tentacle to his empire, he also kept his options open by participating in other schemes in the area. Incidently the O&A Tramway only saw the light of day in 1871 as the minor Wotton Tramroad from Quainton Road on the A&BR.

Metropolitan shareholders continued to be fed crumbs of information wrapped-up in euphemisms – 'the Extension line' – 'breaking through the iron barriers the large railway companies have constructed' – 'connecting with other important towns' – 'increasing the amount of freight traffic'. Watkin was always careful to say just the minimal amount so that the record would be straight and agreement implied, but actually shareholders attention would be drawn more by his emphasis on other matters, such as the inflated dividends that continued to be paid. At the time of the first push to Finchley Road in 1874 he had already incorporated the Harrow & Rickmansworth Railway and started acquiring the relevant land, this was then activated in 1885 and the line opened via Harrow to Rickmansworth in 1887. As the town only had a population of some 1800 the passenger traffic was meagre and to bolster it a horse bus service to Chesham was started on the 1st September 1887. The Rickmansworth goods traffic was now facilitated by completion at the London end of a connection to the MR at Finchley Road and encouraging freight traffic in coal was established as well as ballast from the nearby gravel pits owned by Lord Ebury.

Forward to Chesham

By 1880 Watkin had become firmly committed to pushing on to the north-west and the Metropolitan Board had obtained authorisation for an Aylesbury & Rickmansworth Railway on the 6th August 1881. It must be remembered that this was purely artificial, but convenient way of creating a company that could be later absorbed into the Metropolitan and that there was no obligation to build the railway at that stage. It was

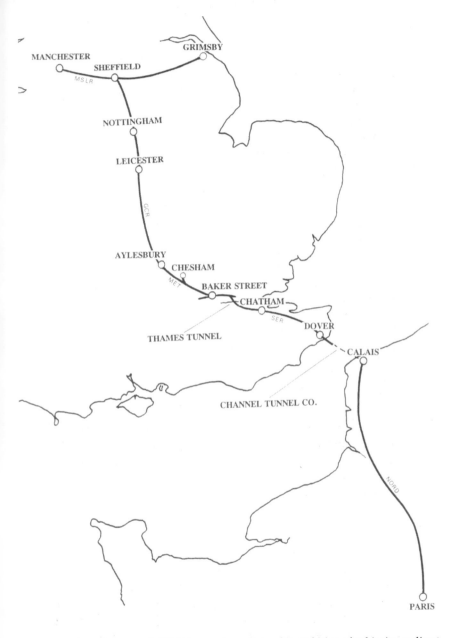

MANCHESTER

GRIMSBY

SHEFFIELD

MSLR

NOTTINGHAM

LEICESTER

GCR

AYLESBURY

CHESHAM

MET

BAKER STREET

CHATHAM

SER

THAMES TUNNEL

DOVER

CALAIS

CHANNEL TUNNEL CO.

NORD

PARIS

The map shows how nearly Watkin was to realising his ambition of achieving a direct rail link between Manchester and Paris.

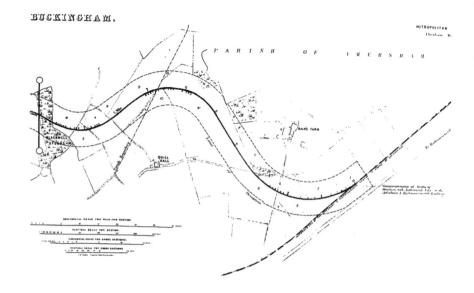

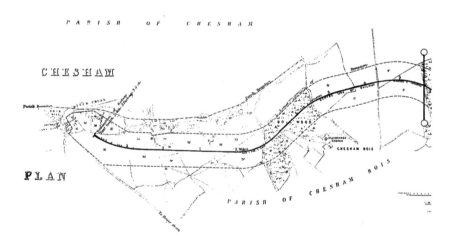

Parliamentary plan deposited by the Metropolitan Railway in 1885 for the branch to Chesham which would have terminated outside the Town.

normal for many such companies to be formed and a large number of speculative surveys were undertaken accompanied by the opportunistic purchasing of land, before any final decision.

Indeed Watkin was exploring the possibilities of at least two routes from Rickmansworth to the north-west based on the gaps in the Chilterns along The Misbourne via Wendover and The Chess via Chesham. If feasible, he wished to reach his MS&LR in the north but the exact route would depend on the outcome of negotiations with the A&BR and others. Whilst the A&BR would be an attractive choice, they had also been approached by the GWR with whom they shared Aylesbury Station. At the same time Watkin had also reached tentative agreement with the LNWR (where his friend the Duke of Buckingham was on the Board) to swing the Metropolitan 'extension' more to the north to join their line between Watford and Tring to give them an alternative loop into London and the south – whilst in the process providing extra transit business for him. By 1882 Chesham had been identified as the only town of any importance, then having a population of over 6500, compatible with meeting both options. It therefore seemed prudent to seriously consider a line to there from the Aylesbury & Rickmansworth Railway and Watkin started to talk to the key landowners with a view to acquiring the necessary land. The land needed for the line and station at Chalfont was bought from the Duke of Bedford, and amounted to 28 acres at a cost of about £100 per acre. As we know the people of Chesham had long agitated for a railway and as the Metropolitan approached they began to lobby harder. Watkin now sought to turn this to his advantage when visiting the town in November 1884 and telling a meeting that it might be possible to build a railway to Chesham and on to Tring with the LNWR, if they were prepared to sell the land for a 'reasonable' amount. The necessary land through Cheham Bois was bought from from the Duke of Bedford, D Darvell, the trustees of Mrs Garrett & J Hayes, whilst that to gain access to the ouskirts of Chesham came from W Darvell, H Webb, J Fuller, W Lowndes, Miss

Hepburn & M Birch. As might be expected the town itself was enthusiastic and Watkin then obtained provisional agreement with the LNWR that they would fund half of the cost of the line in exchange for running powers to Rickmansworth. To facilitate this the Metropolitan obtained the necessary Act in 1885, but subsequently the composition of the LNWR Board changed and they became less keen on the idea. Nevertheless by 1887 the Metropolitan had acquired most of the land from Rickmansworth to the outskirts of Chesham at Mill Field and determined to build this section.

With his mind still on the MS&LR to the north, Watkin arranged a survey of the route from what was to be Chalfont Road (later Chalfont & Latimer) Station along the A&BR to Quainton Road. In August 1888 he convinced the Metropolitan Board to implement this line, thereby turning the line to Chesham into a branch. Consequently, the A&BR was now a vital part of the jigsaw and when their negotiations with the GWR lapsed the Metropolitan seized the initiative, leading finally to acquisition in 1891. Further to the north Watkin encouraged the MS&LR to put forward an intentionaly ambigious bill which provided cover for a strategic extension south to Annesley, near Nottingham.

Thus the gap was slowly closing whilst plans were still being drawn up for the new line to Chesham. Not suprisingly the local people were becoming increasingly upset that station was to be built on the outskirts of the town at Mill Field near The Moor but, by the time the preparations for the station area were well underway, including a railway hotel – now the Unicorn – a public subscription was launched to pay for the land necessary to bring the line the final ½ mile into town. In this effort the leading people are mentioned as 'Squire' W Lowndes, Messrs J W Reading, J&E Reynolds, and G&W Webb. Nevertheless, whilst Watkin had certainly intended to put the station at Mill Field, by 1890 he had already embarked on the purchasing land beyond and along The Vale towards the LNWR at Tring.

The first railway to pass through the Chilterns was the L&BR from London which reached Berkhamsted in July 1837. The early railways needed a relatively level route and therefore, like the earlier turnpikes and canals, tended to follow the line of the river valleys. This shows the first station at Berkhamsted with the Grand Junction Canal to the right of the picture.

For Chesham, access to the railway at Berkhamsted involved using horse-drawn carriers or coaches. Some coaches also made the longer journey to Watford in order to connect with the faster trains. Here such coaches wait outside The George Hotel in Chesham High Street and were a well-established feature as the local people had to wait over 52 years for their own railway. (Ray East Collection)

The route to Berkhamsted was hilly and exposed and whilst it cost 3d to ride outside the coach, the charge was 1/- for travelling inside. (Ray East Collection)

When the original stone 'sleepers' from the L&BR at Berkhamsted were replaced they were acquired by some Chesham businessmen for use in an abortive scheme for a local tramway and now rest in Lowndes Park. (Clive Foxell)

Sir Edward Watkin (1819-1901) was one of the last of the railway 'barons' and his wider ambition for a grand trunk railway from Manchester to Paris was to result in bringing the Metropolitan Railway to Chesham as part of a possible route to the north. (National Portrait Gallery)

ust before the coming of the railway, the workers from Webb's brush factory have come out to ook at the photographer in the centre of the Broadway in Chesham. Later an access road to the station was driven through the houses on the right.
(Ray East Collection)

Firbank the contractor used several light 0-4-0 tank engines in the construction of the branch to Chesham. This shows 'Groombridge' working on the line down the side of the Chess Valley with large buffer stocks to accommodate the varying heights of the motley collection of wagons. (Ray East Collection)

Most of the chalk excavated from the cuttings which were made to ease the climb along the side of the Chess Valley was used to create the embankment across the Moor. (Ray East Collection)

The site of the terminus the MET intended at the Moor on the outskirts of Chesham. However local people gave the necessary land to bring station into the town and here the new line continues to curve across the Moor towards Waterside. (Ray East Collection)

The railway crossed the Moor over the famed watercress beds and two roads before entering Chesham. This shows the bridge over the River Chess which gave the Railway Inspectorate some concern in 1889. (Ray East Collection)

In the final approach to the station the contractor had to make a cutting through the tiered cultivated strips created by the Saxons, known as the 'baulks'. (Ray East Collection)

The goods shed was of the standard MET design. The carpenters working on the roof appear to be of three grades, the most senior are appropriately wearing bowler hats, the next cloth caps and lastly an apprentice stands on the ladder. In the background is Lowndes Park still with it's avenue of trees. (Ray East Collection)

Building the line cost more than expected, partly due to the expense of laying temporary track in order to provide an early trip for the benefit of some Directors and local dignitaries from the partly-built Chesham Station. (Ray East Collection)

Although neither formal Parliamentary nor Railway Inspectorate approvals had been given, the MET organised a celebration on the 15th May 1889 to mark the completion of building works. A special train of MET coaches headed by two contractor's locomotives, preceded by a pilot, left Chesham at 11.30am. (Ray East Collection)

Another view of the special train with a large crowd of onlookers and a man who appears to be checking the clearance between the platform and the running board of the coach.
(Ray East Collection)

On the return from Rickmansworth a lunch of many courses, wines and speeches was held in the goods shed which was suitably decorated for the occasion. Here the townsfolk crowd outside whilst one of the bands plays beneath the bunting. (Ray East Collection)

Public services started on the 8th July 1889 and this shows a typical passenger train of this period headed by a class A 4-4-0T no.4. These engines had been built to work in the confines of the underground lines and were thus fitted with condensing apparatus, but they had no protection for the crew against the rigours of the weather in the Chilterns. (Ray East Collection)

Chalfont Road (Junction for Chesham) around 1900 with the staff proudly grouped around an item of goods. In the background the 'shuttle' of 8-wheel rigid coaches has arrived behind class B no. 59, whilst on the up line a GCR express approaches. This is a handsome Robinson 4-4-0 class 11B in its original condition and unspoilt by subsequent alterations. (Colin Seabright)

A down train enters Chalfont Road headed by a GCR 4-4-2T class 9K probably built around 1905. The lack of shelter for passengers that was to be an ongoing source of complaint for many years is clearly evident. (Clive Foxell Collection)

The station staff posed on the down platform at Chalfont Road. The name was not changed to Chalfont and Latimer until November 1915 and it was 1925 before proper access was provided to this platform from the new village of Little Chalfont. (Colin Seabright)

On the 19th August 1909 an A class tank was derailed near Hodd's Wood due to a broken axle. Nobody was injured and a service was maintained by trains from Chesham and Chalfont running to either side of the accident. Like most of its class, no.46 now had a full cab in order to protect the crew from the weather. (Ray East Collection)

A view of Chesham Station from the coal stage used for replenishing the locomotives. One A class tank has come off the 'shuttle' whilst another moves to the front to take it out. (Ray East Collection)

After ill-health forced Sir Edward Watkin to give up control of his two creations, the MET and the GCR came into confrontation but in 1906 this was resolved by the formation of the Metropolitan & Great Central Joint Railway to run the 'Extension' line. As a result GCR trains operated the branch and here a GCR class 9L 4-4-2T engine is entering Chesham over the bridge at Waterside around 1910. (Ray East Collection)

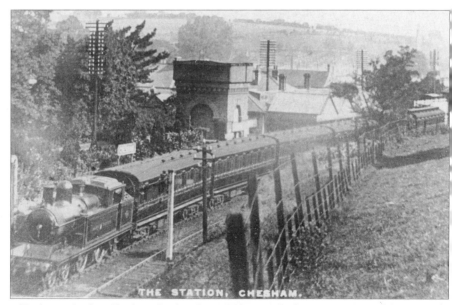

THE STATION, CHESHAM.

Having arrived at Chesham Station the same locomotive has now run round its train of the latest GCR suburban coaches with a clerestory at the rear. The 9L engines had a distinctive raised portion of the cab roof to give more headroom for the crew, as well as larger side tanks and coal bunkers than the earlier class 9K. (Ray East Collection)

picture of about 1908 from a field near the Amersham Road and looking towards Waterside at the start of the 1 in 66 climb towards Chalfont Road. The train consists of a GCR class 9K 4-4-2T hauling an ex-MS&LR suburban coach and a set of the new longer GCR suburban coaches. (Ray East Collection)

No.46 after surviving the accident in 1909, with a train in Chesham goods yard during the First War. The load consisted of sectional wooden buildings destined for the army in France. (Ray East Collection)

Robert Geary collecting passengers' luggage from Broad Street in Chesham to be sent on in advance. His father helped to build the branch and then maintain it, whilst Tony his son became a signalman on the MET. (Tony Geary)

A general view of Chesham Station showing how the water tower dominates the scene. (Ra East Collection)

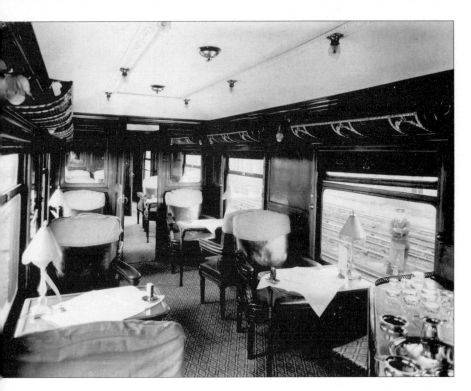

To emphasise its claim to mainline status the MET introduced two Pullman Cars which ran until the outbreak of war in 1939. For the supplement of 1/- businessmen used it in the morning to travel to the City, whilst at night theatregoers found it convenient for returning after a show. (LT)

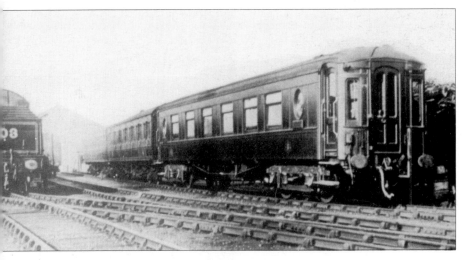

After arriving behind H class no.103 the Pullman rests in Chesham yard on a Saturday before being returned the next day to Neasden for cleaning. (John Gercken Collection)

Robert Hope Selbie (1868-1930) who consolidated the operations of the MET after Watkin's excesses and created MetroLand. (National Portrait Gallery)

Apart from the logo, posters and publicity one of the best remembered features of the MET was the engraved brass plate on every coach door. (Clive Foxell)

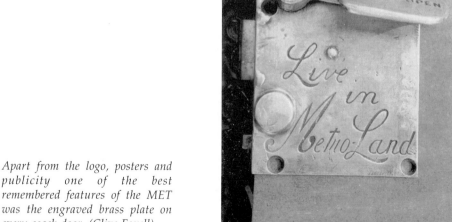

Construction proper started in late 1887 and a separate Bill to authorise the extra 71 chain extension was put to Parliament, but it did not receive Royal Assent until only just 3 days before the public opening of the line.

CHESHAM SHUTTLE

4

COME AT LAST!

For the railway beyond Rickmansworth the contractor was James Firbank and the supervising engineer was a colleague of Robert Stephenson, Charles Liddell, who was also surveying the possible route across The Vale of Aylesbury. The 4½ mile main line to Chalfont Road ('road' invariably indicated that it was a long way to the place, and 'Chalfont' was suitably ambigious to cover both parishes!) was laid to the south of the Chess Valley in order not to lose height for the subsequent climb of the projected main line to Aylesbury through the Wendover Gap over Dutchlands summit. Leaving Chalfont the single line to Chesham of some 3 miles 56 chains, after running beside the expected tracks to Amersham and Aylesbury, curved northwards in an 'S' bend to the edge of the Chess Valley descending down the brim at a gradient of about 1 in 66 to a level suitable for crossing the river by a 31ft wide bridge of two spans. Then after crossing the road to Waterside by similar bridge, a sharp curve of 1 furlong 2 chains radius brought the line along 'the baulks' and a rising incline into the station close to the High Street. To achieve direct access a road was built from the High Street which involved demolishing some houses, and today there remains a gap in the numbering sequence.

The construction of the line seems to have been fairly straightforward, being mainly the excavation of some deep chalk cuttings along the side of the valley with the resulting spoil being employed to build an embankment across the Moor, and the extraction of ballast which created more watercress beds. The contractors used at least three different

35

locomotives and, in contrast to some other lines, the navvies who were imported to do the manual work appear to have had good relations with the local population.

The stations beyond Rickmansworth were built to the same basic appearance, Chorley-Wood and Chalfont Road had most facilities on the up side and with underground passages to ease access to the down platform. However this sole exit on the up side at Chalfont was to be the cause of much complaint from passengers who had to make a lengthy detour in order to reach the village on the other side of the track. Although a footpath was added in 1925, it was not until 1933 that a proper approach road was created to give full access to the down platform. All the stations had goods yards, whilst Chalfont's layout later included a bay platform adjacent to the up platform for interchange with the shuttle train on the by then Chesham branch. In order to ensure that the engine on the shuttle could always be at the front of the train, a loop in the track was provided so that it could run round the coaches after each trip. Unfortunately this was installed beyond the end of the bay platform so that the train had to be taken out of the station again in order to perform the manoeuvre. Activity was controlled by a signal box (Saxby:22 levers + 8 spares) on the down side at the north end of the station using single token operation for the branch. The box at Chesham (Saxby:20 levers + 5 spares) was built opposite the single platform dominated by a large elevated water tank which fed a water crane at the south end of the platform. This track layout also had to incorporate a run-round loop together with a coaling stage and turntable for the locomotives, the latter was installed because the railway inspectorate were unhappy about the essentially underground locomotives running bunker-first over the Extension lines. The 30ft turntable had an exciting life, having been moved from Harrow to Rickmansworth and then on to Chesham as the end of the railway advanced north. However it is doubtful if it was used to any extent and the facility was removed in 1900.

The whole layout at Chesham was made compatible with an onward push along the Vale to the LNWR at Tring and the housing development in Victoria Road (named after the then Queen) was delayed, whilst beyond this a space was left in the homes being built on either side of Eskdale Avenue and the route laid out as far as Francis Wood, some 1½ miles to the north along the route of Watkin's proposals of 1880 for an Aylesbury & Rickmansworth Railway.

The actual cost of the line exceeded the estimates due to the extra costs of bridging the watercress beds and overtime working to complete within the statuatory period. An unexpected cost was that for the provision of the temporary track with a locomotive and wagon to give the directors and some others a trial trip over the branch. This event early in 1889 has added to the confusion over the date of the openning of the line as it is sometimes mixed-up with the private events surrounding the 'Inspection and Informal Opening' on the 15th of May 1889 and also with the intense local interest in the start of the public train service on the 8th of July.

Celebrations

The events organised by the Metropolitan on the 15th of May were intended to mark the completion of work by the contractor with a demonstration of the line to the Directors, subscribers and local dignatories by a trip on the railway and a traditional expansive lunch with numerous speeches that marked such occasions. In that the line had not yet been handed-over by the contractor or approved by the Railway Inspectorate, the Metropolitan regarded it as an internal event and asked the local authorities to postpone their celebrations to when the line opened for public service. However after such a long wait for the railway, people's expectations had been raised to a high level and, particularly as the schools were closed for the day, crowds gathered along the lineside and around the station which had been bedecked with flags by the Company. The events of the day were eloquently described in The Bucks Flying Post & Chesham Express of the 18th of May:-

"The Provisional Opening of the Metropolitan Railway
– One motto which hung upon the station singularly
reflected the feelings of the people. It was – "Long looked for,
come at last".

Soon after 11.30 o'clock, the subscribers to the Railway, and members of the Local and School Boards who had been asked by the Directors to join them at Rickmansworth began to enter in the special train, which had been sent down from London expressly to carry them to Rickmansworth. This train was composed of two carraiges drawn by two engines, Henry Appleby and Walsal[note. the contractors locomotives] which were elaborately decorated, one bearing the motto "God shall bless all thy works". In advance of these was a third engine acting as pilot. – The train left Chesham at 11.45, arriving at Rickmansworth at 12.25, stopping at Chalfont Road Junction and Chorley-Wood Station - all along for a considerable distance the highest bank was lined with people, cheering and waving hats and handkerchiefs, as the train passed by. A special train conveying the Directors to Chesham left Baker Street at 11.45, arriving at Rickmansworth at 12.30, and by which the passengers from Chesham returned, arriving there at 1.20. As the first train to Chesham wound its way slowly down a gradient of 1 in 66 into the town , from amongst the beautiful hills, overlooking a scenery of almost unparalleled beauty; it was heralded by the firing of guns from the Waterside and by almost unbroken cheers of the people who lined either side of the line until, steaming into the newly erected station, a loud burst of hurrahs rang in the air from the hundreds of people gathered there, intermingled with the almost drowned strains of the Town Band, as it struck up, "See the conquering hero comes". – the Directors and friends proceeded to the Goods station, which was decorated so effectively that the illusion of a banquetinq hall was complete. Before entering the warehouse the opening ceremony was performed by Baron F. de Rothschild, in the unavoidable absence of the Right Hon. Sir Harry Verney. Baron

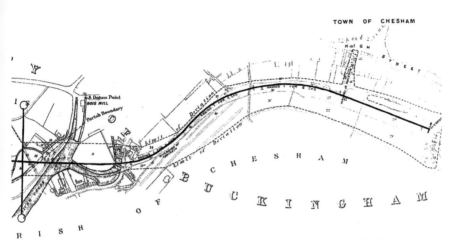

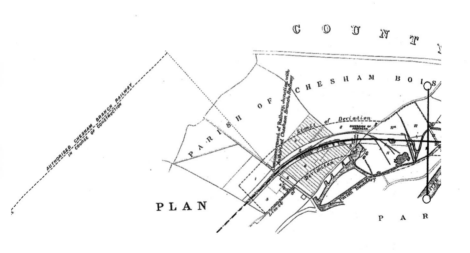

Parliamentary plan deposited by the Metropolitan Railway in 1889 for the extension into the centre of the Town.

The Chairman and Directors of

The Metropolitan Railway Company

request the pleasure of the company of

Joseph Reynolds Esq

at an Inspection of The Chesham Extension Railway,

and its Informal Opening by

The Right Hon. Sir Harry Verney, Bart.

on Wednesday, the 15th instant, preparatory to the opening

of the Extension to the public early in July.

Luncheon will be provided at Chesham after the Ceremony.

An early reply addressed to the Secretary of The Metropolitan Railway 32 Westbourne Terrace W. will oblige

May 4th 1889.

Ferdinand de Rothschild and Sir Edward Watkin mounted a temporary platform in front of the goods station"

Sir Edward Watkin introduced Baron de Rothschild who declared the railway open, observing that the splendid weather was good omen for the future. The party of 200 then entered the Goods Warehouse where an excellent cold luncheon awaited them, provided by 40 staff of Messrs. Spiers and Pond, the operators of the Metropolitan refreshment rooms. Afterwards Baron de Rothschild proposed the toast to the Queen, followed by one to the Duke of Buckingham and then spoke about the problems that had delayed a railway reaching Chesham which led to a toast to Mr Reading and Mr Reynolds, who had done so much to bring it to the centre of the town. An unprepared Mr Reading responded, acknowledging that the land from Waterside had indeed been given to the company and hoping that the line would be "carried through to Tring". Mr Reynolds followed hoping that "the sooner the goods traffic is got into working order the better". The 'Squire' Mr W Lowndes then spoke, also reflecting on the delay and how the LNWR came near to building a line, and thanking the Metropolitan for the extension.

Sir Edward Watkin responded by commenting he had hoped, and still hoped, that "the great companies who had made this splendid district" might still contribute to the line being built through Bucks. He then went on to thank the various officers of the Company whose efforts had led to the success of the work, afterwards proposing the toast to the visitors. Sir Archibald Miller a railway commisioner, replied by saying that " the neighbourhood of Chesham was not altogether new to him, although for some 14 or 15 years he was a regular follower of the O.B.H." and proposed a toast to Baron de Rothschild and then toasted the 'Press' "after which the proceedings terminated. As the company left the Goods Warehouse the Town Band, which had played during the luncheon, struck up with vigour 'Auld Lang Syne'. The Drum and Fife Band were also in attendance. The directors, officers and visitors shortly afterwards left the Station, amid the cheers of hundreds of spectators lining the hill slope above the line. A number of inhabitants got into the train, and proceeded as far as Rickmansworth, and returned on a another train, for the benefit of the drivers of which a collection was made. At Rickmansworth, as the special was returning to London, a very amusing incident took place."

Apparently a number of Cheshamites thought that they recognised Sir Edward Watkin and surrounded his carriage trying to shake his hand and shouting "You've made Chesham". The gentleman concerned responded in good part and kept up the illusion until the real Sir Edward came past!

The line was formally inspected and approved on the 1st of July, the only caveat being the marginal deflection of the main bridges under load, and following statutory approval on the 5th of July the railway opened for public service on the 8th of July. These initial trains were comprised of either A or B class 4-4-0 tank locomotives in their new dark red MET livery with brown four-wheel coaches. Again the Bucks Flying Post & Chesham Express covered the event. "There was no additional ceremony, or demonstration, though this, we understand, many people in the locality , fully impressed with the importance of the event had for some time been advocating. Beyond the departure of the first goods train from Chesham at 6.55 for the Baker-Street terminus, there was nothing to make any deviation in the ordinary business of the town. The good people of Chesham, however, were by no means unappreciative of their newly acquired importance in the possession of a railway station "all of their own", and when the goods train left in the morning many of them assembled to cheer lustily and bid God speed to the new venture. The Town also was highly decorated for the occasion with a profusion of flags and banners – the approach to the station was naturally the gayest with bunting, and over the entrance was a flag with the words 'Long looked for day arrived at last'. Throughout the day crowds of the curious, principally children flocked towards the station to see the departure of the various trains. "The bells of St. Mary's Church rang forth joyous peals, and in the evening one or two small but convivial gatherings celebrated the event with due festivity"

"According to the timetable 17 trains leave Chesham starting at 6.55 am and running at regular intervals of one hour. The average time for the journey between Chesham and Rickmansworth is about 25 minutes – A special convenience for business men is the fast train which leaves at 8.48, and reaches Baker-street at 9.38. The service on Sunday comprises 12 trains from Chesham, the first leaving at 8.50 am and the last at 9.50. The trains are at usual hourly intervals with the exception that there is no departure at 10.50 am, or at 11.50 am."

It is interesting to note this gap in the Sunday morning activities which was provided by the Company so that staff could attend worship. The stationmaster was a Mr Webster who was in charge of two ticket inspectors, two clerks, two collectors and two porters.

METROPOLITAN RAILWAY

—— o ——

Inspection of the

CHESHAM EXTENSION,

WEDNESDAY, MAY 15th, 1889.

· MENU ·

Clear Mock Turtle.

Mayonnaise of Salmon.   Lobsters in Shell.

Dressed Crabs.

Fore-Quarters of Lamb.

Roast Surrey Capons.   York Ham

Ox Tongues.

Pigeon Pies.   Sirloin of Beef.   Pressed Beef.

Galantine of Chicken.

Wine Jellies.   Maraschino Jellies.

Blancmangers.   Maids of Honor.   French Pastry.

Neapolitan Ices.

Cheese.   Watercress.

DESSERT AND COFFEE.

Sherry.   Claret.

Champagne : { Perinet et Fils.
{ Moet et Chandon, Brut Imperial.

Spiers and Pond, Limited,
Refreshment Contractors.

METROPOLITAN RAILWAY.

CHESHAM SECTION.

WEEK DAY TRAINS. — FROM LONDON.

	a.m.	a.m.	a.m.	a.m.	a.m.	a.m.	p.m	p.m.	p.m.	p.m.	p.m.	p.m.	p.m.	p.m.	p.m.	p.m.	p.m.
BAKER STREET ......dep.	6 12	7 29	8 29	...	11 52	1 29	a2 27	d5 29	5 27	6 3	d5 29	6 22	a7 29	8 29	p.m.		p.m.
Rickmansworth	7 3	7 13	8 13	10 13	12 13	2 13	3 5	4 13	6 3	4 13	6 13	7 13	8 13	9 29			11 49
Chorley Wood	7 8	8 19	2 19	10 19	12 19	2 19	3 11	4 19	7 6	4 19	6 19	7 19	8 19	9 19			12 3?
Chalfont Road	7 13	8 24	9 24	10 24	12 24	2 24	3 16	4 24	6 14	4 24	6 24	7 24	8 24	9 24			13 4
CHESHAM ......arr.	7 23	8 34	9 34	10 34	12 34	2 34	3 26	4 34	6 24	6 34	6 34	7 34	8 34	9 34			12 54

a Fast Train, Saturdays only.   a Saturdays only.   e Not on Saturdays.
a Saturdays only.   e Wednesdays only.

WEEK DAY TRAINS. — TO LONDON.

	a.m.	a.m.	a.m.	a.m.	p.m.	p.m.	p.m.	p.m.	p.m.	p.m.	p.m.	p.m.	p.m.	p.m.	p.m.	p.m.
CHESHAM ......dep.	7 30	8 43	10 0	11 0	1 0	3 0	4 5	5 0	7 0	8 0	9 0	10 6				
Chalfont Road	7 41	8 53	10 15	11 11	1 11	3 11	4 15	5 11	7 15	8 11	9 11	10 11				
Chorley Wood	7 45	8 57	10 20	11 20	1 20	3 20	4 20	5 20	7 20	8 20	9 15	10 15				
Rickmansworth	7 50	9 2	10 30	11 26	1 26	3 26	4 26	6 26	7 26	8 26	9 20	10 20				
BAKER STREET ......arr.	8 35	9 37	11 6	12 6	2 6	4 6	5 6	6 6	8 5	9 6	10 5	11 6				

f Fast Train.   g Saturdays only.

SUNDAY TRAINS. — FROM LONDON.

	a.m.	a.m.	p.m.	p.m.	p.m.	p.m.	p.m.	p.m.	p.m.
BAKER STREET ......dep.	8 47	9 47	2 0	5 16	6 16	7 16	8 16	9 16	p.m.
Rickmansworth	9 30	10 30	2 40	4 0	6 0	8 0	9 0	10 0	2 16
Chorley Wood	9 35	10 35	2 46	4 6	6 6	8 6	9 6	10 6	
Chalfont Road	9 40	10 41	2 51	4 11	6 11	8 11	9 11	10 11	
CHESHAM ......arr.	9 50	10 51	2 21	4 21	6 21	8 21	9 21	10 21	

SUNDAY TRAINS. — TO LONDON.

	a.m.	a.m.	p.m.	p.m.	p.m.	p.m.	p.m.	p.m.	p.m.	p.m.
CHESHAM ......dep.	9 50	12 40	2 40	4 40	6 40	8 52	9 40	10 4	10 29	
Chalfont Road	10 10	1 0	3 0	5 4	7 0	9 0	10 4	10 2	10 40	
Chorley Wood	10 14	1 4	3 4	5 3	7 3	9 15	10 9	...	10 44	
Rickmansworth	10 19	1 9	3 9	5 9	7 9	9 15	10 9	10 54	10 49	
BAKER STREET ......arr.	11 4	1 54	3 54	6 54	7 54	9 53	10 54			

Runs to Neasden.

5

BECOMING A BRANCHLINE

For three brief years Chesham basked in the glory of being the farthest terminus of Watkin's Metropolitan 'Extension' some 25.7 miles from Baker Street. On the first day some 1500 people travelled on the line but, as might be expected as the excitement wore off this fell to about 600 on the next day. Indeed many on that second day were booked on an excursion to the Crystal Palace for a Temperance Demonstration. Nevertheless, the total number of passengers in the first week was about 4300 and although dropping to 2800 in the second week this made an encouraging start.

The LNWR admitted defeat and terminated their coach service to Berkhampsted Station. The townspeople now had much easier access to London with a journey time of about 54 minutes to Baker Street. Their horizon was extended in many ways, for not only was there ample time for business meetings in the City, but even daily commuting was now feasible. Now longer distance journeys were also possible for even ordinary folk and excursions took them to the seaside and other attractions. An early outstanding example of this new-found freedom was the trip by two men from Chesham to Calais and back within the day! Goods traffic prospered as expected with milk and other products being distributed further afield, but this also marked the start of an ongoing battle over charges. However parcels were now moved more quickly and the daily papers now arrived on the 7.28 am train for an early delivery. Thus at one step Chesham had taken a leap forward to a level of communications not dissimilar to that we enjoy a century later.

Meanwhile, Liddell and Firbank continued to build the 16 miles of main-line onwards from Chalfont Road to Aylesbury and although they encountered difficult soil conditions, particularly with some heavy clay at Amersham, the double tracks were opened to a temporary terminus at Aylesbury on the 1st of September 1892. Chesham was thus relegated to branchline status and Chalfont Road now sported a notice 'Junction For Chesham', although connections to the mainline services were often made by attaching the branch coaches to the end of the Baker Street 'up' train and removing them from the 'down' trip to be taken into Chesham by another engine. However this arrangement soon changed to the present regime where a few 'through' trains at peak times are supplemented by the branch shuttle service, thereby leading to endless arguments over suspected imbalances in the services to Amersham and Chesham.

During this initial period trains were hauled by the ubiquitous Metropolitan A and B class 4-4-0 tank locomotives. Although built at least 10 years apart by Beyer Peacock, they were both to the same basic design which had been originally developed for overseas railways. For use in the original Metropolitan underground system no protective cab was thought to be necessary for the crew, but condensing apparatus was incorporated in order to minimize emissions in the tunnels that would affect the passengers. Now an increasing part of the engines work was on the 'Extension' and thus quite open to the weather, but fully enclosed cabs were not provided until 1895.

Although the A & B class locomotives gave sterling sevice until well into the next century their riding qualities left much to be desired at the higher speeds scheduled on the 'Extension'. In going to a hopefully better design the MET, as became their norm in locomotive matters, tried to take a short-cut and obtained some to an SER design (another Watkin company) which worked to Rickmansworth from 1891. Unfortunately this C class of 0-4-4T were not good performers and sometimes were relegated to the Chesham branch.

The weather on the exposed 'Extension' line not only sorely affected the engine crews but also the passengers, and so in the wintertime footwarmers pre-heated at the station were provided as an expedient until steam heating was fitted in the coaches from about 1895.

Like the engines, most of the coaches also dated from 1870, being made by the Oldbury Carriage Co. to a 4-wheel design closely coupled in pairs, but the short wheelbase of about 16 feet gave a bumpy ride and although the first class compartments were suitably upholstered with 4 padded seats abreast, the third class passengers had only wooden benches. Indeed, in light of their suspect safety record they were replaced by the 'Jubilee' coaches from Craven Bros., but as these were still on a 4-wheel chassis the inevitable oscillations still caused complaints and even a second batch with a 17 feet wheelbase only gave a marginal improvement. There were also some sets of longer straight-sided coaches which at first sight appeared to be mounted on bogies but which in fact had two sets of rigid axles at each end of the coach, albeit with considerable side-play in the axlebox mountings to allow for traversing curved track.

These longer journeys also invited invidious comparisons with the accomodation provided by existing mainline railway companies and as a result longer wheelbase coaches about 42ft overall were obtained from the Ashbury, Railway, Carriage & Iron Co. and Cravens around 1899. These were mounted on conventional bogies and lit by electricity, rather than gas. After their spell on the 'Extension' they were to have an eventful life, only to return to Chesham some 40 years later.

The Watkin Legacy

In 1890 Watkin had built a new station at Wembley Park to serve the Tower he was building nearby to complement his grand design for a Manchester-Paris link. But soon after he fell ill and although he was quickly back in harness, it was a sign that he was coming to the end of his career. His main prority remained raising the substantial finance necessary to implement the expansion of the MET and the MS&LR and which he only achieved by diluting the value of existing shares. The parallel task was still pushing forward the operational collaboration between the MET and the MS&LR, which resulted in an agreement on running powers and profit sharing on the lines to be joined together. Whilst the two General Managers, John Bell of the MET and William Pollitt of the MS&LR bent to his will, there was an underlying animosity between them going back to their rivalry when working together in junior roles in the MS&LR.

As it turned out the connection between the railways took longer than expected by the shareholders due to the practicalities of establishing the MET at Aylesbury and working trains over the primitive A&BR to Quainton Road. There were also ongoing disputes with the GWR over the use of the joint station at Aylesbury, which led to the withdrawl of their light engines needed to work the line which was in practice little more than a single-track rural branchline. Eventually, the MET achieved access to Aylesbury station in 1894 but they had to borrow some suitable Webb 2-4-0T locomotives from the LNWR for £2.05 per day as a stop-gap. It has been reported that one of these found it's way onto the Chesham branch on the 8th July 1894. In the longer term the problem was solved by obtaining six 2-4-0T D class locomotives from Sharp,Stewart similar to some already supplied to the Barry Railway, as well as rebuilding all the bridges and double-tracking.

Thus in 1897 the MET had reached 50 miles from Baker Street, but in 1894 Watkin had suffered a stroke and, although he remained a nominal director of several companies, it brought his influence to an end and he died in 1901. Nevertheless the considerable momentum he had created for the new route carried the MS&LR forward in their construction of the last link from Nottingham to Quainton Road, and in line with Watkin's wider ambitions this was built to accomodate the more generous continental loading gauge. But the pressure that he had exerted on the MET and the

MS&LR to achieve his ambitions was in the end to prove counter-productive in provoking antagonism between them. With Watkin's waning powers it became apparent that the objectives of the partners were diverging and it was becoming obvious that track capacity would make the Watkin proposition of a co-existing terminus at Baker Street impractical. So it was decided to build parallel tracks for the MS&LR from Harrow to a new terminus at Marylebone, and consequent upon this was a change in name from the MS&LR – or 'money sunk and lost' as it was known in the City - to the Great Central – or 'gone completely' in view of the paucity of dividends!

Bell had now replaced Watkin as Chairman of the MET, and freed of his restraint, embarked upon a confrontational course with Pollitt of the GCR over the extra tracks into Marylebone and the desire of the GCR to divert their trains over the GWR after Aylesbury thus depriving the MET of London traffic. This culminated in a major incident in which Bell personally turned a GCR train back at Quainton Road Junction. Although this was eventually resolved, Pollitt remained unhappy over the minor portion that they received from the profit-sharing agreement and soon entered into negotiation with the MET's old enemy, the GWR, which was to result in combining to create a major new route into London. The GWR had been considering for some time a shorter route to Birmingham in order to compete with the LNWR and by forming a joint company with the GCR they were able to extend north from Acton to High Wycombe and beyond. By also connecting just to the north of Quainton Road and a building new line from Northolt to Neasden the GCR were going to be in a position to to bypass the MET, and the effect of Bell's intransigence was at last apparent to his Board. They restarted negotiations with the GCR and with arbitration on compensation a more equitable agreement was reached in 1906 on a Metropolitan & GC Joint Railway which ensured that some GCR traffic passed over the old route. However, the intended spur from Marylebone to join the MET west of

Baker Sreet, which would have brought to fruition Watkin's objective of GCR trains traversing London via the MET, was quietly dropped.

By the time this came about both Bell and Pollitt had retired and were succeeded by two more compatible characters in the shape of Abraham Ellis and Sam Fay who recognised that more could achieved by collaboration. As part of the accord the management of the joint lines north of Harrow was alternated between the partners every 5 years. This meant that at times the Chesham Shuttle and new through-trains to Marylebone were worked by GCR engines such as their 2-4-2T's for passenger work and 0-6-2T's on goods trains, whilst their superior coaches provided a vivid contrast to the ancient MET passenger stock. However the MET had introduced two new types of locomotive specifically for 'Extension' work, the classic E class 0-4-4T built in 1896 which will always be associated with the 'Shuttle' and was in effect an enlarged version of the C class, and the F class 0-6-2T freight engines supplied by the Yorkshire Engine Co. in 1900.

The lot of the engine crews on the class A/B locomotives was also improved by the addition of cabs to give some protection from the Bucks weather. But unfortunately there were two accidents in succession on the Chesham branch in 1909. The most serious occurred on the 6th of November about 12.32am as a goods train was entering Chalfont Road station when there was a 'blow-back' through the open door of the firebox which enveloped the driver, Robert Prior, in flames. The fireman turned on the blower to control the firebox, beat the flames out on the driver and took the train on to Chesham so that he could be taken to the Cottage Hospital. The Driver died from extensive burns two days later and at the subsequent inquest held at The Red Lion Hotel where, following evidence on the condition of the controls and the driver's failure to turn on the blower before closing the regulator, a verdict of accidental death was recorded. The type of locomotive involved is not mentioned, but it was probably a Class D 2-4-0T which were apparently prone to suffering from backdraught enveloping the cab in flames.

Shortly before this on the 19th of August the 7.53 am train from Chesham was badly derailed due to a class A locomotive, no. 46, breaking an axle near Hodd's Wood. Driver Herbert and the fireman were unhurt and the coaches remained on the track. The passenger service was maintained by trains being run from both Chesham and Chalfont Road to within a few yards of the accident with the passengers transferring by walking along the track. One of whom remarked " we have always wanted a stopping place at Chesham Bois"!

Royalty also had some problems on the 'Extension'. King Edward VII used the line through Chalfont Road several times in a private capacity and the inclusion of the obligatory special train in the dense MET & GC timetable raised operational dificulties. Cockman states that in 1901 the King travelled by ordinary train to Wendover in order to visit a lady friend; on the return journey a MET signalman allowed a slow goods train in front of the King's train which arrived 10 mins late at Marylebone. Apparently the King called for the Stationmaster and gave him a very severe dressing down. Also Mrs James de Rothschild has recounted how in 1898 the Prince had broken his leg during a visit to Waddesdon and was returning via Aylesbury Station in an invalid chair. Whilst he was being carried in the chair over the footbridge the chair collapsed and he was thrown on the floor only to be engulfed in thick smoke from a locomotive beneath!

6

STABILITY WITH SELBIE

Ellis, the new Chairman, also came to realise the need to work with the other London underground railway companies and to embrace electrification in London, but soon ill-health forced his resignation in 1908 thus leaving the way for Robert Selbie to succeed him as General Manager and shape the Metropolitan as it is probably best remembered.

Like Watkin, Robert Hope Selbie was from Manchester and had a railway training, but in his case with the Lancashire & Yorkshire Railway, before joining the Metropolitan and then quickly becoming involved in their electrification scheme. Whilst the advantages of electrifying the underground sections were obvious, the choice of the type of power and pick-up arrangements were to produce more acrimony between the London railways. This ended in another arbitration, this time in favour of an American 600v dc 4-rail system instead of the MET's preferred European 3kv 3-phase ac supply with overhead pick-up. Nevertheless the MET rapidly implemented the agreed system on its underground routes and by 1905 electrified as far as Harrow.

Selbie was appointed Secretary in 1903 and by the time he took over from Bell as General Manager in 1908 he had carefully analysed the strengths and weaknesses of the MET he was to control for over twenty years. Although like Watkin he was autocratic, in contrast he was somewhat retiring and relied for his authority on clear objectives supported by a detailed knowledge and observation of all the activities of the MET and a watchful eye on its competitors. His Board were concerned over the escalating costs of electrification on top of the financial burden inherited from Watkin's excesses. Selbie realised that competition in London was going to increase from both the Underground railways and the motor buses, and that steps had to be taken to optimise the role of the MET in this area and develop the considerable potential of the Extension as a feeder of both passenger and goods traffic. To achieve this aim he planned to refurbish the whole system by making the MET more visible, improving services and reliability and developing the country around the Extension with new branches to Uxbridge, Watford and Stanmore in order to increase its catchment area. In implementing this policy he drove operating costs down relentlessly but maintaining investment caused problems and he was fortunate to have a sympathetic Chairman, Lord Aberconway, throughout his rule.

The appearance the MET was uplifted by refurbishing the surface buildings of the London stations and matching the house-style used by the competitors under the UNDERGROUND logo by adopting MET signs based on a diamond and bar shape with a consistent approach to all material from maps and posters. Around 1915 this found expression in the concept of MetroLand to describe the desirable countryside for leisure and homes so convenient to the West End and the City by courtesy of the railway. Whilst much of this material may strike us as somewhat naive, the arcadian image conjured up by this early marketing campaign was most effective and Selbie recognised that the MET had a unique ability to exploit it. As a consequence of Watkin's enthusiasm for expansion he had acquired a vast amount of extra land along the Extension in order to cover any possible outcome of earlier machinations, but in contrast to all other railways Watkin had ensured that the MET was able to retain the surplus. So, whilst their aquisition had almost ruined the MET, this land could now be used for large scale building development and the Metropolitan Surplus Lands Committee was turned into the nominally independent Metropolitan Railway Country Estates Ltd to undertake this task. In all, some nine estates were created from Neasden (Kingsbury

HUNTING

IN

BUCKINGHAMSHIRE AND HERTFORDSHIRE.

For the convenience of HUNTING GENTLEMEN a Train now leaves BAKER STREET at 9.5 a.m. for

Rickmansworth arr. 9.50 a.m.

Chesham . . arr. 10.14 a.m.

Amersham . . arr. 10.9 a.m.

Great Missenden arr. 10.19 a.m.

Aylesbury arr. 10.38 a.m.

Hunters to be Boxed at Finchley Road by 9.0 a.m.

FARES AND RATES.

| | Fares from BAKER ST. | | | | | | Rates for Hunters from FINCHLEY ROAD. | |
| | 1st Class. | | 3rd Class. | | | | | |
	Single	Return	Single	Return	Single	Return	Single	Return Same day.
RICKMANSWORTH ...	2/6	3/9	1/3	1/11			5/0	7/6
CHESHAM ...	3/10	5/9	1/11	2/11			7/0	10/6
AMERSHAM ...	3/6	5/3	1/9	2/8			6/6	9/9
GREAT MISSENDEN ...	4/4	6/6	2/2	3/4			7/9	11/8
AYLESBURY ...	5/10	8/9	2/11	4/5			10/0	15/0

For Horse Boxes apply to any of the Stations or to the Superintendent of the Line, 32 Westbourne Terrace, W.

B

THE HUNTING SEASON.

THE following are the packs of Hounds hunting in the neighbourhood of the METROPOLITAN RAILWAY, with the Masters, hunting days, and most convenient towns for visitors:—

STAGHOUNDS.

Lord Rothschild's.—LORD ROTHSCHILD—Monday and Thursday. Aylesbury.

Berkhamsted. Mr. J. RAWLE Wednesday. Berkhamsted, St. Albans and Tring.
(For Berkhamsted leave by the 9.50 Station, thence by road conveyance.)

Bucks and Berks Farmers'. SIR ROBERT WILMOT Tuesday and Friday. Amersham and Chalfont.

FOXHOUNDS.

Berkeley Old (East).—Mr. R. B. WIBBER—Monday and Thursday. with a bye day. Rickmansworth and Chorley Wood.

Berkeley Old (West).—Mr. ROBERT LEADBETTER—Wednesday and Saturday Amersham, Chalfont and Missenden.

Bicester and Warden Hill.—Mr. J. P. HEYWOOD LONSDALE—Monday, Tuesday, Thursday and Saturday. Banbury, Bicester, Brackley, Buckingham *via* Verney Junction and Quainton Road District.

Whaddon Chase. Mr. W. SELBY LOWNDES—Tuesday and Saturday Aylesbury, Buckingham, Leighton and Winslow Road.

Grafton.—Hon. E. S. DOUGLAS PENNANT—Monday, Wednesday, Friday and Saturday. Buckingham, Brackley, Towcester and Weedon.

The above meets are advertised every Friday, with name of place, in the *Bucks Herald.*

BEAGLES.

Berkhamsted (13½ in. Stud Book Beagles).—Wednesday and Saturday. Mr. W. J. PICKIN. Berkhamsted.

Bushey Heath (14 in. pure Beagles).—Saturday, alternate Wednesdays. Mr. R. MAJOR. Bushey Heath, Rickmansworth.

Shardeloes.—Mr. E. S. S. DRAKE—Shardeloes and Amersham.

Winslow and District (Foot Beagles).—Thursdays. Rev. T. SHARPE.

DRAGHOUNDS.

Greenford Drag.—Mr. PERKINS—Harrow-on-Hill, Greenford District. Saturday.

GOODS & MINERAL TRAFFIC

THE METROPOLITAN RAILWAY COMPANY deals with Goods and Mineral traffic at the following Stations for conveyance by **Goods Trains** at through rates, viz. :—

Finchley Road	*Northwood	*Wendover
*Willesden Green and	*Rickmansworth	Stoke Mandeville
Cricklewood	Chorley Wood	*Aylesbury
Kingsbury-Neasden	Chalfont Road	Waddesdon Manor
Wembley Park	*Chesham	Quainton Road
*Harrow	*Amersham	Grandborough Road
*Pinner	*Great Missenden	Verney Junction

where facilities are provided for loading and unloading station to station traffic, including Coal, Coke, Lime, Cement, Bricks, Tiles, Stone, Timber and other Building Materials; also Grain, Flour, Oil Cake, Manure, Groceries, Farm Produce and other Merchandise.

At Stations marked * the Company undertake the Collection and Delivery of Goods by Carts and Vans.

London traffic to and from the above-named Stations is dealt with at Metropolitan Company's **WILLESDEN GREEN and CRICKLE-WOOD STATION**, also by the **Midland Railway Company** at St. Pancras, Somers Town, Whitecross Street, City, Poplar Station and Dock (for riverside and dock traffic), Victoria Docks Station (for river and docks traffic). Bow, West Kensington, Hammersmith and Chiswick, and other Midland Railway Company's depôts in London.

THE METROPOLITAN RAILWAY is in direct communication with the Railways of the London and North Western, Midland, Great Central and Great Western Companies. Goods and Mineral Traffic can also be forwarded direct between Metropolitan Stations as shown above and the Stations of the Great Northern, Great Eastern, Lancashire and Yorkshire, North Eastern, North Staffordshire, Cambrian, London and South Western, London, Brighton and South Coast, South Eastern and Chatham, and other Railways in Great Britain

ARTICLES OF MERCHANDISE intended to be sent by Goods train should be distinctly addressed " Per Goods Train," and it is particularly requested that all Goods to be forwarded should be specially directed "**By Metropolitan Railway.**"

LIVE STOCK

to and from all parts of the Kingdom can be loaded and unloaded at—

Finchley Road	Pinner	Great Missenden
Willesden Green and Cricklewood	Northwood	Wendover
Kingsbury-Neasden	Rickmansworth	Aylesbury
Wembley Park	Chesham	Waddesdon Manor
Harrow	Amersham	Quainton Road

Special arrangements are made for the rapid transit of Live Stock for the London Markets to Kentish Town (Midland Railway), where exceptional facilities are afforded for dealing with Stock.

Full information as to rates and conveyance of Goods, Minerals and Live Stock may be obtained from the **Goods Manager's Office, 28 Craven Road, London, W.,** or from the **Company's Station Agents.**

Garden) to Rickmansworth (Cedars), Chorleywood (Chenies), Chalfont & Latimer (Beechwood) and Amersham (Weller) which included private plots, builder's developments and shops. The scale of the activity is shown by the fact that some 4600 homes had been built by 1939 and new towns, such as Amersham on the Hill, were created in the process. This not only generated extra freight traffic for the building work, but also valued ongoing commuter and season ticket business.

It was an idealised image of fresh air and the tamed hills and valleys of the Chilterns studded with picturesque villages, in conjunction with the availability of reasonably priced housing within reach of London, that resonated with the optimism and aspirations of so many people after the First World War. This was thought to be 'the war that ended all wars' and sentiments like 'a land fit for heroes' and 'returning to a better world' helped make the slogan 'Live in MetroLand' so powerful. The new freedoms of the post-war era also found expression in the healthy outdoors via rambling, hiking, cycling and outings for many more people, and both this aspect and the housing developments were brought together in a new annual guide under the MetroLand banner.

To match these demands Selbie moved to enhance the Extension with new stations, such as at Wembley Park to serve the 1924/5 British Empire Exhibition and Sandy Lodge(Moor Park) for the golf course. A branch was built to Watford in 1925 and the main line electrified as far as Rickmansworth, where the change was now made to steam haulage for MET trains going north. This coincided with the replacement of the original 600 hp electric locomotives by the well-known 1200hp Metropolitan-Vickers Bo-Bo type, which complemented the new comfortable coaches which were quickly nicknamed 'Dreadnoughts' in view of their impressive and bulky appearance.

Whilst the main target of the MET was the new middle class, there was a conscious effort to attract what they regarded as the upper class in order to enhance the status of their new estates and maintain a tenuous claim to mainline railway status. Therefore First-Class traffic was encouraged by publicising suitable building plots with nearby golf courses and hunts. The Old Berkley Hunt met regularly at Latimer and for this and similar events like point-to-points the MET provided horse vans and facilities at most stations. Another ploy to attract this clientele was the introduction in 1909 of two Pullman cars – Mayflower & Galatea (named after competing yachts in the 1896 America Cup races) which were attached to some trains from the City to Chesham, Aylesbury and Verney Junction up to 1939. For a supplement over the first class fare of 1/- (beyond Rickmansworth) businessmen used it breakfasting to work and theatregoers found it convenient for returning after a show. A meal cost 2/- and a gin & tonic 6d in the luxury of the only MET stock fitted with toilets.

Against this background an appropriate headquarters was deemed to be needed and about 1914 the opportunity was taken of a drastic improvement to the track layout at Baker Street to redevelop the whole site as Chiltern Court. It was completed in 1929 with over 1000 rooms configured into different flats plus a hall and resturant, attracting tenants such as H G Wells and Arnold Bennett.

The new layout at Baker Street improved the bad congestion at the junction with the Circle line and formed part of Selbie's plan to cope with the extra traffic now being generated. Another step was the quadrupling of the tracks from Harrow to Finchley Road, but his intention to relieve the main bottleneck from there to Baker Street was never realised. On the electrified section capacity was also raised when the original multiple-electric stock was replaced by the MV and MW units – or T stock – from 1927 onwards. Goods traffic was also increasing and to deal with this some larger 0-6-4T engines were obtained from the Yorkshire Engine Co. in 1915/16. These G class tanks were named Brill, Lord Aberconway, Robert H Selbie and Charles Jones (one of the few living Chief Mechanical Engineers to have an engine named after him!) By 1925 sidings had been extended and so there was a need for even more powerful locomotives to deal with the longer goods trains and in the MET's usual economical way some surplus components to an SECR design by Maunsell were bought from Woolwich Arsenal and turned by Armstrong Whitworth into the impressive K class 2-6-4 tank engines. Consequent upon the earlier introduction of the Pullman cars, new locomotives were produced by Kerr Stuart in 1920/1 to haul such prestige Extension trains. To an overall design by Charles Jones, the 4-4-4T H class were handsome engines said to be capable of over 75 mph down to Chorleywood, yet able to negotiate the sharp curves at Chesham. However they were prone to slipping in careless hands.

In broad terms it could be claimed that Selbie achieved most of his aims, certainly by comparison with other railways, for under his leadership the passengers carried rose from 95 to 135 M/yr, train miles from 2 to 6.5 M/yr and freight from 3 to 4.3 M tons/yr. Even shareholders saw their dividends improve from about 2 to 5%, but towards the end of his tenure the effects of the General Strike followed by the Depression produced a downturn in all results.

The momentum of his creation - MetroLand - has continued to today, immortalised in many peoples minds by the works of Sir John Betjeman. However, even his nostalgic poems hint at the inevitability that such a development grew to destroy many of the initial attractions of space and freedom. The MET effectively suburbanised NW London and Middlesex, and turned Bucks into a commuter belt, but if it had not happened in this way the result could have been much worse.

Chesham in MetroLand

By comparison with the burgeoning traffic on the main line, this was a period of stability for the Chesham branch. Although Chesham had developed early on into a thriving town, and the coming of the railway had expanded it's horizons, in essence it remained a focus for a large number of local trades and crafts, and the community did not grow substantialy. Indeed by 1921 the population had only grown by less than 2000 since the opening, and in the next 10 years by only a further 225. In this respect the area had become something of a backwater of MetroLand on the route to nowhere in particular. Although it was featured in the MET publicity as an attractive place to visit, somewhat surprisingly it did not host one of their commuter estates, even though they owned land in the vicinity. Indeed they sold much of the land they owned at Nasleigh Hill to the Council for a recreation ground, and who themselves were also creating estates at Pond Park and elsewhere, but although their construction provided a lot of goods traffic, they were mainly for local people in existing industries. That is not to say that commuting was not encouraged, for the local Council lobbied successfully in 1914 for the introduction of cheap 'workmans' fares before 7.30 am. Nevertheless the plateau in commuting by the Branch is shown by the following comparison of monthly season ticket takings:

Chalfont & Latimer + Amersham		Chesham
1921	£4,736	£4,683
1928	£11,116	£4,994

A contributory factor in this lack of passengers was probably the perceived deterioration in the quality of the service provided by the MET over the years. The GCR and later the LNER at least provided comfortable coaches on their own through trains to Marylebone, but by contrast the MET had used the original 4 & 8 wheel rigid coaches on the shuttle with an operating regime that meant that the engine had to run round it's coaches after each journey and also fit in any shunting of wagons that was required. This caused disruption to the schedules to London, which in any case had worsened since the opening in 1889, first due to becoming a branch, and then at the 1925 electrification to allow for the change of motive power on MET trains at Rickmansworth. In this era there were about 30 trains a day which were supposed to take between 52 and about 60 minutes to Baker Street, but there were cancellations and with frequent delays the passengers on the popular 7.44 am rarely got to work in the City before 9 o'clock. Then returning in the evening they were often confronted at Chalfont & Latimer Station (the name being changed from Chalfont Road in 1915) by the absence of the connecting shuttle and a wait on the exposed platform with few facilities and filthy lavatories.

This treatment, which compared badly with the caring image perpetuated of MetroLand, inevitably led to vociferous protests from the disgruntled passengers directly to Selbie as well as via the local Councils and newspapers reaching peaks of anger in 1908-11 and 1927. For example the editorial in the local paper during 1925 reads: 'The great claim of the Metropolitan Railway is that it is progressive' but 'it is equally fair to point out that the railway service to Chesham has not made that progressive improvement which the place needs and justifies. We have more trains to and from Chesham daily, certainly, but what of the speed, the general accommodation, etc,? And the timetable is not the only criterion, for frequent morning and evening users of the line complain (it was stated at the Urban District Council recently) of the non-running of trains as scheduled and delays between Baker Street and Chesham which make a long and tiresome journey. There are bitter complaints too, about Chalfont Road Station. That station is bleakly situated, and it would take a great deal to make it "cosy", but more shelter (upon the local side), a less sparing use of coal, and better light (the electric cable now runs close to the station and electric light will be available) would make the place a little more cheerful and comfortable, and the waiting time there would not be such a deadly dull and benumbingly cold business as it is now. - all representations to the company are met in a courteous spirit, but that is cold comfort for us at Chesham. During the past quarter-of-a-century Chesham and district has made rapid strides – but the 1918 and 1925 time table comparison shows that the railway facilities have not kept pace with the needs of Chesham.'

Direct appeals to Selbie had some effect but the LNER remained reluctant to match any expenditure that had little benefit for them. However in 1927 the shelters were extended and the waiting rooms refurbished, coinciding with the replacement of the ancient branch coaches by the new 'Dreadnought' stock. By this time motor coaches were begining to compete for the commuter business and although taking longer on the journey, were much cheaper and attracted significant numbers. This added to the vicious cicle of lower traffic inclining the MET to reduce their service and with further Chesham 'through' trains being diverted to meet the demands of growing Amersham.

By contrast, as Watkin had anticipated, Chesham did generate considerable freight traffic amounting to typically some 5000 tons/month and about a 10% of all that handled by the MET&GC. Between 1898 and 1900 the freight faclities were increased, replacing a mobile 5 ton crane by a fixed 8 ton version and modifying the layout of the yard with an extra siding and access. As would be expected this freight was dominated by by coal, mostly from the South Yorkshire pits, for the local gas and electricity works (until it closed in 1925). Such was the value of the gas company's trade that they could threaten to remove it to the LNWR when the station was due to change to electric lighting. Domestic coal merchants were prominent in the goods yard and some such as A H Rance did enough trade to justify owning their own wagons. Coal was also used by the brewery who received their hops and sent out beer by train. Fresh produce, such as fish and fruit, came from the London markets and were more than matched by large outward shipments of the famed local watercress to all parts of the country. The goods traffic at Chalfont & Latimer also grew substantially, with a large coal depot operated by Darvell's and later in the 1940's National Benzole built an oil depot on the site of the present lower station car park.

Tank engines handled all the traffic on the branch and as mentioned earlier, after the reign of the original MET A&B class engines for all tasks the C class were occasionaly used on passenger trains until the larger E class took over for the rest of the MET era. However from 1921 the new powerful H class which could negotiate the sharp curves on the branch began to be used on the heavier through trains. For freight work the D class gave way to the more powerful G class. In the first periods of GCR control they employed their 9L class and later when the LNER took up the operation of the through trains to Marylebone changing to the A5 ex-GCR 9N class of 4-6-2T.

Life at CHESHAM STATION

A fascinating picture of life on the MET is given by Ernie Woodstock, a highly respected figure within Chesham, who rose from a humble delivery boy to stationmaster during his career of 50 years with the railway.

In 1927, he started work at the age of 14 at Chesham station in the goods yard for a wage of 16 shillings per week, of which he gave 15 shillings to his mother in order to help clothe and feed a growing family. In those days such a job was highly regarded as the railways offered the prospect of permanent employment, a free uniform, paid holidays, privilge tickets and a pension upon retirement. His first duties at the bottom rung of the ladder included checking the incoming and outgoing wagon loads -- mainly horsedrawn – of goods and making out the weighbridge tokens to calculate the charges for transport. All this had to be entered up into the numerous records which Mr Cauldrey the Chief Clerk expected to be neatly and precisely kept. The yard was very busy as at that time the majority of goods and parcels were transported by rail. There were more than 16 factories in Chesham who regularly used the goods facilities, many making wood products ranging from clogs and brushes to sheds and even cricket bats. The supply of willow for the bats now came from Earls Colne in Essex and increasingly the finished goods leaving Chesham relied on bringing in the raw materials by rail. As mentioned earlier, there were the substantial train loads of coal from the north destined for the gas works and, whilst it operated, the electricity generating plant. The contents of these 10 ton wagons had to be transhipped by hand into the high sided carts of the local coal merchants, such as Holts. In addition most of the bricks for the new council estates being built in Chesham came by rail from north Bucks and these had to be transferred by hand into horse-drawn carts and the few lorries that had begun to appear, however both found it difficult to tackle the numerous hills in the district with such loads and two horses were often needed. Horses and other livestock were also transported by rail, using designated vans and the cattle loading bay in the goods yard.

Apart from coal, the local brewery also relied on the railway for the delivery of the hops. Perhaps it was because the young Ernie was teetotal that his colleagues sent him to the brewery to check-off the delivery notes, knowing that he would be offered a sample of the local brew. As always he refused the drink, and his workmates thereafter kept that particular duty to themselves.

At that time they were employees of the Met & GC Joint Rly. and the staff were fiercely loyal to this hybrid. Whilst on the bottom rung of the ladder he inevitably had to undertake a number of tasks that no one else wanted to do. Even at his age he was given the job of walking along the track to Chalfont if the train crew reported anything suspicious during the journey. This was particularly gruesome at night, when only equiped with a weak oil lamp there was always the prospect of finding a body, as a few local people sometimes used the track as a convenient short-cut. One such instance happened at night on a snowy Boxing Day in 1927 when following a drivers' report he found, much to his relief, only a bag of track chair bolts beside the line.

After two years he was promoted to parcels boy in the passenger station where his duties covered not only organising the packages and a wide variety of perishable goods sent by the ordinary trains, but also ensuring that the passengers were seen on and off the trains. The day started at about 5.30 am with the arrival of the newspaper train, which had left Marylebone at about 4 am, and which returned later in the day as a pick-up goods. The volume of parcels often necessitated dispatching early every morning a trolley load of about ½ ton of goods which had been collected the previous night from factories around the town. Twice a week there

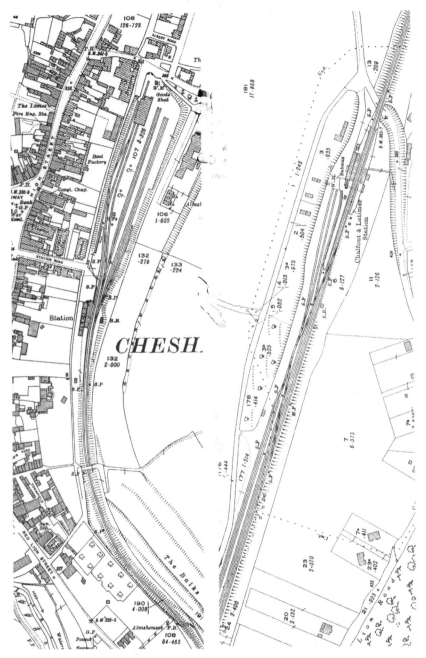

*1925 Ordnance Survey map showing the track layout
at Chalfont & Latimer and Chesham Stations.*

CHESHAM

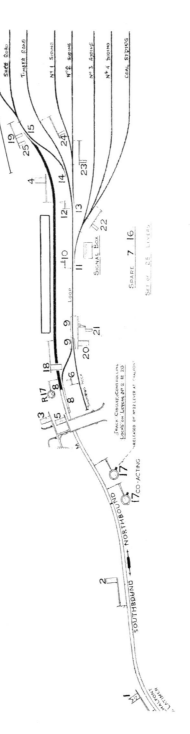

The Met & GC J R signal box diagram for Chesham of 1922.

were deliveries of fresh fruit and fish from the London markets which had been loaded into vans at the MET goods depot near Farringdon and marshalled at the front of the train. After unloading at Chesham the van was sometimes used to convey money from the local banks back to London, accompanied by a parcels boy for security. Special vans were also provided for milk being sent to London for processing and distribution. Again speed was essential to prevent degradation of the milk and from the staff's viewpoint there was a knack in handling the full and heavy churns from the platform into the van. From autumn to spring the watercress was sent in large quantities by passenger train to the London markets, hotels and many cities in the Midlands and the North. It reached a peak around Easter and was packed in special wicker baskets of two sizes and usually loaded on the fast Marylebone of about 5 pm. Another dispatch that was a regular feature of the service provided by the railways was the carriage of racing pigeons to a distant staion for release by a porter at a predetermined time. At Chesham, Ernie had to receive some 20-25 crates of pigeons every Friday for their journey. However, the strangest livestock was handled at the Chalfont & Latimer yard where for many years a circus brought by train their animals from lions to elephants to go to their winter quarters nearby. However Chesham had its share of exceptional loads such as boilers and machinery, but the largest was probably the delivery in 1936 of a massive 15 ton steel girder to support the 'circle' of the new Embassy cinema.

On the passenger side, a collection service was offered for 2 shillings for those sending their luggage on 'in advance' to await them at their destination and it's subsequent return. In practice this sometimes meant that Ernie had to go to their house and wheel it back on a trolley through the town to the station. Often he had the job of giving the 'right away' to the guard when the train was due to leave. Those catching the business trains to London in the morning gave the greatest problems and the son of an ironmonger in the Broadway was the worst offender – although he lived nearest to the station –

and Ernie would go to the top of Station Road to urge him on. This consideration for passengers certainly paid handsome dividends in the case of one regular traveller, a Mr Murdoch of Botley Road who was the well-off owner of a music shop in Regent Street and was driven by his chauffeur, Sid Thorn, in an Armstrong-Siddley car to the station in order to catch the morning Pullman train to town. Ernie would recieve a tip from Sid if he held the train when Mr Murdock was late or, if the train had departed, for going down to the Broadway to signal the car to go on to Rickmansworth station. Tips for such services could boost the 40/- weekly pay of a porter by half again.

The station porters were also expected to help with the uncoupling of the engine on the arrival of the Shuttle and re-coupling after it had run-round the coaches for the return trip. Then there was a gap in the service for an late afternoon tea break and it appears that on a couple of occasions the re-coupling was forgotten and the engine departed without the passengers!

At the age of 20 he was promoted to goods porter at Rickmansworth at wage of 44/- per week where his duties included looking after Moor Park station on Sundays. Then this was built largely out of old sleepers without gas or electricity supply and he had to collect the drinking water from the nearby Sandy Lodge Golf Course. There were plenty of passengers on a Sunday with guests for the large houses and servants going on visits.

He then moved to Watford station as a lorry driver transporting goods to the local factories and in the late 30's unloading the gas cylinders from Billingham destined for the barrage ballons at Stanmore. In 1943 Ernie tranferred to Great Missenden where deliveries seemed to be mainly cattle food and fertilizers in 2 cwt bags. Thence by promotion to Harrow in 1949 as head shunter at 64/- per week on shifts and soon back to Rickmansworth as station foreman at an extra 3/- where he also passed out as a qualified signalman. At times of staff shortages he undertook almost every task at

Rickmansworth, including the tricky coupling that was needed to achieve the less than 4 minute changeover from steam to electric traction. This was followed by becoming successively station master at Great Missenden, Amersham, Chalfont & Latimer and finally Harrow before joining the senior management with broader responsibilities for the MET.

With his experience Ernie always looked at the total situation and took the lead in solving operational and staff problems with understanding and humanity, and away from the MET this led to his appointment as a local magistrate and an elder of his church. However this approach also enabled him to solve many difficult railway problems, for example on one occasion at Harrow the signalman mistakenly diverted the up 'South Yorkshireman' express onto the wrong track so that it ended up in the goods yard instead of the line to Marylebone. Ernie rapidly devised a series of manoeuvres, possibly within the rulebook, involving shunting the entire train in and out of the goods yard via platform 6 to rejoin the Marylebone track, incurring a delay of only 10 minutes. He had fears of a reprimand, but in fact received a letter of commendation: one of many in his 50 years with the MET.

Into London Transport

At the start of the first World War all the railways came under the control of the Government and although afterwards they reverted to private ownership, the experience showed that greater efficiency could be achieved by rationalisation of the multiplicity of companies. This led to the grouping of the mainline railways into the 'big four' in 1923, with the GCR becoming part of the new LNER. This highlighted the anachronistic status of the independent MET, for although it maintained its claim to a mainline role, much of the operations were in London and interleaved with the Tube companies.

Selbie fought hard against the growing pressure to merge with this increasingly assertive Underground group now led by Lord Ashfield. By 1930 matters had come to a head with the Ministry of Transport urging the Underground case with successive Governments. Without doubt Selbie would have continued his stuborn fight, but tragically he suddenly collapsed and died in St Paul's Cathedral on the 17th May 1930, whilst at a confirmation service which included his son. Perhaps recognising the reality of the situation, the Board established a management committee under their solicitor John Anderson, who became General Manager next year. The nature of this appointment indicates that they had accepted that being subsumed into the proposed London Passenger Transport Board was inevitable, and that the fight was now over compensation.

Thus whilst the MET contiued to oppose the Government Bills their Chairman, Lord Aberconway, negotiated to improve the settlement for shareholders. At last in 1932, the Board obtained their agreement to a conversion to LTPB shares with a guaranteed dividend plus the independent existence of the Metropolitan Railway Country Estates Ltd for housing development. The relevant Bill was soon passed, but Lord Aberconway died just before the LTPB was formed in 1933, thus ending the existence of the MET after some 78 years.

The LPTB now embraced almost all London's trains, buses and coaches but, although this reduced the past competition from commuter coaches, the 'Extension'and in particular the Chesham branch were increasingly regarded as an anomaly to their core business. From this point the LTPB and its successors have tried to extract themselves from this part of their operations. The MET signs were replaced, the MetroLand concept dropped, the Brill branch closed in 1935, passenger services ceased between Quainton Road and Verney Junction in 1936 and all steam operations beyond Rickmansworth transferred to the LNER on the 1st November 1937. They took over some 18 of the 36 MET locos plus 270 wagons to run the inherited services, whilst the LTPB retained the rest for service trains on the tube lines. These were based at a new shed on their Neasden site whilst those acquired by the LNER moved to their existing shed on the other side of the tracks, where the ex-MET crews retained their uniforms, employment conditions, worked the same trains and

The H class 4-4-4 tank engines usually worked the 'through' trains, but here no.110 is at Chesham changing the composition of the Dreadnought coaches for the 'shuttle'.
(H C Casserley)

A view of Chesham goods yard indicating the wide variety of traffic. Including that associated with the traditional 'boots, beer & brushes', a substantial 4,000 tons of freight was handled every month. (Ray East Collection)

The MET shed at Neasden with a group of firemen and cleaners posed around no.97 'Brill', a 0-6-4 G class tank engine, in order to celebrate one of them being promoted. Most of these men lived on the Neasden estate for railway families and at some time worked over the Chesham branch. (Tony Geary)

After prolonged complaints about the poor quality of the 'shuttle' coaching stock eventually some of the new Dreadnought coaches were allocated to the service. Here one of the classic class E 0-4-4T's, no.80, brings a set into the bay platform at Chalfont & Latimer. (Clive Foxell Collection)

A K class 2-6-4 tank locomotive no.114 shunting in the sidings at Chalfont & Latimer. In the background are open fields and some good examples of the telephone poles of the time. (K R Benest Collection)

Soon after the MET was absorbed into the LTPB in 1933, an E class tank no.80, still in MET livery, heads the 'shuttle' into Chesham Station. (H C Casserley)

An ex-GCR class 9N 4-6-2T arriving at Chesham Station with on the left the fine example of a MET signal box, which still graces the station today. (Len's of Sutton)

In the early 1930s an ex-GCR Director class 4-4-0 heading an express from Marylebone passes Chalfont and Latimer, probably bound for Manchester.
(John Gercken Collection)

e goods yard at Chesham after absorption into the LTPB with a mixture of rolling stock. This is now the site of a Waitrose supermarket. (Ray East Collection)

The use of steam power was anathema to London Transport and they explored more radical ptions. In particular a new diesel railcar was loaned by the Great Western Railway for trials on the 20th March 1936 and is seen here in the yard at Chesham with attendant officials. (Ray East Collection)

*The LTPB passed all steam and freight operations over to the LNER in 1937and here an ex-ME
G class 0-6-4T has been renumbered by them as 6157 and had the height of its chimney reduced
enable it to work further afield. Chesham Brewery can be seen in the background on the right.
(Ray East Collection)*

*The LTPB also developed the 'down' side of Chalfont & Latimer Station in 1933
by providing a proper access road. (LT)*

A 1938 aerial view taken looking to the north across Chesham with the railway crossing the River Chess at the bottom left, curving round over Waterside and passing through the 'baulks' into the station. In the distance is St Mary's Church next to Lowndes Park still with its magnificent avenue of trees. (Aerofilms)

The booking office at Chesham Station during the LPTB/LNER period of 1944. (LT)

The quintessential 'shuttle' passing Ranns Bridge hauled by an ex-LNER class C13 4-4-2T 67418 soon after rail nationalisation in 1947. In order to economise in 1940 the LT had resurrected some vintage MET coaches built by Ashbury in 1898 and converted them for auto-working. In this way the train could be driven from either end and thus avoid the need for the engine to run-round the coaches after every trip. (Clive Foxell Collection)

Another photograph of the 'shuttle' headed by 67418, with the later British Railways logo, passing Raans Farm before running beside the main line into Chalfont & Latimer. (Clive Foxell Collection)

BR later replaced the LNER C13s by Ivatt 2-6-2 tank engines, and here 41270 hauls the ancient Ashbury coaches over the original bridge at Waterside. (Ray East Collection)

Very few photographs exist of a train on the most difficult part of the climb up the side of the Chess Valley but, in the last phase of steam operation on the 31st August 1960, 41272 has steam to spare. (LT)

The 'shuttle' approaches Bell Lane bridge over track ready for electrification on 15th August 1960. (LT)

On the last day of steam operation 41284 nears Raans Road bridge with the traditional wreath mounted on the smokebox. (Clive Foxell Collection)

Three forms of motive power at Chesham Station during the trials before start of the electric services. In the new bay platform an Ivatt 2-6-2T no.41284 stands at the head of the normal 'shuttle' whilst the trial train of MET multiple electric T stock is at the main platform which has been suitably lengthened. Finally, the pick-up goods train waits in the loop with BR 4MT 2-6-2 76040. (LT)

Appropriately the final steam shuttle was hauled by ex-MET class E no.L44 whilst Dr Arnold Baines leads the dignitaries for the last ceremonies. (LT)

A consequence of the electrification was the demise of the polished manouvres at Rickmansworth for the changeover between electric and steam haulage in less than 3 minutes. In 1956 an ex LNER class C13 is in position whilst a stationman tackles the couplings whilst standing over the electrified track. (LT)

Until the new A60 multiple electric stock was ready the 'shuttle' was operated by MET T stock and the 'through' trains were hauled by the veteran MET Bo-Bo electric locomotives. Here at Chesham is no.7 which carried the name 'Edmund Burke'. (LT)

ABOVE:
The coaches employed in the early days of the branch were the rough-riding rigid 8 wheelers. The roof shows were the lamps were inserted for each compartment, but ventilators were only provided for first class passengers. (LT)

LEFT:
The interior of one of the long-serving Ashbury coaches which will always be associated with the 'shuttle' at Chalfont & Latimer on 18th March 1948. (LT)

After the war LT started development of the stock needed for the electrification of t *'Extension' and replacement of the ageing T stock. The first experimental coach in 1946 was hybrid corridor/compartment concept, but with sliding doors for the first time on the MET. (L'*

Car 17,000 followed in 1950 with a more modern appearance to the interior and 2+3 seating (LT)

The exterior of Car 17,000. As the rest of the trial train was comprised of ordinary T stock an extra guard was required in order to operate the sliding doors of the new coach. (LT)

The experience of Car 17,000 led directly to the construction of Car 20,000 with conventional LT upholstery and fluorescent lighting and this resulted in the final design of the production A60 stock. (LT)

The first 4 car set of A60 stock undergoing trials near Northwood Hills on 8th March 1961 during the widening and electrification works. (LT)

The financial saga over the replacement of the unsafe Chesham bridges, which might have led to closure of the branch, was at last resolved by the GLC. The new bridge at Waterside is here ready to be slid across sideways on the 24th March 1986.
(Clive Foxell)

remained fiercely proud of their individuality. The E class MET engines continued to work the Shuttle, but the larger types were dispersed around the LNER system and replaced by their N5 class ex-GCR 0-6-2T locos hauling the through trains.

The LTPB did make some minor improvements to the passenger facilities, with a better booking office at Chesham and platform shelters plus a proper approach road to the down side at Chalfont & Latimer. It would also seem that a free season ticket was given to a London commuter on his 92nd birthday.

Whilst the LNER were prepared to provide the steam locomotives and a goods service, they did not want to take overall responsibility for the line and so LTPB, seeking ways of reducing their dependence on steam haulage, drew up plans in 1935 for electrifying the line to Amersham under the Government 'New Works' programme to ease unemployment. The Chesham branch was excluded from these proposals and in wishing to eliminate steam the LTPB noted the progress the GWR had made in introducing diesel railcars and approached them for a trial on the Chesham branch. On the 20th March 1936 the newly completed No.16 was diverted from delivery to Newport for a number of experimental runs on the branch. It was one of the earlier fully streamlined railcars with a Gloucester Railway Carriage & Wagon Co. Ltd. body on an AEC chassis incorporating bus transmission systems. Aparently it coped satisfactorily with the sharp curves and gradient, but there is an apocryphal story that the replacement of noisy loco by the relatively quiet railcar caused mayhem at the lineside Chesham Gasworks where the workers timed the processes by the regular noise of the train passing! Apart from the fact that the railcar was unable to haul more than one or two wagons, the main disadvantage was felt to be the capacity for only 70 passengers. Therefore LTPB embarked on the design of a larger railcar based on one of their coach bodies mounted on a AEC/GWR chassis but by the end of the year the project had been scrapped in the light of a decision to extend the 'New Works' to the electrification of the Chesham branch.

Although some preparatory construction for modernisation beyond Harrow was started in 1939, the outbreak of war brought work to a halt.

The war had an immediate effect on the railways. Again, they were brought together under Government control. At local level station nameboards were obscured in order to hinder any enemy, whereas in practice it certainly confused the passengers who were also restricted by mesh over the carriage windows plus blinds and minimal lighting to meet blackout regulations. Travel for pleasure was discouraged and first-class tickets were withdrawn by LTPB on the 1st February 1941, although astute travellers could still identify the now un-marked compartments and travel in comfort. In those early days of the so-called 'phoney war' a number of special trains ran to Chesham with evacuees to be billeted in the vicinity and goods traffic of materials for the war effort began to increase. The need for economies gave the LTPB another chance in 1940 to show its disdain for the branch when they converted the Shuttle to auto-working in which the train could be driven from either end . Obviously this gave the advantage of avoiding the need for the engine to run round the coaches after every trip, but the LTPB used the oldest coaches they had – the 'Ashbury' 3-coach sets of 1898. These had been converted for electric traction from 1906 onwards and were now reverted back for steam working with the driver's cab having optional control of the steam engine's regulator and brake. To operate the push-pull trains the LNER replaced the long-serving MET E class engines by 3 of the ex-GCR 4-4-2T C13 locos which were made compatible for auto-working and were of sufficiently ancient appearance to complete the ensemble of a vintage train.

There were two sets of coaches and each spent a week at a time in traffic from the Sunday morning, after cleaning at Neasden and having been brought by one of the electric locos as far as Rickmansworth. The complete train was kept at Chesham overnight and work started with the 6.30am up and finished after some 28 shuttles at 1.10 am. On Sundays there were just 20 trips, the first being to Rickmansworth to return the coaches to Neasden.

From 1940 the war caused many disruptions to the service, mainly due to bombing of Baker Street and the City stations. Marylebone was also hit and for a time trains terminated at a temporary station at Neasden. The closest attack on the branchline came in 1940 when a stick of 8 bombs were dropped across the Chess Valley with one falling in Holloway Lane. The C13 engines and Ashbury coaches survived the war, only for the locomotives to be re-numbered by the LNER towards the end of its existence eg. 5002 to 7420, 5115 to 7438, 5193 to 7418.

7

STEAM SUNSET

In the immediate post-war period the established routines continued, but the organisation changed dramatically with the nationalisation of most of the transport in the UK on the 1st January 1948 in which the old LTPB and LNER were placed under the strong central control of the British Transport Commission. In becoming respectively the London Transport Executive and the Eastern Region of British Railways the pattern of passenger and goods traffic remained much the same except for 'BRITISH RAILWAYS' in large white letters eventually appearing on the tank sides of the engines, followed later by evolving BR logos. There was also re-numbering in order to harmonise all BR motive power and a '6' was added as a prefix to the C13's (at this time 7416 replaced 7438). Other engines such as the ex-GCR N5 and ex-LNER N7 0-6-2T's were seen on the branch either substituting for the C13's or hauling the 'through' trains to and from Rickmansworth.

However by 1957 the power of the BR regions had increased and there was a fundamental rationalisation of territories in which the old MET & GC was transferred to the London Midland Region of BR with a significant change in culture. Everything, including bridges, were re-numbered and the ex-LNER/GC engines were replaced by ex-LMS and some of the emerging BR standard types. The branch locomotives became the Ivatt 2-6-2T's, usually 41270/272/284/329, but still hauling the old Ashbury coaches. The goods traffic continued under BR auspices, declining from road competition and the 'Beeching' rationalisations to the point that coal for the local merchants was virtually all that remained. Nevertheless this by now skeleton service was allocated any engine that was spare and so brought a number of esoteric visitors to Chesham like the BR 4MT 2-6-2 76040 - and it is rumoured an ex-LNER 2-6-2 V2. By this time the decision to electrify the line had been taken and so the days of the 'Shuttle' were numbered. The last day of the steam service was operated by the regular 41284 and the final passenger train left Chesham at 12.11 am on the 12th September 1960. On that day some 1917 people used the 'shuttle', compared with about 100 on a normal Sunday. On the previous evening LT had arranged a commemorative trip, fittingly headed by ex-MET no.1 class E (L44), in the presence of Councillors, Railway Officers and many local well-wishers.

The now redundant Ashbury coaches had each covered some 800,000 miles and 4 went into preservation on the Bluebell Line, 1 was cannibalised and the last put on display at the London Transport Museum with the MET class A tank engine no. 23. The Chalfont & Latimer and Chesham main goods yards were closed in 1966 in order to make way for car parks, and the last steam working was by a LT maintenance train hauled by L99 (ex-GWR pannier locomotive no. 7715) on the 26th September 1967 which removed the lifted track. Since then any service trains have been hauled by LT battery loccomotives. The removal of the ex-GWR water tower near the signal box to go to the Dart Valley Railway appeared to sever the final link with steam. The last relic of the old order was the traditional early morning newspaper train (03.55 ex Marylebone arrive Chesham 05.38), by now a diesel multiple unit, which ran until the 14th October 1967.

By this time steam locomotives had disappeared from the old GC line with the withdrawl of passenger services north of Aylesbury, Marylebone ceasing to be a mainline terminus, and the commuter service provided by type 115 diesel muliple units. At that point few would have predicted that steam power would ever be seen again at Chesham!

Electrification

The earlier LPTB plans for electrifying the 'Extension' were revived after the war, but also with the old doubts about their role beyond Rickmansworth. This led to a further attempt to introduce diesel railcars in 1952 when a 3-car set of 4-wheel 125hp ACV vehicles replaced the 'Shuttle' for 2 weeks from the 13th October. However, as might have been expected they were not successful and in 1957 work at last started on implementing most of the original plans for doubling the track to Rickmansworth, electrification to Amersham and Chesham and the provision of new rolling stock. The main omission was the creation of a new 4-platform station at Rickmansworth with the 4 tracks converging to the north of the station. At Chalfont & Latimer the platforms were extended, the junction layout modified and the signalling modernised with control from a new signal box at Amersham. The branch was powered from a 3MW sub-station just north of Chalfont and Latimer but its distance from Chesham meant that care had to be exercised by drivers to limit the power demand of their train on leaving that end of the line. To accommodate a 4-car 'shuttle' in addition to 'through' trains a new bay platform was built at Chesham and the relief road electrified.

The development of new multiple unit electric stock to replace the ageing 'T' stock for the Watford, Rickmansworth and Uxbridge services and the new line had been underway since the end of the war. In 1946 the first trials took place of such a prototype carriage on a 'T' stock underframe which featured a full-length corridor, 3 large compartments and - for the first time on the MET – sliding doors, but the decor and prominent luggage racks were still reminiscent of the 'T' stock. This was followed by the experimental 'Car 17,000' which was run in 1947 of more modern appearance with an open 2+3 transverse seating arrangement, although the seats were still individually shaped. As a result of experience with this unit a 'Car 20,000' emerged with conventional LT upholstery and fluorescent lighting which was clearly the basis for the production of the A60 stock, deliveries of which began in 1960. These were made by Craven's and were the largest trains on London Transport with the typical laden weight of the 4-car shuttle being 130 tons. However deliveries were too late to inagurate the newly electrified line and on 16th August 1960 trials began with a 'shuttle' comprising a 3-car set of 'T' stock, leading to replacing the steam service on the 12th September. At the same time the LTB passed all reponsibility to BR for services north of Amersham. During this interesting interlude before the A60 stock took over in June 1962 the 'through' trains were hauled by the MET Bo-Bo electric locomotives. Service was disrupted for some time on the 23rd of September when the track was short-circuited by two boys dropping a coil of wire across the rails.

The train schedules had lengthened during the electricification and provision of the new fast tracks between Rickmansworth and Harrow but when completed, and even with the removal of the change-over at Rickmansworth, the best time to Baker Street from Chesham only recovered to some 48 mins.

The infrastructure continued to be simplified when on the 29th November the new bay line and the remaining sidings were removed at Chesham. At the same time the signal box was closed and the signalling reduced to a one train in occupation basis. The system was modified again in 1978, as a result of the lessons from an accident at Moogate station, to ensure that trains approaching the buffer stops at each end of the branch had to slow to a safe speed.

Bridge over the River Chess

In the 1970 the LTB became the LT Executive and the original optimism for electrifying the 'Extension ' began to wear thin, particularly in respect to the Chesham branch which generated little income and remained an operational oddity. With the inevitable increase in commercial pressures they were reluctant to cross-susidise the remoter lines in Bucks and Herts and fares were raised by about 40%, so that a monthly season from

Chesham to Baker Street became £43. Although LTE claimed loses of more than £1.5M pa for these lines the financial accounts to substantiate this were never revealed and, whilst there must be higher costs due to the nature of the services, the overall figures will be dominated by an arbitary allocation of overheads. In that London Transport have never been enthusiastic about their inheritance of the 'Extension' it is suspected by some that the apportionment of these overheads was made to justify closure

By the 1980's the services were being maintained with subsidies of about £500,000 pa from public sources ie the GLC, Bucks CC and the Ministry of Transport. However with a shifting political background it became difficult to get all these plus London Transport to agree on any issue! The key matter was whether a subsidy should be used for capital expenditure or reducing fares and in 1982 it was directed to lower fares significantly (Chesham-Baker Street return was reduced from £6 to £5) as a result of the GLC's 'Fares Fair' policy to increase the usage of public transport. However the basic dilemma was brought into focus again by the urgent need to replace the deteriorating original railway bridges over the River Chess and Waterside. In some ways it is suprising that they had lasted so long, as before the opening of the line in 1889 the Inspector had noted an excessive deflections when under load. Now, unless the bridges were replaced, at an estimated cost of £1.2M, the branch would have to close in 1986.

The national policy at that time favoured roads and in this area British Railways were seeking to close Marylebone and the line to Aylesbury, leaving those trains to run into Paddington via High Wycombe. Against this background Bucks CC in 1982 refused to continue their subsidy, or pay for replacing the bridges, suggesting that the line could be terminated at The Moor – ironicaly at the site originally proposed by the MET! The GLC subsidy was also in doubt as the body was about to be disbanded and their responsibility passed in 1983 to the new London Transport Executive. Thus Chesham again found itself fighting for the survival of its railway and local leaders such as Dr Arnold Baines and others intensively lobbied all who could avert closure. Meanwhile a speed restriction of 15mph was imposed on trains crossing the bridges and although London Transport started some preliminary design work on replacements this created a dispute as to whether they had authority to do this. Literally at the eleventh hour, Chesham's pleas were answered when the GLC, as one of its last acts approved the expenditure of £1.18M for the new bridges on the grounds that it would benefit those who travelled to work in London.

After all this the actual replacement of the bridges was something of an anti-climax but nevertheless was a considerable civil engineering task due to the restricted space and need to minimize closure of the roads. The opportunity was taken to employ single spans which were assembled beside the existing bridges so that road traffic was only suspended when they were rolled sideways into position. The Waterside bridge was replaced on the 24th March and that over The Chess on the 14th April 1986.

The late 1980's were marked by yet another deterioration in the quality of the service, particularly affecting the through City trains where a combination of autumn leaves on the line, signalling failures and quirky operational decisions meant that many trains were an hour or more late. The Chesham users had numerous meetings with the LUL managers but to little avail, their only suggestion being to eliminate the through trains and increase the frequency of the Shuttle!

However 1989 saw a resurgence of interest with the introduction of Travelcards to encourage journeys to London and the creation of a 'Metropolitan Line' management group within LUL. This team took-up the suggestion of a local character, Bob 'Stormy' Gale, who proposed that there should be a centenary celebration of the opening of the railway line into Chesham in 1889. This idea was enthusiastically developed by the Town Council and many local organisations culminating with an agreement with the Buckinghamshire Railway Centre at Quainton Road for the use of their recently restored ex-MET no.1 class E 0-4-4T locomotive, that had worked the line during the classic steam days. At the last moment this was joined by a privately preserved 0-6-0 (no. 9466) pannier tank engine designed designed by Hawksworth in the final years of the GWR. In addition LUL provided their preserved MET Bo-Bo electric locomotive 'Sarah Siddons' to provide some extra braking for the train of BR coaches. Unfortunately the garish colours of these coaches was something of a distraction from the authentic maroon livery of the ex-MET motive power.

Thus on the weekends of the 1-2nd and 8-9th of July 1989 a steam 'shuttle' was run between Chesham and Watford over the little used north junction at Rickmansworth. With the removal of all the steam servicing facilities, water was provided from bowsers and coal in sacks. It proved a tremendous success for the railway and town, attracting 9000 to travel on the train, a large number of visitors and recreating the magnificent sight and sounds of the heyday of steam as the class E headed over the bridge at Waterside and climbed towards Chalfont with the sound of its whistle echoing across the Chess Valley. Indeed such was the impact that this inspired the management of the MET to organise similar events in some subsequent years under the banner 'Steam on MET', although mainly centred on Amersham due to the increasingly restricted signalling facilities on the Chesham branch. These remain very popular and have brought a wide variety of steam power to the 'Extension' (ie: ex-LMS 4-6-0 'Black Five', ex-LNER N7 0-6-2T, ex-GWR pannier 0-6-0T and a 73XX 2-6-0, ex-BR Ivatt 2MT 2-6-0, Class 4 4-6-0 and a Class 20 Bo-Bo diesel) complemented by some ex-BR coaches which have been acquired by LUL and painted a tasteful maroon reminiscent of the MET livery.

Many excursions from Chesham were arranged by the MET and also afterwards by London Transport, particularly to Southend, but subsequently the most notable was a special train to Wembley Park for those attending the FA Amateur Cup Final in 1968 to watch Chesham United. As might be suspected a number of railway enthusiast trains have also appeared on the branch in recent years with varied motive power, including the 'John Milton' on the 3rd of June 1966 hauled by ex-MET class E no.L48, a set of LT multiple-electric 'Q' stock for the centenary of the District Line on the 24th August 1969 and later a DMU 'bubble' car and also a ex-BR class 20 Bo-Bo diesel locomotive.

The most recent visitor to the branch was a consequence of the privatisation of British Rail and involved a route inspection by Railtrack on the 18th March 1996 in which a class 33 diesel locomotive propelled an ex-Southern Railway general manager's saloon over the old 'Extension' lines – thereby causing some disruption to the service trains!

8

EPILOGUE

By the 1990's railways came back in favour to some extent and BR decided not to close Marylebone and instead to modernise their lines in Bucks with new 'Chiltern Turbo' class 165 multiple diesel units and signalling systems coming into service in the autumn of 1992. This now provides at attractive option for travellers from Chalfont & Latimer with a journey time of about 33 mins to Marylebone. About this time the Government put forward the Crossrail project which would link the route Aylesbury - Rickmansworth (with a new station on the present sidings) – Neasden South Junction – new line to Old Oak Common - Paddington – new tunnel to Liverpool St - Shenfield. At first sight it appeared that the Chesham branch was excluded on the grounds of the costs involved in replacing bridges and other work for the proposed 25kV overhead electrification system, but yet again local lobbying helped to reverse the decision. However, after considerable work on planning the route and even making a mock-up of the proposed type 341 rolling stock the Government bill was defeated in 1995, although it could well resurface in the future.

Reminiscent of a century ago new railways are being proposed, sometimes in relation to the Channel Tunnel. The only one in the vicinity has been put forward to link the BR and LUL stations at Croxley Green, thus allowing MET trains to run to the centre of Watford and on to Watford Junction. However as far as the Chesham branch is concerned the current developments are more mundane including the refurbishment of the, by now 35 year-old, A60 stock which work the line and further simplification of the signalling arrangements which, by installing pressure plates near Chalfont, counts the axles of the train 'in and counts them out again', thus allowing the starting signals to be removed.

For the past few years the 'Extension' has been newsworthy for its share of the problems caused by tree leaves falling on the rails at autumn resulting in slippage and interuption of track circuits. This was at first countered by various rail-mounted track cleaning methods and even a strange road-rail machine carrying several large blowers, which was parked for some time near Chalfont & Latimer Station. In the end, the source of the trouble was tackled and a lot of the undergrowth and over-hanging trees have been cut back. However in the autumn some 4 mins recovery time is added to the journey to Rickmansworth to allow for any such problems.

Recently the appearance of stations on the 'Extension' has been improved by tidying-up and re-decoration. In particular this has improved Chesham which retains its MET water tower and signal box to the extent it won an ARPS award in 1993. But the real uplift has come from the efforts of the staff who have created magnificent prize-winning gardens and floral displays which have echo the achievements of the staff in MET days. Over the period 1991 to 1995 the number of tickets sold by Chesham Station has been steady at around 115,000 daily and 5,000 period issues each year, which probably corresponds to some 800 people using the branch on a weekday.

Indeed a trip along the Chesham branch is still a delightful experience, with the its curve around Raan's Farm, its views of the Chess Valley and the entry over the bridges above the Town, but as always the past seems to have been favoured with more memorable incidents and characters.

For instance:

My first journey to work on the 'shuttle' in steam days with the smells of the carriage – the wood, the leather, the dusty upholstery, the smoke and grit. Being warned off a particular empty seat because a 'regular' always sat there.

Then there was the passenger who habitually tore interesting pieces out of his newspaper, until it resembled a colander: and the new commuter, who in his efforts to get to Wembley, forgot to change from the shuttle at Chalfont and Latimer and was therefore returned to Chesham and by the end of the day, and a series of wrong connections, had managed briefly to visit Baker St., Uxbridge, Harrow, Marylebone and Amersham before deciding to give up and try again the next day.

To this day I can see an umbrella hanging on the window of a T stock coach after an alighting passenger had slammed the door shut and sliced-off its end.

I recall the sight of a very large Christmas tree being forced into a narrow MET compartment already packed with passengers.

How could one forget the slick change-over from electric to steam power at Rickmansworth during which a particular regular traveller still managed to find time to nip across to the buffet for a swift half that the barmaid had ready.

Then there was the tale of the American airman based at Bovingdon during the last war who bet the train crew at Chalfont that his Jeep could beat the 'shuttle' to Chesham. The airman just won , but the green faces of his passengers as they staggered out of the Jeep told another story.

Also the Chesham shop assistant that married a lady who wished to remain in Southend and for the rest of his career became a daily commuter – except on early-closing days!

All these and many more are the shuttle tales that could be told, and even if we complain these days of rough rides down the branch line these are as nothing compared to those days of steam. For by the time the evening 'through' steam train reached Chalfont & Latimer, after it had slogged up-hill from Ricky with a worn and failing N7, the crew would be anxious to recover time and so would make the most of the down hill run into Chesham on what was left of their water and steam. To the passengers this could be at the same time a nerve racking and a thrilling experience particularly as the train hit the reverse curves at the bottom of the valley at speed, before bending round over Waterside with the flanges of the wheels screaming in protest against the rails, and with the glow from the firebox lighting up the cutting. The train drew into the station rather quicker in those days with many of the carriage doors already flung open and the passengers were soon jostling their way through the narrow booking office heading for home. No wonder the other name for the 'shuttle' was the 'Chesham Flyer'.

SELECT BIBLIOGRAPHY

KEY WORKS

Baker, C : The Metropolitan Railway, Oakwood Press 1951

Edwards, D & Pilgrim R

: Metropolitan Memories, Midas Books 1977

: The Romance of Metroland, Midas Books 1979

: The Final Link, Midas Books 1982

Jackson, A A

: Chesham's Branch, Railway World vol 45 p454 1984

: London's Metropolitan Railway, David & Charles 1986

Lee, C E

: The Metropolitan Line, London Transport 1972

RAILWAYS IN THE CHILTERNS

Baines, A & Birch, C

: A Chesham Century, Baron 1994

Barrie, D S

: The Hemel Hempstead & Harpenden Railway, Railway Magazine 91, 556 p67 1945

Birch, C

: The Book of Chesham, Barracuda 1974

Birch,C & Armistead J :Yesterday's Town: Chesham, Barracuda 1977

Bradshaw's Railway Manual, Shareholders' Guide & Directory, 1848

Cockman, F G

: The Railways of Hertfordshire, Hertfordshire Library Service 1983

Cockman, F G

: The Railways of Buckinghamshire, Unpublished 1971 held at the Bucks Record Offfice

Davies, R & Grant, M D

: Forgotten Railways: Cotswolds & Chilterns, David & Charles 1975

Hepple, L W & Doggett A M

: The Chilterns, Phillimore 1992
Lewis, H L
: The Uxbridge & Rickmansworth Railway, Railway
Magazine vol 91, 555 p7 1945
Oppitz, L
: Chiltern Railways Remembered, Countryside Books 1991
Reed, M
: A History of Buckinghamshire, Phillimore 1993
Rothschild, J de
: The Rothschilds at Waddesdon Manor, Collins 1979
White, I
: A History of Little Chalfont, Alpine Press 1993
: A Companion to Chesham Almanacks 1844-1847
: MetroLand : Metropolitan Railway, 1915-1932
: Chesham Metropolitan Branch Line Centenary, Chesham
Town Council 1989
: Steam on the MET, London Underground booklets 1992-96

PHOTOGRAPHIC BOOKS WITH RELEVANT TEXT

Casserley, H C
: The Later Years of Metropolitan Steam, Bradford Barton
Coles, C R L
: Railways Through the Chilterns, Ian Allan 1986
Seabright, C J
: Chesham in Old Picture Postcards – Vols 1,2 & 3,
European Library 1985/89/95
Shannon, P
: British Railways Past & Present – Buckinghamshire,
Bedfordshire & West Hertfordshire, Past & Present
Publishing 1995
Waters, L
: Celebration of Steam: The Chilterns, Ian Allan 1995

ROLLING STOCK

Benest, K R
: Metropolitan Electric Locomotives, London
Underground Railway Society
Gadesden, E J S

: Metropolitan Steam, Roundhouse Books 1963

Goudie, F
: Metropolitan Steam Locomotives, Capital Transport Publishing 1990

Hardy, B
: London Underground Rolling Stock, Capital Transport Publishing 1983

Huntley, I
: The London Underground Surface Stock Planbook, Ian Allan 1985

Rowledge, J W P
: Metropolitan Railway Locomotives, Locomotives Illustrated no 65, Ian Allan 1989

− : Fowler's "Ghost", Railway Magazine 8, 43 p63 1901

− : Experimental Coach for London Transport, Railway Magazine 92, 562 p104 1946

− : Electric Trains Replace Vintage Stock to Chesham, Railway Magazine 106, Nov p799 1960

OTHER SOURCES

Bucks Flying Post & Chesham Examiner

Bucks Examiner

The Times

Metropolitan Railway, Met & GC Joint Railway and London Transport public and working timetables.

Kelly's Directory

CHESHAM SHUTTLE

Later on the night of the 14th April 1986 the two span bridge over the River Chess was also replaced by a single span. (Clive Foxell)

The Centenary of the opening of the branch was celebrated in style by the town, LT and railway enthusiasts. Fittingly, E class 0-4-4T locomotive ex-MET 1 had just been restored at Quainton Road and was able to work over the line with a 'shuttle' to Watford in July 1989. (Clive Foxell)

For the Centenary LT were able also able to loan their preserved MET Bo-Bo electric locomotive no. 12 'Sarah Siddons' to provide extra braking for the train of BR coaches, here in Chesham Station. (Clive Foxell)

The branch has always been a popular location for special trains arranged by enthusiasts and on the 3rd June 1966 another ex- MET E class engine LT no.48 hauled the 'John Milton' over the line. (Clive Foxell)

After electrification a set of LT multiple electric Q stock visited Chesham on the 24th August 1969. (Len's of Sutton)

Preserved BR class 20 diesel locomotive no.20227 on a brief visit to Chesham on the 20th May 1995 organised by the 20-20 Society. (Clive Foxell)

DMU 'bubble' car no. l123 took over the 'shuttle' service on the 20th May 1995 during the annual Steam on MET event. (Clive Foxell)

Following the recent refurbishment of the buildings at Chesham Station, the staff led by Barbara Brown and Mark Stephenson have developed the gardens and flower displays to greatly enhance the station and winning many prizes. (Clive Foxell)